MERMAI

CW01604819

To
Rosemary
Best wishes,
Lilian Gray
13/7/97

For the three men in my life;
My sons - Keith and Jamie
and my strength - 'Ray'.

MERMAID MEWS

LILLIAN JAY

NAVIGATOR BOOKS

Published by Navigator Books
Ringwood, Hampshire

Copyright © Lillian Jay 1994

ISBN 0 902830 21 X

All rights reserved. No part of this publication may be reproduced, stored in a retrieval system or transmitted in any form or by any means: electronic, mechanical, photocopying, recording or otherwise, without the prior permission of the publishers

This book is a work of fiction and no resemblance to actual places or persons living or dead is to be inferred. Any such resemblance would be entirely coincidental.

Printed in Great Britain by
Antony Rowe Ltd, Chippenham, Wiltshire

PROLOGUE

If she had been able to talk, the small statuette would have held an audience enraptured with tales of yesterday.

Once, she had been glorious; all shiny black marble, her tail dipping into a rippling pool where water had flowed down the rock upon which she sat. Her long tresses cascaded around her bare shoulders and modestly shielded her breasts from view. In her hands she held a delicate mirror and shell-shaped comb. Arms held high, she gazed for eternity at her smiling image, perpetually frozen in time as she raised the implement to her hair.

Now the water was stagnant; it no longer danced across the rock or rippled in the pool. The fountain had long since ceased to function, some forgotten hand had cut the water supply and her beautiful scaled tail rested in a dirty puddle. The surface of her ebony frame was dull and pock marked, her mirror cracked and the comb chipped and broken. Her expression had become almost cynical over the years as she watched her changing countenance. The mythical mermaid had lost her elegance; she was no longer the splendid figure of her youth.

Locked within her staring, glassy eyes were pictures of war torn London and the erratic bombings that filled the air with smoke and dust. These same eyes had watched as blast after blast shattered the windows about her, spraying fragments of glass, splinters of wood and whole bricks at her slender frame. Her ears held tight the memory of shrill, urgent notes of warning as the young lads of the Boys' Bugle Brigade sounded the alarm. Of clanging bells as huge, red fire engines invaded her sanctuary. The angry, crying, desperate sounds of man still echoed in her head. And finally, the welcome sound of the 'All Clear' signal and the hush which followed.

There had been happy times that she could also recall. Flags and banners had waved in her face as singing bands of people, straying from the main thorough fare, paraded around her. Voices raised in relief, as victorious celebrations were held and the war to end all wars was over. Then, her body had been adorned with streamers, children had paddled in the fountain below her and peace reigned.

It had not lasted. Again she had been hurled into the fray of yet another of man's battles and she became witness to a repeat performance of man-made devastation. But this time the air attacks were made with deadly precision. The whistle of falling bombs became a nightly occurrence and the explosions which followed had shook her foundations to their very roots. After each onslaught, when the air had cleared, and still she remained intact, the locals had begun to look upon her as their lucky mascot. If she could survive, then so would the folk who lived around her. When the last bomb had fallen and the last war office telegram had been delivered and wept over, the square had rung with laughter. The fountain was the focal point as jubilant cockneys gathered, raising their glasses at the now empty skies.

The silent sentinel had sat for the past fourteen years in relative harmony, safe and secure except for the passage of time and mother nature.

Holding her lonely vigil, the mermaid sat in the centre of a small, cobbled square. To her left and right and at her back were six two storied terraced houses, badly in need of repair, while before her lay the entrance to her namesake; Mermaid Mews.

In its time, Mermaid Mews had housed the horses and servants of a large estate which still stood across the road, in front. Eventually the Mews had fallen empty until the advent of council housing when the London Borough had cast its net and bought the six dwellings for the homeless.

Each house contained six rooms, a kitchen and a recently converted bathroom. They had been built to accommodate the large families of their era; the reigning Queen of that time, Victoria, having instigated this particular fashion, and they had become the palaces of the poor.

It was 1959 and over the years, the little mermaid had witnessed the comings and goings of numerous families. She had viewed the personal tragedies and joys of her residents, the ups and downs of their lives and today she watched as yet another family took up new residency within her domain. No doubt they would bring their own history with them, their own dramas, but it would not be anything she had not seen before. It would, perhaps, run a different sequence, but the finale would still remain the same; the people of Mermaid Mews left either in a removal van or a hearse.

But for now, the statue would follow the meandering path of the new inhabitants, she would watch this new play, based on the time weary theme of life.

CHAPTER 1

"Ellie! Put that down, if I've told you once, I've told you a dozen times. If I have to tell you again, you'll feel the back of my hand."

The tall, slim figure of Catherine May Treist, stood glaring at her small daughter. It had been a terrible day. The removal van had been late and they had lost their way amongst the back streets of the labyrinth of London. On their arrival, the workmen had unceremoniously rid the van of its load, leaving all her furniture in the middle of the square and sped out of the Mews, late for their next delivery.

"Oh, Mum! I'm only looking for my doll. You said you'd put her in the big box with the cross on it but she's not there. I told you she'd be safer with me up front in the van and now she's lost! I'll never see her again. Poor Lulu! How's she going to find her way home? She doesn't even know where we live." Wiping a grimy hand across her face, Ellie whimpered and looked accusingly at her mother.

"Don't talk to your mother like that. Now, that's enough, Ellie. Go into the house and stay there, I don't want to hear another whine out of you today, do you hear?"

John (Jack to all and sundry) Henry Treist surveyed the jumble before him. It would soon be dark and this lot would have to be shifted before then. Being a big man, it would not take long for him to clear the square of his household goods, as long as everyone kept out of his way. His eyes slid sideways to the forlorn figure sat on a tea chest in the far corner. How his mother, Sal, irritated him! Why didn't she go indoors instead of sitting there looking dejected? Jack knew he should have more tolerance. After all, his mother had just left the house she had been born in and all her friends. But how could she forget the outside lavatory that iced over during the winter months? Or that no-one could have a proper bath, except if you pulled out the heavy iron tub from underneath the worktop in the small damp kitchen. And as for the mildew that grew on the inside walls of every room, well, you only had to listen to the hacking coughs of most of the inhabitants of her old neighbourhood to realise how bad that could be. Anyway, they were pulling down the whole street next week, so all her old friends would be rehoused elsewhere. Still, it must be an awful upheaval for the old girl. He'd have to be a bit patient with her, just until she settled down.

"Why don't you go on in, Mother? We'll put the kettle on in a minute, I've only got to connect the cooker and we'll be away. Come on, don't sit there getting all cold, let's find you a place to sit indoors." Gently, Jack took his mother's arm and led her into the house.

"I'm alright. Don't shove me about, I'm not one of your sticks of furniture you know, and I'm not dead yet. I can find my own way, leave off, Jack." Grumbling loudly, the old woman entered her new home for the first time on her only son's arm.

Cathy watched their retreating backs. God, they'd only just arrived and they were at it again. She couldn't have five minutes peace before they started. She had hoped that the move would bring Jack and Sal closer but she should have known better. How could you break the habit of a lifetime? Since the day she had married Jack and he had taken her home to his mother's house, the bickering had been constant. Cathy couldn't say they fought. No, the two niggled at each other, like a dog worrying a bone. At the beginning she had tried to stay neutral, but slowly, over the years, she had been brought into each argument and appointed arbitrator. Sometimes, she had fled the house and walked the streets in a vain effort to escape their harsh words but no matter how long she stayed out, when she returned they would still be going, hammer and tongs. Cathy's gloomy thoughts were interrupted when an excited voice said:

"Cor, it's great here, Mum! You should see the back garden! And it's all ours, we haven't got to share it with anybody, it's just for us. There's bushes in it as well! I'll be able to play cowboys and Indians for hours out there, come and see it, Mum!"

Smiling fondly, Cathy tousled the hair of her one and only son. Billy had such a loving temperament, easy-going and placid. God knows, he didn't get that from his father or his grandmother! At ten, Billy was secretly his mother's favourite unlike his two sisters who never stopped whining and harping on about something or other.

Ellie had not emerged from the house since her father had banished her there, but Cathy's other daughter, Fay, who was at that awkward age of twelve, had been hovering around the front door, sullenly observing the scene before her.

Her arm about Billy's shoulder, Cathy entered the house, saying as she passed her, "Take your fingers out of your mouth, Fay. One of these days you'll wake up with your arms bitten down to your elbows."

Twilight was descending before the square was cleared of their belongings and the family could sit down to a cold tea. Each member had been allocated a room and it was Sal who rose first from the table.

"I'm off to my bed, that's if anyone has put it up yet. Don't you lot stay up half the night shifting things round and keeping me awake. We all need a good night's sleep, there's lots to do tomorrow."

Jack and Cathy exchanged glances. Well, it hadn't taken her long to find her feet. Obviously, she meant to rule this particular roost the same as she had ruled the last.

Gradually the children retired to bed and left their parents sitting in the semi-gloom of the living room.

"So. This is it, then." Hugging his wife to him, Jack continued. "It'll all be fine once we've got everything in it's place, love. We're going to be happy here, I can tell. There's a nice feeling about the place. It feels like it's our house and not my mother's."

"Yes, Jack. We will be happy here, we'll make sure of it. Just one thing. Do you think you could try and get on with your mother? I know you've always carried on that way with her, but this is a new beginning and we should all turn over a new leaf. I really want to make this work, Jack and I don't think I can cope with another thirteen years of you two getting at one another."

"OK. I'll try. I can't promise anything. After all, it takes two, you know. Talking of taking two, what about an early night, eh love? We'll pretend we've just got married. No kids, no mother, just you and me, what do you say?" Jack kissed the top of Cathy's head.

"Just married? You must be joking! Have you forgotten how old you are, Jack Treist? You'll never romp all night again, my love, like you used to!" Laughing, Cathy rose from the couch and ran lightly up the stairs to their bedroom.

"Cheeky mare! Old am I? I'll show her!" Switching off the lights, Jack followed his wife up to bed.

The square settled down for the night. Lights were turned off all around, dogs stopped barking and cats began screeching. The little mermaid was left staring into the darkness. Another day had passed in Mermaid Mews and the first day of the rest of their lives for the Treists.

CHAPTER 2

All had not been as quiet on the Treist's first night in Mermaid Mews as one could be led to believe.

Privacy has always been one of the key words in the working class community, especially if there was trouble afoot. 'Mind your own business' is probably the most used phrase amongst these people and although Londoners, in particular Cockneys, are a friendly breed, poking one's nose into their affairs is definitely taboo. Many friendships have been lost due to one or the other parties overstepping the mark. It is a very fine line that is drawn between concern and consideration for one's neighbour and being just plain nosy. The inhabitants of Mermaid Mews paid strict attention regarding this unwritten law, going out of their way to avoid any misunderstanding. Therefore, when the usual commotion began at No. 1, everybody became suddenly deaf.

The Ridley's home had been peaceful until Seb, the master of the house, had returned, drunk, from one of his long drinking sessions with his cronies. His loud, ranting voice could be heard long before he entered the square.

"I don't know why you love me like you do, I don't know why but you do. La la la la, de da de da de da, I don't know why, but you do!"

Seb's rendition left a lot to be desired as he swayed, then tripped over the cobblestones, saving his fall by grasping the edge of the mermaid's fountain.

"Vera, Vera, you old cow! I know you're in there, hiding behind the door. Come out! Give your old man an hand." His voice reverberated around the Mews. "Bloody dried-up prune! Don't know why I married her in the first place, just because she was up the spout. Who's to say the brat's mine anyway? Mind you, it must have been mine, who else would want to get in that one's drawers? Only someone as stupid as me. Never could refuse, especially when it's waved in my face and I've had a few. Led me a life of misery, so she has, always moaning saying 'Don't you think you've had enough, Seb?' Enough? If there was an ocean full of it, that wouldn't be enough! Driven me to drink, that's what she's done and who can blame me? It's like getting into bed with a lump of ice or a plank of wood. And what's ice and wood good for? One for crushing and the other for chopping! So, I think I'll get along now and do just that!" Raising his half empty whisky bottle to his lips, Seb took a long swallow.

"If you know what's good for you, woman, you'll open that door, because if I have to break it down, I won't stop there! Oh no! You'll be next and it'll be no good you screaming your head off like a stuck pig because no bleeder round here's going to help you. They wouldn't give you the wax out of their ears, not this lot!" Brandishing the bottle, he made his unsteady way to his front door. As he raised his arm to strike at the obstacle before him, it opened, silently and slowly.

Seb staggered through the portal, the frame quivering as he slammed shut the door and turned to his wife, who stood shaking and shivering at the foot of the stairs.

"And now, you! I'd better teach you a lesson or two. Don't you know by now, how to treat your husband? How many times have I got to beat this into you? God, you'd think you'd learn, wouldn't you? Get up them stairs, now! I'll teach you, even if it kills you, I will."

The object of this, as yet, verbal abuse was a small, thin woman. She had not fared well over the years and the constant beatings by her husband had left their mark.

Only thirty years old, Vera could be likened to a woman fifteen years older. Her hair was prematurely streaked with grey and on closer inspection, one could determine patches of baldness where Seb had repeatedly dragged her from room to room, his hand entwined in her once shiny locks. Lined and wrinkled, her face spoke volumes of the hardships she had endured, caught in a trap of a marriage to an evil, brutal husband but was unable to break loose from the ties which held her to him. Vera was a sweet natured, timid being and had been taught at an early age that all she could expect from life was to marry and bear children. This last directive was the only good thing to emerge from her marriage. Angela had been born just nine months after Vera's wedding day and she would be the only child Vera managed to carry full term and survive. There had been many, too many, miscarriages during the first ten years mainly due to the 'accidents' that frequently occurred at home.

"What are you going to do? Seb, don't hit me again, I'm still black and blue from the last time. I'm sorry Seb, really I am. I try to be a good wife to you, and I'll try even harder from now on, only don't hit me, please Seb!" Vera had dropped to her knees, her arms clasped around Seb's lower legs and her face was raised to his, beseechingly.

"Get up! For Christ's sake woman, take your punishment and stop grovelling. Let go of me, you silly cow! You're making it worse for yourself, you know how I hate it when you whine and snivel. Stop your racket, do you hear? Shut up!" With that, Seb bent down and bringing his arm back, he swung with all his force to strike at the pleading face before him. The blow resounded through the silence of the house and sent Vera sprawling across the hallway, skidding over the bare floorboards and coming to a bone crunching halt as her frail body hit the far wall. The crumpled form lay still. She had learnt that to move after one of Seb's 'lessons' would only antagonise him further. Eyes shut tightly, her mind began its exploration of her battered body. Slowly, she mentally examined all parts of herself and found she had come off lightly this time. Apart from the ringing in her ears and the dull throb in her temple, nothing else seemed to be amiss.

Vera willed her breathing to return to normal and waited for the next onslaught. For once, it did not come. It appeared that Seb had had more than his usual intake of alcohol and, muttering obscenities, he began to haul himself up the stairs, pulling at the banister as he mounted each step. She waited until she heard the thump of his boots as they fell to the bedroom floor after removal, then carefully and quietly she stood up.

She lent for a moment against the wall and waited for her head to stop spinning and for the stars to vanish from her still closed eyelids. When everything returned to normal, she opened her eyes and made her way down the hallway and into the small kitchen on the left. Going to the sink, she picked up the kettle from the stove and filled it with water.

"A nice cup of tea, that's what you need, a nice, hot, sweet cup of tea." She knew she was talking to herself and realised that she could be in shock, but nobody would hear her and the sound of her voice was somehow comforting.

Sitting at the kitchen table, she waited silently for the water to boil. Already, she could hear the sound of Seb's snoring and could picture him lying, face upwards, mouth gaping, fully clothed and unconscious on the bed. He would likely remain in that same posture until the morning, when he would stumble from the house and make his appearance at the glue factory where he worked on the line. She must remember to rise before him and warn Angela to keep quiet and not turn on the radio until he had left the house.

The shrill whistle of the kettle made Vera jump. Pushing herself up from the chair, she crossed the room and began to automatically make her tea. Piling three heaped teaspoons of sugar into her cup, she poured the steaming liquid into the milk at its base, then returned to her resting place at the table.

As she passed the dresser, she glanced up into the mirror on the second shelf and caught sight of her face. A livid, red, angry welt was already appearing on her right cheek. It ran from her hair line down to the corner of her mouth, which was cracked and bleeding. Hands shaking, she placed her cup and saucer upon the table and reaching into her dressing gown pocket, she retrieved her handkerchief and dabbed at the open wound.

She slumped once more, into her chair and let her head drop onto her arms resting on the table. She still felt dizzy and her vision was blurred. Slow tears fell on her sleeves and her thin shoulders heaved from her wracking, silent sobs.

How would she be able to keep this from her daughter? The bruise on her face would tell its own story. As this latest attack had been swift and relatively quiet, she had hoped to protect Angela from the knowledge that her father had beaten his wife, yet again. So many times, Vera had pleaded with her daughter not to confront Seb or berate him for his cruelty as the fear of him unleashing his anger on the girl was becoming more real as each day passed. Gladly, Vera would have stood between Seb and Angela and taken the beating aimed at the young girl, if needs be, but presently, this had not been called for. Seb had shouted and raised his fist, but as yet, he had not caused any bodily harm to his daughter.

How much longer could she continue with this farce? If Vera's family had survived the last war, she would have fled home to them. But they had all perished in one of the last air attacks on London. Her mother, father, sister and brother had all been taken from her in one fell swoop as their home took a direct hit and reduced the whole street to rubble. Vera had been out with a girlfriend and when the warning siren sounded, she had ducked into an air raid shelter, just two streets away from her home. After the 'All Clear' signal had abated, Vera had ran from the shelter, aware that the bombings that night had been nearby. Even after all this time, she could still see the smoking pile of brickwork that had been her home, still recall the acrid smell of burning masonry and the unfamiliar sickly, sweet taint of scorched flesh. She had scrambled among the debris, calling out the names of her family and had dug with her bare hands in a vain effort to free their tortured remains.

They had led her from the bomb site, her finger nails ripped and torn and her mind unhinged. She had remained in this state for close to a year, secluded in a rest home for the emotionally shattered victims of one of the worst wars of our time.

When she had emerged from her cocoon, she had found herself alone in a ruined city. She had no home, no family and no point to her life. Unfortunately, Seb had made his appearance just at this time and she had clung to him, trusting that he would put aright her world.

In those days, Seb had cut a dashing figure. Fresh from the army, he was confident that he could re-enter 'civvie street' and become successful in whatever field he decided to turn his hand to. The stocky built frame, deep brown eyes, thick wavy brown hair and easy charm were as a beacon to Vera. He radiated confidence and a devil may care attitude and she was smitten at once. So what if he liked a drink or two? Most men of that time were apt to drown the memories of war and who could blame them? But as time passed and Seb became more disillusioned, so he took more refuge in the bottom of a bottle.

At first he had not struck her, but his threats were terrifying to the timid woman. Seb found pleasure in tormenting her and the more she cowered the better he liked it. When the time came that he actually raised his hand to her and used it, he discovered that the feeling of power was as an aphrodisiac. He was a man again. Someone was frightened of him for a change. And always, after the beatings, he would throw her down and take her by force, this being the ultimate in securing his manhood.

As drink became Seb's master, the rapes had stopped. His body would no longer respond at will and this further frustration was also vented on his wife.

Vera sat on into the night, remembering and regretting. Where would it all end and where would this path lead her to?

CHAPTER 3

Spring time in Mermaid Mews is a busy season. Rugs and mats are brought out into the square and vigorously beaten, the dust and dirt of the past year rising in small puffs after each stroke of the wooden carpet beaters. Curtains, covers and bedding blow in the breeze, anchored to clothes lines in back gardens. And the grime and grit of a year's accumulation are sought out and banished from dark corners and from the depths of cupboards and wardrobes. All manner of household articles are aired before the front section of each house, arrayed in public for all the world to see.

"Look at the state of her settee! It looks more battered than she does and that's saying something. I never could understand why she lets him get away with it. Pissing his money up against the wall, then coming home and taking it out on her. He wouldn't do it in this house, I can tell you. No man's worth it, girl, and don't you forget it."

Ruby lived at No. 2. She had moved her family, a daughter, Brenda and a son, Gary, to the Mews directly after her husband had up and left without a word some five years since. Shortly afterwards Seb and Vera Ridley had moved in next door and Ruby had listened as night after night Seb had taken out his frustrations on his wife. Sometimes, as she lay in her bed, unable to sleep for the sounds coming from No. 1, it became unbearable and Ruby would bang on the wall, hoping that Seb's conscience would be pricked. It never worked. Seb would only pause long enough to shout obscenities at his neighbour, then continue with his favourite pastime of wife beating.

"God knows why she stays with him. He hasn't got a streak of decency in him and never a good word to say to anyone. I've always thought that if you looked hard enough, you'd find some good in a person, but not with that one. Mean and evil, he is and she's a fool to hang around, always there at his beck and call. You listening, Brenda? I'm not saying all this because I like the sound of my own voice and neither do I enjoy other people's misfortunes. But you should learn by it all and steer clear of blokes like him." This lecture had continued as Ruby and her daughter had cleaned and aired their own home and now Ruby stopped, wiped her brow with the corner of her apron and stood surveying her handiwork.

"Alright, Mum. I hear you. Not that you've got anything to worry about. They're not exactly queuing at the door, begging for my hand are they? Just stop and take a look. I'm big and ugly and I'll probably still be here, living with you, long after he's beaten Vera to death."

Some of what Brenda said was true. She was the spitting image of her mother. Large framed, with a square, plain face, she would never set the world on fire. These days, women took more care of their appearance and men were aware of this. It was not enough to be able to cook, sew and bring up your husband's children any more. You had to look like Vera Lynn or Marlena Dietrich and above all you had to be sexy, but only for your husband. Fat chance! Brenda was under no illusions. There were no fancy clothes or make-up that could transform her into a sex symbol. She was basically a homely soul and if only a man would take a long enough interest in her, he would find she held a heart of gold. Like Ruby, Brenda did not mince her words and called a spade, a spade. Unfortunately, her outspoken attitude had put off the few would be suitors that had crossed her path.

"That's enough of that Brenda. No point in wallowing in self pity, God gave you what you've got and you'd better make the most of it. Some bloke'll come along, one of these days, and he'll see beyond the shell and realise that good looks aren't everything. I only hope he's not like your father and does a disappearing act. You'll see, Brenda, there's someone out there for you, it just takes time for you to find each other." Ruby was understanding of Brenda's dilemma, as the same worries had plagued her teenage days. Ruefully, she thought it might have been better if she had not found 'Mr. Right'. She might have been happy in her ignorance and she believed the same applied to her daughter, although Ruby would never have voiced this opinion. Let Brenda have her dreams, she thought. There was time enough for her to wake up and realise that all men were alike. Once they'd got what they wanted, they soon became bored. Women were just playthings and were discarded like an old toy once a better one came on the scene.

She would never be sure, but Ruby suspected that her own husband had stumbled across a better proposition. After all, it was too much of a coincidence that at the time of her husband's leaving, the young Wilcox girl, Freda, had also been conspicuous by her absence. And, in Ruby's opinion, if a newer version couldn't be found, then they stayed around and made your life a misery. Like him next door.

Gary, Ruby's son, was in her mind, the exception to the rule. He did not resemble his sister or his mother, neither in looks or character. His was a happy go lucky disposition and his face portrayed an optimism and good natured humour that was appealing to everyone he came in contact with. Gary could be prone to devilment, but he was mischievous rather than spiteful and he meant no harm to any fellow human being. At twelve years of age, Gary was the younger of Ruby's two children and both females of his family doted on him. He had come along at a time when Ruby had given up hope of bearing more children, some eight years after Brenda and although he could vaguely remember his father, he did not miss him and considered himself fortunate to have two such obliging women for his mother and sister.

Lounging against the door post, he now called out jokingly, "How much longer are you two going to be? Where's my tea? I'm starving! Look at me, all skin and bones, I am, wasting away before your very eyes. Come on, Mum, get a move on, I've got football practise tonight."

"Hold your horses. Me and Brenda have been working like Trojans since early morning. What's your hurry? You've got a couple of hours until you have to be down at the grounds and we're having two minutes sit-down. Be a love, and put the kettle on, Gary. I could kill for a cuppa."

Ruby had parked herself on an old discarded tea chest and was enjoying the last of the day's sunshine looking pleased with her endeavour's of that day.

"You out tonight, Brenda? Going to the dance, are you?"

"Yeah, Carol's calling round at seven. Mind you, I'll probably do what I always do on a Saturday night. Make like a bleeding wallflower and watch all the blokes swarm round her, as usual. Don't know why I bother. It's no fun coming home on your own week after week, dodging all the other couples and pretending not to care."

"Well, you'll not find anyone sitting indoors and Saturday night's for you young ones. Get out and about and do all the things you'll not be able to do once you get hitched. And you'll never meet anyone in that stuffy old library, will you? Only young boys and old men get in there. Go on, get yourself ready and I'll do the tea." Rising from the tea chest, Ruby made her way indoors. She had not been pleased when Brenda had chosen to work as an assistant librarian and encouraged her to go out as much as possible, meet new people and enjoy herself. Ruby wanted her children to have all the things she had not had; nice clothes, lots of friends and the freedom to enjoy everything. Gary was not a problem, he would always find his feet no matter what life had in store for him. But Brenda was another story. She would always need a push, always need bolstering and Ruby intended to fill that particular post to the utmost.

On entering the kitchen, she glanced out of the window, watching as her son stood talking animatedly over the back gate. A young girl, perhaps six or seven years old, was standing on the path that ran around the outside of the Mews, beyond the back garden gates.

The young, high voices of the two children rang clear and vibrant in the early evening air.

"That's a nice name, that is. I like it. Ellie? What's that short for? Eleanor, is it?"

"Yeah. My aunty's name is Eleanor, that's my Mum's sister. She lives a long way away, down south in a place called Cornwall and we don't see much of her. So my Mum said I was called after her so's Aunty wouldn't feel so far away. Have you lived here long, Gary?"

Swinging back and forth on the gate, Gary pushed the hair from his eyes and scrutinised the figure before him. He had seen her wandering past his garden only moments before and had rushed outside to introduce himself to his new neighbour.

"About five years. Have you met everyone yet? The Ridley's live at No. 1. Funny lot they are, keep themselves to themselves, at least the mother and daughter do. He's horrible. Likes to hit people when he's had a drink. You'd best keep out of his way. Then there's us, the O'Shea's. That's me, my Mum and my sister, Brenda. And next door at No. 3 are the Carmichael's. There's five of them. The three boys; Frankie, Toby and Jacob and their Mum and Dad, Eileen and Frank. They're a rowdy lot, but good fun and always ready for a laugh. And next to them is your tribe and then at No. 5 is Mr. and Mrs. Verwood. They haven't got any kids and they're really old, at least fifty. We don't see much of them, except in the mornings when he goes off to work. She always stands at the door and waves him off, like he's never coming home again. The last house, No. 6, belongs to Grandma Lottie. Her real name's Charlotte Goodbody and she's really nice. When she gets to know you, she'll ask you to pop up the shops for her and then she'll give you some sweets or a few coppers for your trouble. It's sad about Grandma Lottie. Her husband and her son were both killed in the war, only two weeks apart as well. My Mum says she's really brave and it's a wonder she keeps smiling everyday and hasn't stuck her head in the gas oven."

Gary was like a walking, talking version of 'Who's Who' and Ellie smiled widely at him as he described each family in the Mews, marvelling at his knowledge and trying desperately to remember who lived where, as she knew her Nan would want to hear all the gossip about everyone.

Cocking her head to one side, Ellie listened as she heard her name called.

"That's my Mum. I'll have to go in for my tea now, bye."

"Bye Ellie, see you tomorrow. Come round and call for me and I'll show you and your brother and sister around, if you want. I'm usually up by eight and we've got all day to go exploring as it's Sunday. OK?"

"Great! I'll tell Fay and Billy. They'll be grateful to have someone to show us the ropes. We haven't had time to make any friends yet and none of us knows where to go. See you in the morning, bye." With that, the small girl ran along the path and disappeared from view through her own garden gate.

Gary stayed swinging to and fro for several more minutes, before jumping down and going indoors in search of his tea, thinking she seemed alright and wondering if her sister and brother would be nice too. Well, he'd meet them all tomorrow and he had a lot to think about, planning the day, making sure he showed them everything on his patch.

CHAPTER 4

"You can think again, my girl. There'll be no gallivanting off around the streets, up to God knows what. Besides, it's church first thing tomorrow and well you know it. Just because we've moved, it doesn't mean we don't go to church any more. What would Father O'Connell say if we didn't show up tomorrow? This family has always worshipped at the Oratory and nothing's about to change. And don't think you can go crying to your Mum and Dad, they'll back me in this. And the same goes for Fay and Billy. The four of us will be going to the nine o'clock service as usual."

Ellie stood before her Nan, head bowed, fighting back the tears of disappointment. Why did her Nan always insist on the family attending Mass every Sunday? And why didn't her Mum or Dad go with them. Perhaps it was because they were grown up and could choose what to do with their free time on Sundays. Well, when she was older, her children wouldn't be made to go to church. They wouldn't have to traipse the half mile in all weathers, then sit in a cold draughty building on a hard pew. She wouldn't mind but the whole service was spoken in Latin. Most of the time, the people who attended Mass at the Oratory recited the words parrot fashion and many times Ellie had looked around her only to find that a large number of the elderly were dozing quietly, heads nodding, an occasional snore breaking forth.

"But Nan, we could still go with Gary after Mass, couldn't we? We won't get up to anything, honest we won't. He's only going to show us around, just so's we know where we are. Please, Nan?"

"Well, you'll have to ask your Mum. If I was your mother I wouldn't let you go wandering all over without an adult, but no doubt your Mum'll say it's alright. Just remember; no matter what else you do tomorrow, Church comes first." Sal admonished her youngest grandchild.

Turning about, Ellie scampered from the room, racing down the stairs and entered the kitchen breathlessly, crying:

"Mum, Mum, is it alright if me and Fay and Billy go exploring with Gary O'Shea from No. 2 tomorrow? Nan says we've got to go to church first and then after that it's up to you. Can we, Mum?"

"Hold on a minute! You're always in a hurry. Now, what's all this about a Gary O'Shea? How old is he and does his mother know about all this?" Cathy turned from the stove where she was preparing the evening meal and watched as Ellie pulled out a chair and sat down, legs swinging, her elbows resting on the table.

"He's twelve, Mum. And he's allowed to go out on his own, his Mum doesn't mind. He knows where to go and he's asked us to go with him. Go on, Mum, we'll be ever so good and we'll come back when you tell us to. Can we go, please Mum?"

"Oh, alright, but only for the afternoon. You tell this Gary to come round here at half past one, after we've had dinner. And you've got to be back before five, understand? No later." It might be nice, Cathy thought, to have some time alone with Jack on a Sunday afternoon. Sal always had a kip after dinner, so they could curl up together and listen to the wireless without any interruptions.

"Thanks, Mum. Can I go round and tell him now?"

"Yes, yes. But be quick, tea's nearly ready and your father will be home any minute." No sooner were the words out of Cathy's mouth, then the small girl jumped down and ran out of the back door and down the garden path, heading for the O'Shea's gate.

As Ellie left the house, so Jack entered.

"Hello? Anyone home?" The front door slammed shut and the soft clump of Jack's boots could be heard as he made his way down the hall and into the kitchen.

Even though Jack rose at 5.00am every weekday morning and did not return home until 6.00pm, he always managed to be cheerful. His energy was apparently endless and whereas most men would be tired and irritable after a twelve hour shift, Jack appeared fresh and alert with no trace of weariness. He had worked with the same company, The London Water Authority, since leaving school at fourteen, gradually climbing up from the position of Boiler Boy to Maintenance Supervisor. This was as far as he could expect to go with the limited education he possessed. Without a college degree he could not take the next step into the world of engineering and for the same reasons he would never be allowed to enter into 'Management'. However, this did not cause him any great anxiety as he considered himself fortunate to hold the position he had. Jack was not ambitious for himself, only for his children. Unlike other men of his age, he foresaw a future in which everyone would have equal opportunities; a time when women would hold positions of authority and would work side by side with men. Adamant in this belief, Jack held a deep respect for education, knowing that this was the key to his children's futures. As for himself, he was more than content with his lot, happy to have a secure job which provided food on the table and a roof over his family's heads.

"There you are. Everything alright? What's for tea?" His arms about Cathy's waist, he lent forward and kissed her cheek.

"Now, what's more interesting? Me or your stomach? It seems to me, that it was a lucky coincidence that I was standing here, otherwise I reckon you'd have gone straight to the stove and ignored me." Her head resting against his, Cathy smiled at the thought.

"Since when have I come home and not kissed my wife first? You know what they say, Cathy: 'The way to a man's heart, is through his stomach' and you've certainly got that off to a fine art. There's not a better cook than you in all of London." Jack nuzzled his wife's neck, his arms tightening around her slim frame.

"Jack Treist! You know what you've got off to a fine art, don't you? How to get round me, that's what! I swear there's Irish in you, because somewhere along the line, one of your lot must have kissed that Blarney Stone. Go and get washed, this'll be on the table in five minutes and then you'll be moaning that it's cold."

Suddenly the back door was flung open and Billy and Ellie tumbled into the kitchen.

"Look at the state of you two! If I didn't know better, I'd think you were from one of those Jamaican families. Whatever have you both been up to? Black as coal, you are. Get yourselves up them stairs and get washed. Quick, now! Up you go!"

"It wasn't me, Dad. Billy pushed me from behind and I fell into the coal pile at the bottom of the garden." Pointing her finger, Ellie stood glaring accusingly at her brother.

"I was only playing! And look at me! As she fell, she grabbed me and I went in after her. It was an accident, Dad, honest!" Grinning from ear to ear, the boy stood before his father, palms held upwards, in a gesture of innocence.

"I don't care who did what. You should know better, Billy, frightening girls. And Ellie, you should know that two wrongs don't make a right. Your mother's going to have a hell of a job getting those clothes clean. Now, scoot, before I clip your ears." Jack was having some difficulty in repressing his laughter. His children were a great joy to him and he could always see the funny side of their antics.

As the two soot covered children left the room, giggling and pushing one another, Cathy turned to her husband, admonishing:

"Don't encourage them, Jack. Honest to God, I've got my hands full enough without you laughing with them whenever they get up to something. You'll laugh on the other side of your face when I have to come to you for new clothes for all of them. And Ellie shouldn't act like that. She's a proper tomboy and now she's only gone and made a friend of that boy at No. 2. God knows why she can't have girls as friends. We never had that trouble with Fay. She always liked to play with her dolls and wear pretty dresses. You wouldn't catch her coming in looking like that."

"And what's she like now, eh? Fay hardly has anything to do with us. She's always round at someone else's house and sometimes I think she feels she's too good for us. We'll have to keep an eye on that one, she's turning into a right little snob with all her airs and graces. Anyone would think she was doing us a favour just living here!" Turning from his wife, Jack stomped out of the room and up the stairs.

Cathy sighed. The only things that she and Jack disagreed over were the children and his mother. She knew that Jack was right where Fay was concerned, but what could she do? Her eldest child was coming into that 'funny age'; neither child nor woman. You didn't know where you were with her from one minute to the next. Still, once she started her periods, Fay would settle down and become human again. Cathy could still remember her own adolescent years and how even everyday situations could be fraught with imaginary traumas. No matter what Fay said, Cathy would make sure that she accompanied her brother and sister tomorrow and perhaps that would appease Jack. He liked to see his children doing things together. Being an only child, Jack had never had the opportunity to share a close brother/sister relationship and he imagined that this would have been a wonderful experience.

On the other hand, Cathy came from a family of four and she knew that it was more likely that one would not even like one's brothers or sisters, at least not at a young age. More often than not, a friendship would evolve in later years, as had happened between her sister, Eleanor, and herself. All Cathy could remember of her childhood were the constant squabbles between the four children and the never ending fight for survival. There never seemed to be enough money to go round, thus the children were always hungry. Food and where the next meal was coming from, were priorities, along with keeping warm and having a bed to sleep in at nights. Therefore, Cathy had become a master with household economy. She could make a little food go a very long way and still taste delicious and would become incensed if all plates were not cleared after each meal. "Waste not, want not," was a rule she insisted her family follow and each family member would not have dared to deviate from it. The only time anyone was allowed to leave the table without eating every scrap from their plates, was in dire circumstances. Such as extreme illness or death.

Cathy finished preparing the meal, and called to her wayward daughter:

"Fay! Come and lay the table, tea's ready."

Dragging her feet, Fay slouched into the kitchen.

"Why do I always have to do it? Why can't Ellie or Billy do it? Anyone would think I was the servant around here."

"Look, young lady, Ellie and Billy are upstairs scraping off a life time's worth of dirt and besides, I asked you to do it, so just get on with it. And before the others come down, I want a quiet word with you. Tomorrow, I want you to go along with your brother and sister and that Gary O'Shea for a bit of a walk round. I don't want any arguments. Your Dad's worried that you don't spend enough time with your family and I think it would be a golden opportunity for you to get reacquainted with them, OK?" Cathy waited for the outburst that would surely follow.

"Oh, Mum! You can't expect me to go traipsing round the streets with a bunch of kids. What if any of my friends see me? I'd never live it down! Anyway, they'll only want to play silly games and act stupid. It's bad enough that Nan still drags me off to Church every Sunday, without having to spend the rest of the day with that lot. Besides, I've got homework to do and I promised Caroline Meadows that I'd go to her house in the afternoon, so's we could do it together." Fay was close to tears at this new injustice her mother was putting on her.

"I don't think you heard me, Fay. I said no arguments, didn't I? As for the 'bunch of kids' you're talking about, two of them are your brother and sister and the other is the same age as you. You can do your homework tonight and straight after tea, you can pop round to Caroline's house and make your excuses. I mean it, Fay. No but's, just for once you'll do as you're told. Do I make myself clear?"

Cathy brooked no argument, but knew that Fay would sulk for the remainder of that day, all of tomorrow and probably well into the following week. But this time, Cathy would not back down. If she did not hold a tighter rein over the girl, then she knew, in time, there would be worse to come.

Tea was a quiet meal that night. Each member was deep in their own thoughts. Sal did not agree with her grandchildren walking the streets; Jack hated to fall out with his wife and liked everything to run smoothly in his family; Cathy also disliked conflict of any kind, especially with Jack, and thought longingly of their big double bed where she would make up with him later; Fay believed the whole world was against her and dreamed of escape and Billy and Ellie looked forward with anticipation to the next day's exploration adventure.

Meanwhile, in the centre of the Mews, the Mermaid sat on, smiling benignly on her kingdom.

CHAPTER 5

Angela Ridley watched as the four left the Mews that clear, sunny Sunday afternoon. She peeped from behind the curtain of the front room, not wanting them to see her and envied their friendship and easy banter that could be heard, even from behind closed doors.

"First of all I'll show you the way to the embankment, we're only just over the water from Battersea Park. There's a big fair there all summer and its got a tree walk."

"What's a tree walk?" Ellie enquired.

"Well, it's like walking from tree to tree, except above ground, high up in the branches. You climb up a kind of ladder at one end and then there's a sort of scaffolding between each tree. You know, planks of wood, and you can walk along holding onto ropes on each side. In each tree there's a platform where you can stop and look out and see for miles. It's great! I go there whenever I can, when the weather's OK." Answered Gary.

"Cor, that sounds really good! Come on Fay, hurry up. We haven't got long. We could play Tarzan and the Apes and pretend we're in the jungle." Already Billy's imagination was in top gear as he crouched over, swinging his arms low to the ground, making loud monkey noises.

Fay trudged behind. She really did not want to be with them and was still seething after her Dad had also insisted that it would be a good idea for her to accompany Billy, Ellie and Gary today. No amount of sulking had changed her parents minds but she had formed a plan. As soon as the three others were occupied with one of their childish games, Fay would slip away. There were far more interesting things to do this afternoon, such as hanging around the cafe in Brompton Road, watching the boys as they arrived on their motor-bikes. This was a pastime that Fay and her friend, Caroline, indulged in whenever they could slip away from the confines of their homes. In several weeks, Fay would turn thirteen and considered that she had far outgrown the games of her younger counterparts. "I'm nearly a woman and all the boys say I look much older than I am. Why should I have to trail around with these kids?" She muttered to herself as she left the square.

Ellie was in her element. This was the first time she had been allowed to venture out with Billy and Fay without the watchful eyes of her parents upon her. And there was the additional pleasure of being with Gary. Already the seven year old had formed a crush on the gangly youth and considered him to be nearly as wonderful as her Dad. In Ellie's mind, no-one was better than her father. She loved the other members of her family, but adoration was nearer to the feelings she had for Jack. The two had been close from the start. It was always to Jack that Ellie would confide and he would listen to her attentively, no matter how small her problems. In the evenings, after she was washed and ready for bed, she loved to curl up in her father's lap and listen to the story of her birth. Jack would recount how she had arrived in the middle of the night, taking everyone by surprise. He would describe how beautiful she had been when he had first set eyes on her and how pretty she was now and would be in the future, calling her "the apple of my eye and the light of my life". For the first time in her short life, Ellie had met someone who could challenge her feelings for her father. Gary had quickly become Ellie's hero.

More than content, she walked now between the two boys, not concerned that they chatted together, over her head, seemingly ignoring her. Ellie was just happy to be in Gary's company.

Not one of the foursome were aware of the watching eyes at No. 1.

Seb's daughter let the curtain fall back and stepped back from the window. Sighing, she turned and left the room.

Once inside her own bedroom, she shut the door and lay down on the bed, face down. She was alone in the house. Her father was, no doubt, wending his drunken way back from 'The Worlds End' and his usual Sunday afternoon 'session' and her mother would be washing the last of the glasses at the British Legion in Fulham.

If only she could make friends as easily as the new children at No. 4. They hadn't been here five minutes, and already they were out and about with Gary Carmichael. Whereas, she had lived here for over four years. In fact, she could not remember living anywhere else, except that her mother had told her that they had resided, for a short time, in Putney.

Rolling over on her side, Angela surveyed the room. Being sparsely furnished, her bedroom only accommodated a small chest of drawers, an old single, dark stained wardrobe with the door hanging by one hinge and the old double bed she now lay on. All her worldly goods were second hand; either passed on to her from a kindly neighbour or retrieved, under the cover of darkness, from the rubbish tip.

Staring up at the ceiling, Angela watched as a spider slowly made its way across the cracked and dirty surface. "I'll bet it's going somewhere, off to meet other spiders, not like me." She thought, "Everyone's got someone, except me. I'm always on my own. No one wants to play at my house, because of my Dad. And they don't ask me to go around with them because of him as well."

These thoughts were true, in part, but Angela did not help herself. She had become aloof and distant due to the lifestyle which she led. Deep down, the child was ashamed of her parents. Her father because of his violent and drunken behaviour and her mother because she allowed it to continue. Angela was not immune to the whisperings around the Mews. Although fiercely protective of her mother, another part of her guiltily despised Vera's cowed attitude. How could anyone allow another person to treat them in that manner? And how long would it be before she herself became subject to his abuse? Being aware that her mother would stand between them if the need arose, did not abate Angela's fears. When all was said and done, Vera did not handle the situation for herself, so how could she protect her daughter from becoming his next victim? Just lately, Seb had cast his eyes in a less than fatherly fashion, towards his daughter and Angela was more than aware of his lustful glances in her direction. The girl had taken to wearing loose and baggy clothing, hunching her shoulders forward in an effort to conceal her growing body and she no longer came downstairs in her nightwear to kiss her mother goodnight, if he was about. The only times she felt relatively safe, was on the evenings Seb was out and she and her mother would sit quietly by the fire, talking softly together or listening to the radio.

And too many times, in her short lifetime, she had buried her head beneath the bedclothes and fearfully listened as Seb ranted and raved, heard her mothers pleading responses and waited with batted breath, for her door to crash open. Being an intelligent girl, she was under no illusions that, in the not too distant future, her turn would arrive. Seb would not be content for much longer with taking out his frustrations on Vera. After all, he had been beating the same person for so long now, that his victim was predictable. Angela would be a new challenge. He would be able to play his sadistic games with renewed vigour. For he had determined that Angela would be hard to break. She would not scream for mercy or beg his forgiveness, not having inherited Vera's timid nature. The game would last for so much longer and be so much more enjoyable and the pity of it all was; the child was acutely attuned to her father's thoughts on the matter. But she was too young and inexperienced to cope with the situation and found herself treading in extremely potential dangerous waters.

"Please God, if I can just get through school, then I'll be old enough to get out of his clutches and take Mum with me. We'll go somewhere where he'll never find us and then we can be safe and happy." This was her last silent prayer every night, as she fell into a troubled sleep and her first thought of every new day.

"Oh well, no point in laying here day dreaming, if I don't get the tea on, it'll be something else for him to have a go about." Rising from the bed, she left her room and descended the stairs, just as her mother entered the front door.

"Hello, luv. What you been up to? Your father in yet?"

"No, not yet, Mum. I was just going to start tea."

The two entered the kitchen, chattering quietly together, not once mentioning the expected state that Seb would arrive in. They never discussed it. And if on rare occasions, Angela were to begin to bring up the subject, Vera always managed to change the conversation, skirting round the true issues.

The day would come when neither one would be able to avoid this long overdue discussion, but, for now, their lives followed the pattern they had made; fooling no one, not even themselves.

CHAPTER 6

All the children between the ages of seven and eleven of Mermaid Mews attended the Brompton Oratory School. This was a four storey building situated in the heart of Chelsea, some twenty minutes walk away. It was run by the Catholic church and directly attached to the Oratory Church and all the teachers were nuns. With the exception of the Headmaster. Mr. Pierrana was a devout Catholic and believed that all children should be seen, but not heard. He ruled the school with an iron hand and would allow no 'nonsense' from either pupil or teacher. Being a strict follower of corporal punishment, Mr. Pierrana was always in possession of a small, bamboo stick which he kept concealed up his left sleeve. Should any child misbehave in his presence, he would whip out the stick and smartly strike the offending child on his or her legs. The 'whoosh' sound as the stick was descending would strike terror in each wayward child's heart. Many a youngster's nightmares contained that particular sound.

The Oratory school was peculiar to any other school in London for the older children's playground was on the roof. It was surrounded by a six foot high wire mesh fence and through the diligent supervision of the staff, there had never been a recorded accident due to its situation. Many a child had tried to scale the wire fence, but to date, no one had succeeded in reaching the top. Oratory pupils were proud of their rooftop playground and would boast to others of 'lesser' schools.

Secondary school for the older children was St. Edmunds, Hammersmith. This was also an old established school, serving the Catholics of the surrounding area. Because of the large area this school accommodated, it was a much bigger school than the Oratory and was not solely staffed by the brides of Christ. After attending the Oratory, each child felt that St. Edmunds was far more lenient and looked forward to attending 'big school' and being able to enjoy the relaxed manner of discipline.

So it was, that on the Treist childrens' first Monday of residency in Mermaid Mews, there were two groups leaving the square.

The first group was rowdy and boisterous, pushing each other with shrieks and giggles and was in direct contrast to the second group.

Gary and Frankie took the lead, sauntering up the road bearing an air of soon-to-be adulthood, while Fay followed behind, head down, not willing to be associated with any of them. She was still smarting from the telling-off she had received yesterday from her parents. It had not occurred to her that her story of becoming separated from the group, would not be believed and now she was grounded. Both Jack and Cathy had been extremely angry with her, not so much because of her misdemeanour, but because she persisted in lying to them. Therefore, Fay was not to be allowed out anywhere for the next two weeks and she would be expected to perform extra duties around the house during this period.

At the last minute, before either group left the Mews, the door of No. 1 opened and Angela stepped out. Closing the door slowly behind her, she turned and quietly brought up the rear. Glancing over her shoulder, Fay saw the girl. They were of the same age, although even to the most discerning eye, there appeared to be years between them. Angela was short, slim and blonde dressed in her normal baggy attire. Whereas, Fay was dark haired and tall. Her womanly curves were already in evidence and her clothes spoke of the person within. The uniform of St. Edmunds was navy blue and white and was strictly adhered to. But Fay was rebellious by nature. A bright red scarf was tied into her hair and another, this one canary yellow, hung from her school satchel. Hanging from her ears were forbidden, large gold hoops and on every finger, sparkled the cheap jewellery of which she was so fond. Notes were continually sent to the Treists' household, telling of Fay's constant refusal to conform and Cathy was forever at loggerheads with the girl over this.

Neither girl had anything in common. Angela would naturally shy away from so flamboyant a creature and Fay would have neither the patience nor the inclination to overcome the barriers Angela had erected around herself. Turning away, Fay flounced on, leaving the other girl to trail behind.

Eyes downcast, Angela thought, "I wish I had the courage to wear clothes like her. She looks so sure of herself, all bright and carefree, not drab and old fashioned like me. I'll bet she's got loads of friends as well. All the boy's will like her. I reckon I could drop down dead, and no one would even notice. I wish I was like the Mermaid. Everyone thinks she looks beautiful, even if she does look a bit tatty these days, not that she cares. She just sits there, combing her hair all day long, not a care in the world. Lucky thing!"

Her eyes slid sideways as she passed the statuette. Unbeknown to even her mother, Angela and the Mermaid conducted a strange relationship. When things became too much for her, Angela would sneak out late at night and sit at the base of the fountain and recount all her troubles to the silent figure. Although the girl never received any answers to her problems, she felt a certain rapport with the marble fish-woman and this acted as a catalyst for the troubled girl.

*

Once the men had left for work and the children were safely on their way to school, the women folk of the Mews set about their daily chores, depending on what day it was. Mondays were clothes-wash days, Tuesdays for ironing, Wednesdays were for cleaning windows and front steps, if the weather allowed. Thursdays for general house cleaning and Fridays were baking days. In between their tasks, the women would stand at their front doors, hair in rollers, smoking and passing the time of day with each other. Now and again several women would congregate in a delegated house for a cup of tea. Normally, it would be Lottie Goodbody who would instigate this.

"Ruby? What time are you cleaning at the Dentists today?" She shouted across the square.

"Not until lunchtime, Lottie." Came the reply.

"Well, get yourself on over here and have a cuppa with me. What's Eileen up to? And what about that new woman at No. 4? Give them a knock and see if they want to come over as well. Suppose there's no point in asking Vera, but I'll knock for Mrs. Verwood and see what she's up to."

"Righto, Lottie. Be over in a minute, get that kettle on." Ruby strode across the path separating her house from the Carmichael's and called through the open door. "Yohoo! Eileen? Lottie's summoned us for a cuppa tea. Are you coming?"

"Be with you in a minute, Ruby. Save us a chocolate biscuit!"

Smiling, Ruby continued on her errand. Lottie always put out a plate of biscuits with the tea, but there was only two, perhaps three, of these that were chocolate. Both Eileen and Ruby had sweet tooth's and would pretend to fight over them.

The door to No. 4 was closed. Ruby knocked lightly and waited. Footsteps could be heard coming down the hall and then the door was opened wide and Cathy stood smiling at her neighbour.

"Hello. I'm Ruby O'Shea, Gary's mum. We've all been invited over to No. 6, Lottie Goodbody's house for a cuppa and we was wondering if you'd like to join us?"

"That's kind of you. I'll just take off this apron, hang on a minute." Cathy turned, leaving the door open and returned to the kitchen.

"Where are you off to now? Leaving me on my own again. I don't know anyone around here and now you're going off and leaving me on my jacksy." The grumbling sound of Sal's voice could be distinctly heard at the front door.

"Shush, Mother! You'll be heard. I won't be long, I'm just popping over the way to have a chat with some of the women. I can't take you with me, as they didn't say I could bring another person along. You'll be alright for half an hour. Here, have a read of the paper." Embarrassed that her mother-in-law might be overheard, Cathy grabbed the newspaper and put it into Sal's hands.

"Excuse me? Cathy? Lottie won't mind if your mother wants to come along. Bring her with you." Ruby had heard the exchange of words and thought to pacify the old girl.

Cathy put her head around the doorway, saying, "Oh, thanks, Ruby. Sal doesn't like being on her own." Turning back she continued, "Come on then, Mother. Get yourself up out of that chair. You're invited now."

The two women came down the passageway, Cathy leading, and joined Ruby at the front door.

"It's really neighbourly of you to include us like this. It'll be nice to meet everyone." Holding out her hand, Cathy said, "My name's Cathy, although it seems you already know that and this is my mother-in-law, Sal. We're very pleased to meet you." Smiling, Ruby and Cathy shook hands, both liking the look of the other.

"We standing here all day? Or are we going across? Move yourself, Cathy, I can't stand here for long, my old legs won't take it." Obviously piqued at being left out of the limelight, the old woman pushed herself forward and Cathy with her.

"Alright, Mother, keep your hair on." Cathy stepped to one side and allowed Jack's mother to go on ahead, then in an aside, she whispered to Ruby, "Take no notice of her, she's just put out because she's not queen bee around here. Mind you, you'd all better watch yourselves, because it won't be long before she's got her feet firmly under the table and then she'll try to run things, no matter what anyone says!"

Laughing softly, Ruby answered, "Well, I'd like to see her try! Lottie rules us all and has done ever since anyone can remember. Sal will have a job taking over here, I can tell you. Still, it might be fun to watch them fight over it, eh?"

"What are you two whispering about? Just because I'm old, doesn't mean I'm stupid. Which house is it? Here you, Ruby, lead the way and hurry up about it." Motioning with her hand, Sal waved Ruby to the front and the three crossed the square and entered Lottie's house.

"Hello, Lottie? It's only me. I've brought the two new ladies over, from No. 4. Has that kettle boiled yet? My mouth feels like the bottom of a budgies cage, I'm bleedin' parched!" Going straight to the kitchen, with Cathy and Sal close on her heels, Ruby sat down at the table and looked across at the old woman standing at the sink.

Charlotte Goodbody was a small, bird like woman. Her hair was completely white and gathered in a bun at the nape of her neck. She still favoured the fashion of the Victorian era. A white linen blouse, with high collar and a cameo brooch in the centre, was covered by a black lace shawl. To complete the ensemble, her black skirt swept the floor as she moved from sink to table, setting out cups and saucers and the predictable plate of sweet biscuits, two chocolate ones on top.

"Where's Eileen? Is she coming?" Not waiting for an answer, Lottie continued, "I knocked at Mrs. Verwood's but she said she couldn't make it today. Said something about cooking her husband's dinner. He doesn't come home until 5.30pm, so God knows why she's cooking now. She'll have to plate it and keep it hot all afternoon. That'll be nice, all dried up and looking like what the cat dragged in! Thinks she's a cut above, that one does. Doesn't like to mix with the rest of us, that's her trouble. Something in the oven? Pull the other one, it's got bells on, that's what I think."

Just then, a plump redhead entered the room. Eyes twinkling, and a ready smile on her full lips, she parked herself next to Ruby, saying, "What are you on about, Lottie? You couldn't be talking about our good neighbour, Mrs. Verwood, could you? And her such a nice woman and all! Shame on you, Lottie! What a way to carry on in front of our new neighbours!" Turning to Cathy and Sal who were both now sat at the other side of the kitchen table, she laughed and said, "How do you do? My name's Eileen. I haven't had a chance to introduce myself, but I live next door to you, at No. 3. I expect you've heard us, we make enough racket. Still, if it bothers you, just bang on the wall and yell at us to shut up, we'll soon get the message!"

Returning her smile, Cathy shook her head, "Don't worry about it. We won't hear you over the row that's coming from our place and it'll be no good you knocking on our wall, because we won't be able to hear that either!"

"Well, I hope you two are going to have five minutes silence while you're here. Some of us others mights have a thing or two to say as well. Here, have a biscuit, that should shut you up for a few minutes, girl." Lottie pushed the plate at Eileen, who was now laughing openly.

"Now, how do you like your tea, Mrs. Treist, or can I call you Sal?"

"Oh as it comes, Mrs. Goodbody and please do call me Sal as I hope I can call you Lottie?" Sal was using her 'posh' voice and was smiling winningly at the older woman. There was not more than two years between them, but Sal assumed she could fool people into thinking she was younger than her years, vainly believing she had held her age well. In fact, Sal looked all of sixty seven and some might think she was older.

The morning passed quickly and proved invaluable to Cathy and Sal. The other three women, recalled all the gossip on each of the absent neighbours and, in kinder tones, told of their own histories. When the Treist women left Lottie's house that day, they already felt as if they had lived in Mermaid Mews for years, instead of just days and had invited Lottie, Ruby and Eileen to their house on Thursday morning for a return visit.

As time passed, this became a ritual, with the five women meeting twice a week in one or the other's house to catch up on all the latest gossip. They indulged in mainly harmless chit-chat, passing on recipes and discussing world events as well as affairs of the heart and home. The group soon became known as the 'Grapevine' and the men could often be heard to ask, "What's new on the Grapevine, these days? Who's up to what and with who?"

CHAPTER 7

Time passed. The seasons came and went in the normal fashion and life continued in Mermaid Mews.

The year was 1959 and the fountain was adrift in a sea of leaves, swirling round its base, then lifting with the breeze and laying plastered, momentarily, on the figure of the Mermaid, before the wind brushed them aside and they sailed forth, off in search for other surfaces to cling to. it was late Autumn and Christmas would soon be upon the Mews and its occupants.

The Treists were no longer considered as new residents and had made a place for themselves within the small community.

Lottie and Sal had come to an unspoken, amicable agreement. Neither one would be sole overseer of the square; they ruled together, sharing the responsibility of keeping everyone 'on the right tracks'. Any unsettled arguments were brought to the two, a solution would be arrived at over cups of tea and all parties concerned would leave, firmly convinced that a fair hearing had taken place.

So it was that on a fine November morning, the 'Grapevine' were assembled, in No. 4, debating on an issue which was both baffling and worrying.

"You can't help someone like her. She doesn't want us to interfere and anyway, how are we going to go about it? Short of dragging her, kicking and screaming over here, what else can we do?"

"Oh, Ruby. It's not like that, or at least I can't believe it is. Someone's got to step in and put a stop to it all. I mean, it's obvious. The poor woman can't handle it herself and if we don't help her soon, it'll be too late. I live three doors away and I could still hear him last night. He was knocking seven bells of shit out of her, and I could hear Angela screaming at him to stop. To be honest, I don't know which was worse; the bloody screaming and yelling or that awful quiet afterwards. One of these nights he's going to finish Vera off, good and proper, you mark my words!"

"Well, what do you suggest then, Cathy? The coppers aren't interested, not until he actually kills her, at any rate. I can understand how both you and Ruby feel about it, because there's two sides to every coin. Half of me thinks she's stupid to let him carry on slowly killing her and the other half wants to help her somehow. But the person I really feel sorry for, is the daughter. It's not her fault that neither one of her parents knows how to behave. Like you, Cathy, I could hear everything last night and I had to keep Frank from going over there and giving that sod a taste of his own medicine. Anyway, after it had all died down, I couldn't get back to sleep, so I came downstairs and put the kettle on. I was sort of half asleep and daydreaming out of the window, when I saw something sort of flit across the square and fall down by the fountain. Well, I can tell you, it nearly gave me a heart attack, thought I'd seen a ghost or something! To cut a long story short, after I'd caught my breath and my heart had started beating properly again, I had another look. It was that Angela! She was lying all curled round the bottom of the fountain, her arms sort of cuddling it and I could see her shoulders moving up and down, like she was having a real cry. Then she lifted her head and I could see her lips moving, couldn't actually hear anything because it was blowing a gale last night, but honest, it looked like she was talking to the Mermaid! I watched her for a while, and was just about to go out and bring her indoors with me, when she seemed to calm down. She sat up and wiped her face on her sleeve, stood up and went back to her own house. Something should be done about her. She only had a thin nightie on and she was out there for at least half an hour, she'll catch her death of cold if she carries on like that. One of these mornings, one of us is going to get up and find her draped around that fountain, all cold and stiff and then I'll never forgive myself for not doing something."

Lottie and Sal stared, eyes round with astonishment as Eileen had recounted the event. A heavy silence fell on the group and it was Sal who finally broke it, saying,

"Right. That's it. We can't go on ignoring it any more, we've got to act now. I agree with Ruby and if Vera was the only one involved, I'd say 'let her get on with it, silly cow', but it's not just her. That young girl can't help herself and now it's up to us to put things right."

Lottie looked at Sal, nodding her head in agreement. Then rising, she placed both hands, palms down on the table and addressed everyone present.

"Sal's right. We've sat back and watched it all for too long and now we've got to take the matter in hand. What I suggest is: We get the men to deal with him. Jack and Frank are going to have to have a little 'talk' with the slimy, little bastard. Put the frighteners on him, rough him up a bit if necessary. After all, he only hits women and he'd be too much of a coward to stand up to a proper man."

"That's no problem. Eileen's already said she's had to hold Frank back and I know my Jack would love to have a go. The difficulty is, when and where? We'll have to plan this really carefully, otherwise our men will be had up for G.B.H., then where will we be?"

"Everyone will have to play their part." Ruby took over. "Us women will have to stand sentry. One of us can wait out in the road until he's coming, then run back and warn the others. Best to do it on a Saturday night, because there's always lots of drunks coming up the Brompton Road after the pubs have closed and no one will take any notice if he makes a racket. If Frank and Jack grab him under the archway, it'll be dark there and they won't be seen from either the square or the road. We can keep a watch out to see if anyone's coming and someone will have to watch the houses here, to make sure none of the kids or Vera comes out to see what the commotion's all about. It'd be just like that Vera to try and help him if she saw he was having a good hiding and that's the last thing we need."

The women were all in agreement. This was the only solution to the problem and a certain amount of pleasure would be derived from bringing Seb to justice. Albeit, their own brand of justice. Nevertheless, the plan would be put into operation that coming Saturday, two days hence.

*

"Quick! He's coming! I could see him swaying up the road, singing to himself. Well, he won't be singing for much longer, will he boys?" Ruby stood before the two men, her voice slightly breathless from her short sprint back into the Mews.

Just then, Cathy came into view as she left the square and crept in under the archway.

"What's happening? Is he coming? Eileen, Sal and Lottie sent me to find out what's going on."

"Get yourself out of here, Cathy. He's on his way and I don't want you hanging around watching. It's not going to be a pretty sight and I don't want you accidentally hurt. Tell the others to keep a look out. Don't let anyone from inside the Mews come out here. We'll let you know when it's all over." Jack took Cathy's arm and steered her back into the square and out of harms way.

"Ruby, go back into the street. Go back down the road and hide in a shop doorway until he's turned into here. Then keep watch for any Bobbies and sing out if anyone comes by." His voice deep with an authority that was new to him, Frank pointed down the street in the opposite direction from which Seb was coming.

Everyone was in place and an eerie silence prevailed.

"You made me love you. I didn't wanna do it, I didn't wanna do it. You made me love you. And all the time you knew it, I guess you always knew it. Gimme, gimme, gimme, gimme what I'd die for, you know you've got the kind of kisses that I'd die for..."

Seb's voice was cut off as two pairs of hands reached around the opening to the Mews and pulled him roughly in and under the darkened archway.

"Hey, what's going on? Who's that? Let me go! Get off of me!"

"We just want a word with you Seb Ridley. Now just you stop hollering and listen very carefully to what we've got to say."

Seb could not identify the person who spoke quietly into his ear. It was too dark and the voice echoed slightly within the confines of the archway. His head whipped round as another voice continued from behind him.

"We don't like people like you. You're a vicious little weasel, picking on women and children because you're not man enough to pick on someone your own size. Well, the time has come, Seb, for you to be taught a lesson or two. We're here to warn you to lay off your wife and stop frightening your daughter."

Still struggling, Seb tried to shrug off the hands which held him tight, straining to see the faces of his attackers.

"What's it to you? Who gave you the right to meddle in my affairs? It's none of your business. What goes on in my own house hasn't got anything to do with no one except me and mine. Just let go of me and leave off!"

"This is not a friendly warning, Seb. We've all had enough of you. We mean business and we mean to put a stop to your bullying." The soft voice whispered again, in front of the now quaking man.

Gathering up the last of his alcohol induced courage, Seb blustered,

"Oh, yeah? And just what are you going to do about it?"

Before the words had barely left his mouth, Seb felt all his breath leave his body as a fist slammed into his stomach. Clutching his middle and moaning softly, Seb fell to his knees. He found he was no longer supported by the rough hands which had been clasped around his body and, head almost touching the ground before him, he gasped,

"You bloody bastards! You fucking sods. Takes two of you, does it? You don't think this'll bleeding stop me, do you? I've lived through worse than this in the sodding war, so don't think you can bloody well get the better of me, with one measly punch!"

"Well then, let's see if this'll do the trick then, shall we?"

Coming from behind, a hand reached down and grabbing a fistful of hair, whipped Seb's head up. As the fallen man's eyes came into focus, a bright red light exploded within them, followed by a pain so excruciating that he felt his insides turn to liquid and his gorge rise.

Seb had been hit squarely in the centre of his face and with such force that his nose was immediately broken and his front teeth loosened to such a degree, that he now spat out several of them, along with most of that evenings consumption of beer.

Groaning loudly now, he rolled over onto his side and listened as two pairs of heavy footsteps could be heard making their way out from beneath the cover of the archway. Seconds later, a lighter pair approached from behind him, faltered by his side, then continued on into the Mews.

As Seb slipped into unconsciousness, he vaguely heard whispered voices coming from beyond, in the square, then darkness overtook him and silence was restored, once more, to Mermaid Mews.

CHAPTER 8

During the lead up to Christmas, the incident with Seb Ridley was all but dismissed. As far as the occupants of Mermaid Mews were concerned, the matter had been dealt with. It was not discussed and Seb, not wishing to lose face within his own family, had informed Vera that he had been accosted by persons unknown and for no particular reason other then hooliganism. He stubbornly refused Vera's administrations and would not entertain her insistent pleas that he report the attack to the police. In the weeks to follow, Seb's physical wounds healed, but mentally he harboured a need for revenge. Retaliation was foremost in his mind. But for the moment, he would lie low and appear to be submissive. His day would come, he assured himself, when he would take retribution and then he would make them all pay for interfering in his life.

So followed a relatively peaceful period in the lives of Vera and Angela. They were no longer terrorised and all violence towards them had ceased.

Vera could not believe that her life had changed so drastically. She found herself balancing on a seesaw of emotions. One day she would be optimistic for the future, only to find that the next she would be agitated at the thought of how much longer would the present situation last. How long would it be before Seb returned to his normal self? Being unaccustomed to living with a Seb who was subdued and almost human, even to the extent of being polite to Angela and herself, Vera was in a quandary. She did not know how to behave with this reformed Seb. Her role as the victim of physical abuse had been hers for so long, that she experienced a great deal of difficulty in adjusting. And at the back of her mind, hovered the thought that this could be another of the games Seb liked to play. Perhaps he meant to lull the two of them into a false sense of security. Then, when they became pleasantly used to the new way of life, he would pounce. Their daily pattern would return to the violent way of before, but then it would all seem so much worse. It would all be so much more painful after this reprieve.

On a good day, Vera would berate herself for her suspicions and tell herself to enjoy it, for however long it lasted. In this optimistic mood, Vera imagined that her husband had undergone a major personality change when he had sustained the blow to his head.

Now, she could only hope that he would not revert back to his old habits.

In this somewhat confused state of mind, Vera began her preparations for the coming season of goodwill. She was determined that this Christmas would be special for the Ridley household. If Seb continued to be halfway pleasant, then she would be able to make this a time to be remembered for Angela. For the first time since she had married, Vera looked forward with enthusiasm and hope.

Deep in thought, Vera turned the corner to enter Mermaid Mews, on her return journey from her Christmas shopping. She was smiling to herself as she thought of the pretty red dress she had managed to purchase for Angela at the North End Road market. It had taken quite a bit of juggling of the household bills for Vera to save enough to acquire the dress. The thought of her daughter's surprised face on Christmas morning would be reward enough for all the scrimping and cutting down over the past weeks. So engrossed was she in the pleasant picture of her mind's eye, that the small, slim woman did not notice the other figure rounding the corner. The two collided and as Vera bent to retrieve her packages from the ground, a loud, friendly voice boomed at her from above.

"Bloody Nora! What you doing charging round the place? You're going like a bat out of hell! Who's after you then? Anyone nice?" Eileen laughing as usual, stooped down to help Vera.

"Oh! Sorry Eileen. I didn't see you coming. I was so busy thinking about Christmas and everything, I forgot where I was!"

Sitting back on her heels, Eileen took a good, long look at the normally timid woman. The change in Vera was dramatic. No longer was the hunted appearance apparent in her eyes, her hair was shiny and clean and, most important, there were no bruises visible on her smiling face.

"You're a sight for poor eyes, Vera. What happened? Lost a shilling and found a pound, did you? Honest, you look really happy. And not before time, either. Life treating you good, is it?"

Raising her head, Vera gave a small snort.

"You'd be hard pressed to find a halfpenny, round here, never mind a pound note! And don't look so surprised, I have been known to smile now and again. Though I suppose no-one round here has seen me. You're right, though, I do feel happy. I haven't felt like this in a long time and I have a feeling it might have something to do with you and your other friends." The smile had slid from Vera's face and something very close to gratitude had replaced it, as she continued.

"I know you lot haven't thought very well of me. And I know you all looked on me as some kind of idiot. There's no excuse. You just become accustomed to living the way you do and it's only when things change that you realise how awful things have been." Raising her hand to stop Eileen from protesting, Vera went bravely on.

"No, don't say anything, let me finish. I'm not as green as I'm cabbage looking and even though some don't admit to it, I know that I've had help from people who I didn't think cared. You won't regret doing what you did and if I never get to return the favour, I want you to know that you'll all have my undying gratitude for the part you all played. Well, enough said. Perhaps you'll pass on the message. Tell them, Vera says, 'Thanks'." With that, Vera gathered up her belongings and carried on her way.

Speechless, Eileen stayed stock still, on her knees at the entrance to the Mews. She watched as Vera strode jauntily to her front door and she swore afterwards, she could hear the little woman humming under her breath.

*

Needless to say, at the next Grapevine meeting, Eileen recounted the event, at great length and in a somewhat exaggerated manner.

"You should have seen her! I've never seen such a change in a person in all my life. Blossomed, that's what she's done, bloody blossomed! And her who wouldn't say boo to a goose, says "And you all have my undying gratitude" and I'm to tell all of you lot, thanks. You could have knocked me down with a feather! My mouth was still hanging open when Frank came home. Course, he thinks the worst, thinks I've lost my purse or broken something. And when I tells him, he says: "Oh, yeah. And I came in on the last banana boat, didn't I?" I had to keep on till he believed me and swear on the kids lives and all. Well, when you think about it, I don't suppose she's said as many words in all the time she's lived here, never mind all in one go."

Cathy, Sal, Ruby and Lottie had listened with rapt attention and as Eileen finished the tale, Lottie glanced around the table, saying:

"Good on her! I think it's really nice that she's coming out of herself. And now would be a good time to get her to join in with us.

We'll have to keep her spirits up and not let her slip back into her old ways. What about inviting her to our Christmas do. I hadn't suggested it before, because I didn't think she'd be interested. But in the light of what Eileen's told us, perhaps she'd enjoy it. There's no need for us to ask her to bring Seb. After all, Ruby, me and Sal'll be on our own, so she won't feel left out not having a man with her. Is everyone agreed?"

The chorus of assent was unanimous.

For several months, the women of the Mews had been squirrelling away items of food in readiness for a Boxing Day party. It was to be held at Lottie's house, during the afternoon and was not expected to finish before late evening. Frank and Jack had offered to bring a bottle or two and Sal had volunteered her services as pianist. All and sundry would be present and it was to be the highlight of the year.

"You'll never guess, but even Lady Muck has said she'll grace us with her presence, along with Mr. Verwood and all." Ruby imparted.

A loud guffaw exploded from Sal as she exclaimed, "Oh, well, if we've got royalty coming, we'd best get out the red carpet and don't forget to mind your P's and Q's and for God's sake don't anyone bleedin' swear!"

As the last of the laughter ebbed away in Ruby's small cluttered kitchen, the younger children of the square were leaving school.

"No more school for two whole weeks! And Christmas only three days away, what could be better?" Billy threw his cap high in the air, catching it deftly behind his back.

Running out of the school yard, Billy, Toby and Jacob came tumbling to a standstill at the curb. In unison, they turned as one and watched as Ellie, her small legs pumping, called out to them.

"Wait for me! You always run too fast. I'm only little, how am I supposed to keep up with you?"

Pigtails flying, with one hand anchoring her beret to her small head, Ellie skidded to a halt by the roadside and looked up at her brother.

"Why is it, that you're always the last one out? It doesn't matter what time we get out, you can bet your life that you'll be behind us. You'll be late for your own funeral, you will, Ellie!" Playfully, Billy grabbed the green hat from her head and threw it to the Carmichael boys, giggling at his side.

"If you drop that in the road and it gets all muddy, I'll tell my Mum! Give it back you two or I will, I'll tell on you!" Ellie jumped up, trying to snatch the article from hands held high in the air.

"You'll have to catch us first and then you'll have to give us a kiss if you want it back. Come on, Ellie, how fast can you run?" the two boys dodged across the road, weaving in and out of vehicles and the bodies of other children crossing. As Ellie made to give chase, Billy reached down and yanked her back.

"Mind what you're doing, Ellie! You'll get yourself run over if you don't watch out. Just because those two haven't got the brains they were born with, doesn't mean you have to copy them, does it?"

Taking her hand, Billy walked his sister sedately across the busy road. Once safely on the other side, they set off in hot pursuit of the Carmichael boys and it was in this fashion that they arrived laughing and calling out to one another as they entered the Mews.

"I'm not kissing you, no way. I'd rather kiss a dog's bum, than either of you two. So just give me back my hat. Tell them, Billy, go on."

Just at that moment, Gary turned the corner.

"Well, that's a fine way for a young lady to talk! Eleanor Treist, you should know better than to shout those sort of things in the street. I thought you were a nice girl, but it seems I was wrong."

Ellie was mortified. Here was her hero, looking at her with such a stern expression on his young face. Turning abruptly, tears welling in her eyes, Ellie stumbled blindly over the cobblestones and retreated to the safe harbour of her home.

"Hang on! I was only messing about. Ellie! Come back, I didn't mean it." Gary made as if to follow her, then stopped short and spoke softly to Billy. "My! She's touchy, isn't she? I was only having a laugh with her. What brought all that on, then?"

"Take no notice, Gary. She's always like that with people she likes. Gets embarrassed if they catch her out. Don't worry, she'll be as right as ninepence tomorrow and pretend nothing happened." Billy bent and picked up the offending headgear from the ground where Toby and Jacob had abandoned it at the first sign of trouble.

"You looking forward to Christmas? Got all your presents, have you? The party at Grandma Lottie's should be good, eh?" Not waiting for any answers, Gary continued, "Tell Ellie, I didn't mean to upset her and I'll see you all in the morning. Fancy a walk round the shops? They'll be lots to see, including fifty Santa's on every corner!

How are the young ones supposed to believe in Father Christmas when there's hundreds of them all in the same street?"

Billy agreed with him, nodding his head sagely, whilst all the time realising that Father Christmas was a myth after all. He had, of course, had his suspicions when he had seen his father creep into his bedroom in the early hours of Christmas morning, last year. But he had pushed this to the back of his mind, until now. "I'll have to keep this to my self, otherwise Ellie will get all upset if she finds out. Let her have a few more years before she catches on. And I'll have to keep it from Mum and Dad as well. Best not to let on that I've grown up, yet." Billy thought as he entered his house.

Glancing back over his shoulder, the first flurry of snow drifted down and settled tentatively on the shoulders of the stone figure in the Mews' centre. This year it would be a white Christmas as predicted by the weathermen and there would be much excitement when young cockney children awoke the next day to a frozen, snow covered London.

CHAPTER 9

True to prediction, snow fell steadily over London and most of England during the Christmas period of 1959.

Within twenty four hours of the first snow flurries, England's capital was covered in a bright, white blanket; pretty to view, but treacherous to venture out into. Each day brought a fresh arrival and each night, as the temperatures dropped below zero, the street's were reduced to icy, dangerous places.

For the first time in living memory, the river Thames froze over. It became a huge skating rink for young and old alike and, once dusk had fallen, the embankments were littered with vendors selling their wares. The cries of "Hot chestnuts, buy your hot chestnuts here!" and "Oranges! Get your fresh oranges. Cheap at half the price!" could be heard. And among these street sellers were others plying their trade. All manner of Christmas paraphernalia was available from Christmas tree lights to sprigs of mistletoe.

Wrapped up in hats, scarves, mittens and several layers of clothing, the people of London roamed the shores of the river and an air of festivity prevailed. Families ambled along, children running ahead, slipping and sliding with voices raised as elders called out in warning. Young people gathered in groups, whispering behind their hands for fear of a passing adult overhearing their innermost thoughts; and lovers hid in the dark shadows between the evenly spaced lamp posts, arms entwined, dreaming to the soft strains of 'Silent Night' sung by brave Carol singers.

"No more, Ellie! you'll be sick if you eat another one. Besides, chestnuts lie in your stomach and you'll not sleep a wink tonight. Go on now, find your sister. See? She's over there, talking with her friends." Jack's breath swirled around his face in misty clouds as he bent and lightly tapped his youngest daughter's derriere.

The small girl, eyes alert and still clutching in her hand the last chestnut, made her way gingerly over the slippery pavement and stood quietly by Fay's side, listening.

"So, I said to him: "What do you think you're looking at? Do you want a picture?" And he comes straight back and said: "Don't know what it is, can't see the label and I wouldn't want to take a picture of it, in case I break my camera!" Cheeky sod! Mind you, he's so gorgeous, he could get away with murder. Reminds me of

Richard Burton, he does, with them dark, brooding eyes. What I wouldn't give to have half an hour with him!"

Several young girls were clustered around her and even though their bodies were bulky with extra clothing, Fay still managed to stand out, her young contours enticing beneath her bright red coat. She had pleaded and cajoled her mother until the latter had given in and allowed her to wear the garment tonight, even though it was to be her main Christmas present and that event was still two days hence.

"Did he ask you for a date? And how are you going to get out? Suppose you'll be using me as your excuse again. We've got to be careful Fay. My Mum's getting suspicious. She keeps asking me where we're off to and what we're up to. I'm running out of ideas." Faithful as a puppy, Caroline Meadows waited for Fay to answer. Unfortunately, Fay's best friend was a plain simple girl and next to Fay's sultry beauty, Caroline was a dim and dull contrast. This was no coincidence. Fay had deliberately picked this less attractive girl as her closest friend believing, and rightly so, that Caroline would be more than grateful to trail in Fay's shadow. Also, Fay shone more brilliantly in comparison.

"Yeah, he wants me to go to the Youth Club on Christmas Eve. They're having a bit of a do there. I've told my Mum that me and you are going up the church to help get everything ready for Midnight Mass. Nobody'll check and we'll be home before they get back from the service. You can tag along with me, but make yourself scarce when it finishes, because I want him to walk me home. And for God's sake, keep your mouth shut. We don't want anyone finding out, else we'll be for it." As Fay uttered these last words, she noticed her friend's eyes widen and glance meaningfully to Fay's side.

Looking down, Fay suddenly realised that Ellie had been her silent audience.

"How long have you been standing there? If you repeat any of this, Ellie Treist, I'll knock your block off! Bloody hell! You're like creeping bleeding Jesus! Whenever I turn round, there you are, sneaking about and waiting to get your chance to snitch on me. Well, I'm warning you. If you breath a word of this, I'll sodding kill you! Do you hear?"

Tears of indignation smarting in her eyes, Ellie protested loudly.

"I'm not a snitch! And I don't sneak around. Dad told me to come over here and you was talking and didn't see me. Anyway, I won't say anything, but if you get caught, Mum'll murder you. And don't go blaming me, it'll be your own fault."

"Shut up! They'll hear you. Alright, I'll trust you not to tell. Just remember what I said. If I find out you've let on, I'll get my own back, see if I don't." With that, Fay turned abruptly on her heel and marched off with Caroline in tow, as usual.

Ellie stood there for a moment, scanning the throngs of people, searching for a friendly face. Her eyes rested for a second on her father's smiling profile, but before long someone else had caught her attention. To the left of her parents, Gary was approaching. Beside him, her arm linked in his was a tall, pretty dark haired girl. Heads bent towards one another, the couple passed within a few feet of the surprised little girl. Gary did not see her; he had eyes only for the girl at his side. As they walked by, Ellie turned bodily and watched their retreating backs and heard their ready laughter at some secret, shared joke.

Once more, tears stung her eyelids and Ellie lifted her hand and swiped at her face in an angry gesture. She did not recognise the girl hanging on her hero's arm but for the first time in her short life, Ellie felt a deep hatred for another human being. The alien emotion caught her unawares and she gasped aloud at the sheer force of it.

"Hello, young Ellie. What are you looking so lost and forlorn about? Come along with me, I'm going down on the ice to have a skate."

Brenda O'Shea had been only yards away from Ellie when she had seen the young girl's face turn chalky white as Gary sauntered past with his newly acquired girlfriend. She had recognised Ellie's reaction to the scenario, as she herself knew the feeling of jealousy of old. Brenda had been aware for some time that Ellie regarded Gary as some sort of God and knew that childhood crushes could be just as painful as an adult suffering from unrequited love.

Stretching out her hand, Brenda spoke softly to the child.

"Don't you take no notice. He's only trying out his wings. He'll still be around, foot loose and fancy free when you're old enough for him to take an interest in you. By then, you'll have so many blokes swarming over you, that he won't stand a chance and then you'll wonder what you ever saw in him in the first place. In the meantime, how about me and you having a bit of fun. Come on, I'll give you a hand onto the ice and we'll forget about him for a while, eh?"

Gratefully, Ellie took Brenda's hand, whispering more to herself than to the older girl, "I won't forget him. Not ever, I won't."

Together they made their way down from the embankment and onto the glass-like icy sheet below. Scrabbling over the ice, they slowly reached the centre. Here only the most hardy of skaters were swishing over the frozen surface. Out of the shelter of the embankment, the wind whistled up the river and the temperature was even more daunting.

"Keep moving, Ellie, else we'll end up like Frosty the Snowman!"

Soon Brenda and Ellie were giggling happily together as they fell bumping solidly onto the wet slippery ice, then pulling and pushing each other they would regain their footing and the whole process would repeat itself.

"Look at me, Brenda! I can go right round on one leg. See?"

Twirling round and round, Ellie danced across the ice, becoming more and more dizzy with each circuit. She stumble once, laughed and carried on. She was completely oblivious of the danger which lay in her path.

"Ellie, stop! Look out! Come back, don't go any further!" Brenda's cry of warning could not be heard above the clatter of skates on ice and the small girl continued, gathering momentum with each turn.

The danger which threatened Ellie was in the shape of a small break in the ice. It had been weakened by the current which flowed through the centre of the river and in one place had become so thin that a hole, large enough for a person to fall through, had appeared in the smooth surface.

Ellie's feet, slid on regardless. Arms outstretched and head thrown back, she laughed aloud in giddy abandonment at the black, star studded sky.

Brenda had begun to follow her. Her legs were not as sure footed as the younger girl and her progress was much slower. Looking round, wide eyed and frantic, she began calling out to passing skaters.

"Help! Stop her! Somebody stop her, she's going to fall in! Please, somebody help me!"

Suddenly from the outskirts of the small crowd of skaters, a short, stocky figure detached itself and began gliding effortlessly over the ice. Heading straight for Brenda, he swerved past her, almost knocking her off her feet. Faster and faster he went, arms swinging from side to side, the better to aid speed. Ellie's small figure still twirled in his direct path. The ice hole was just yards from Ellie's feet when the man swooped down, his arm hooked about her waist and as Ellie's left foot dipped into the icy water and she began to totter, he pulled her roughly to his side. Skates flailing, Ellie clutched at the man's upper arm and he swung her easily into an arc, skidded to one side and turned, all in the same movement.

With less speed, the skater slid over the ice, Ellie now tucked safely under his arm,, and with one graceful manoeuvre, tipped his skates sideways and came to a halt before the open mouthed Brenda.

"I believe this belongs to you, Ma'am. You should be more careful where you leave your belongings, strange things can happen to them if they're left unattended." Swinging Ellie out from under his arm, he stood the now shaking girl firmly on the ice. "You OK, young lady? Nearly took a nasty tumble there, didn't you. Still, no harm done and all's well that end's well."

Looking up into his open smiling face, Ellie grinned back.

"Thanks, Mister. I never saw that hole. My mum's always saying to watch where I'm going and that my head's always in the clouds. She was right this time, wasn't she?"

The man threw back his head and roared. "Well, I'll say this for you, you've certainly got some spunk. There you were, dicing with death and knocking on heaven's door and you can still crack a joke. You limey's sure have a strange sense of humour, gets me every time." Glancing sideways at the still shocked Brenda, he held out his hand and said, "Hi. The name's Matthew Goldberg, Junior, but everyone calls me Matt."

Shaking hands, Brenda looked at him with awe. Not more than five feet eight, but possessing a muscular body, Matthew Goldberg was not a heart throb. His spiky crew cut and craggy face were not in tune with each other. But when you saw his deep blue twinkling eyes, one forgot that his nose was slightly too large and his mouth a little crooked. He held an attraction for women that was illusive and Brenda could feel herself falling under his spell.

"Hello. My name's Brenda O'Shea and this here is Ellie Treist. I don't know how I'll ever thank you for what you just did. You probably saved her life, if she but knew it."

The trio skated slowly back to the safety of the embankment and climbed up on to solid terra firma.

"Now perhaps you young ladies will allow me to buy you a hot drink?" Matt had removed his skates and not waiting for an answer dodged between the now thinning crowds and within minutes returned, three steaming cups balanced in his hands.

"What is it with this country? Tea seems to be the answer to everything but you'd have to sell your grandmother for a cup of coffee."

Brenda laughed, saying, "You're not wrong. Britain runs off a tea urn, didn't you know? Coffee? You must be joking, only the rich and famous drink that. Where do you come from, then? And where did you learn to skate like that. I've never seen anything like it in my life. You were so quick, I nearly missed it!"

"Oh, that. Well, I come from Ohio, in the United States of America. The skating comes from vacations taken with my folks in Canada. Not much else to do there except skate, so you soon become good at it. I've been here since the end of the war. I sort of ended up here and never went home."

Ellie stood between the two adults, turning her head to and fro as if watching a tennis match and listened to the easy conversation.

Soon, Brenda, looked around and realised that most people had gone and stalls were being packed away for the night.

"Well, it was very nice meeting you Mr. Goldberg and thanks again for everything. We've got to go now as I'll have to get this one home before they send out a search party. Bye."

"Hang on, don't rush off. Can I see you again? Where do you live? I could pick you up tomorrow night and we could go for a drink, OK? And the name's Matt, remember?"

Blushing, Brenda agreed to meet him the following night, not wanting him to see the shabby house in Mermaid Mews. They arranged to meet in a pub in the Kings Road at seven o'clock and took their leave.

The two girls walked back slowly to the square, hands swinging and as they turned into the Mews, Ellie suddenly exclaimed.

"Oh look, Brenda! Doesn't she look lovely, all covered in ice and snow. It covers up all the broken bits, doesn't it?" Pointing at the Mermaid, Brenda agreed. But already doubts were beginning to surface in her mind. How would she hide her cracks and flaws when she met Matt tomorrow night? Well, tomorrow was another day and she'd just have to face it then.

CHAPTER 10

Just forty eight hours before Christmas, December 23rd, 1959 and the Mews was a buzz with festive activity.

Each resident, from the youngest to the oldest member, was assigned their own special tasks. For the women this involved mostly cooking and cleaning while the men were expected to purchase Christmas trees, put up decorations and generally run last minute errands.

"Oh, Jack! That looks nice, who thought of that?" Cathy, stood at the kitchen sink, was staring with admiration at the Mermaid in the centre of the square. The statuette had been adorned with sprigs of holly and mistletoe and in the dry bowl of the fountain lay discarded branches cut from the various Christmas trees now standing proudly in living rooms of each of the houses.

"That was Frank's brain wave. Soppy sod! Soft as muck he is. Not content with the million and one jobs Eileen's found for him, he has to go and find more work. Mind you, when he'd finished I had to agree with him. Just a few bits and pieces to liven up the old girl and the whole place looks better. Bet she was a cracker in her day. It's a shame she's been left to wrack and ruin. We'll have to see about tidying her up permanent after the New Year."

Jack turned from the window and looked to the table where his mother was sat peeling vegetables. Her head was bent over her task and her iron grey hair looked softer in the kitchen glow. A small frown of concentration could be seen over her glasses perched on the end of her nose and as Jack observed her, he realised with a small shock of surprise, that she had grown old. With this realisation came a picture of her as she was now. She no longer stood ramrod straight and her voice was querulous and somehow less forbidding. Perhaps, at last, she was mellowing. She had carved a niche for herself in the square's community and now her attentions were not focused entirely upon her family. Still diligent with regards to her grandchildren's religious upbringing, Sal had relaxed somewhat. She found she no longer had the time to attend every Saint's Day Mass and now only subscribed to the chosen few. Ellie, Billy and Fay revelled in this new attitude of their grandmother and the bickering between them all had lessened to such a degree that nowadays when summoned to attend church, the children went meekly enough, not wishing to return to the regime of the past.

With a sigh, Sal now laid the small paring knife down and wiped her hands on the ever present apron worn around her waist. She had been aware of her son's scrutiny and was vaguely embarrassed by his attentions.

"Idle hands, Jack? If Cathy can't find anything for you to do, then I'm sure I can. There's still the coal to be brought in and when you've done with that, Lottie'll need a hand over her place. If we're all descending on her on Boxing Day, she'll need things doing over there. She can't be expected to do it all by herself and me and Cathy are too busy here, so that leaves you. Soon as you've finished here, get yourself on over there and make yourself useful."

"Alright, alright, don't nag me Mother. I was only having a breather then I was on my way to Lottie's in any case. God help a man who lives in the same house as two nagging women! I only hope Billy doesn't have to suffer the same predicament." Grinning, Jack endured the slap of a tea towel that Cathy deftly aimed at his head.

"Nagging women? You don't know you were born, Jack Treist. Of course if you feel so hard done by, we can always oblige by living up to our names, can't we, Sal? Now, where shall I start? What horrible things can I find you to do?"

Holding up his hands in surrender, Jack backed out of the room, still smiling broadly at his wife. As soon as she had gauged he was out of earshot, Cathy sat down at the table and reached across to still Sal's hands.

"He's worried about you, Sal. You've not been yourself lately. Is anything wrong? You alright?"

Sal let her hands relax under those of her daughter-in-law's. As her twilight years fast approached, Sal found human contact to be comforting. The need to be strict and unbending had been necessary when rearing her son single handed and then it had become a habit she found hard to break. Lately, she had come to regret her rigorous stance and would have welcomed an occasional hug from any of the members of her family, especially Jack. But the emotional barriers she had erected about herself were too solid to scale and she was too old to change.

Pulling her hands from under the warmth of Cathy's, Sal spoke more gruffly than she intended.

"Stop fussing. I'm alright, never felt better. I'm no spring chicken, you know. You wait until you get to my age, then try being nice all the time. As for Jack worrying about me, he should find something else to occupy his time with. Now, what else is there to do?"

Groaning inwardly, Cathy was reminded of the saying concerning teaching old dogs new tricks and about beating one's head against a brick wall. She wondered why she kept trying. The old woman was the way she was and Jack would never change either. Sometimes, she thought all communications would break down completely between the two if she did not act as their main line. Thrusting aside this depressing thought, Cathy concentrated on the coming events of Christmas and soon, she and Sal were engrossed in their preparations.

*

Meanwhile, Brenda O'Shea was getting ready for the coming evening in a fever of activity.

"Mum? Where's my blue dress? You know, the one with the lace collar and pearl buttons down the front. It was in my wardrobe last time I saw it and now it's gone. And have you seen my new nylons? I left them on the chair here and they've also done a disappearing act. God, I can't leave anything for two minutes and someone comes along and bloody hides it! I knew I should've had my hair done because now I can't get it to do anything and look at my coat? It looks like a dish rag. He'll wonder what the hell he's taking out when I show up tonight. If I show up tonight. I reckon the best thing I could do, is not turn up. Then if I ever bump into him again I can tell him I did him a favour. Mum, are you listening?"

"For God's sake, Brenda, stop running round like a blue arsed fly! I'm ironing your dress, your nylons are on the sideboard, where you left them, I'll help you with your hair when I've finished here and once your coat's had a brush down it'll look fine. And if I have to frog march you down the road, you will be there tonight, come hell or high water, right? Just sit down for a minute, you're wearing me out just watching you. I haven't seen you this worked up since your first date with Malcolm Bradbury when you were fifteen. What's so special about this one, eh?" Ruby stood at the bottom of the stairs and watched as her daughter descended, clad in her dressing gown, a scowl firmly fixed on her face.

"Come on, love. Sit down with me and have a fag and a cuppa. You've got plenty of time before you have to leave, though it doesn't seem right, you going off to meet him in a pub. He should have had the decency to call here for you." Leading the way, Ruby entered the steamy kitchen and put the kettle on the stove.

Brenda followed her in, leaning against the sink as she tried to explain why this particular date was so important to her.

"It's just different. It's not that he's good looking or anything or even as if he's young and dashing. He must be in his late thirties and his face looks well lived in, but he's got a certain something. I think it's his eyes. They're really blue, like the pictures you see of the sea in a foreign country. And they're sort of laughing with you. Not laughing at you like some of the blokes I've been out with, but like having a joke with you. When he spoke, his voice was really deep and he had a lovely accent and he's got nice manners. Instead of letting me get on with it and climb up the embankment on my own, he got up first, then helped me. He must be ever so strong and all, because he pulled me up with one hand, like I was as light as a feather. He can't be much taller than me, but he's stocky and broad shouldered. Really nice, he is." Staring dreamy eyed, Brenda took the cup of steaming tea her mother thrust at her.

"Well, he's certainly made a good impression on you, hasn't he? I've never believed all that rot about love at first sight, but looking at you, I'm beginning to think there must be some truth in it after all. Just be careful, Brenda. Don't do all the running, just walk slowly enough for him to catch you. Men like to do the chasing and if you make it all too easy for him, they get bored and go off after something harder to catch."

"Oh, Mum! I wasn't born yesterday, you know. I have been out with other blokes and I know how to behave. Though God only knows why we have to play these stupid games. If you like someone and you want to be with them, why do you have to pretend you're not all that interested? Think of all the time you waste playing hard to get? If I had my own way, I wouldn't bother with it all, but if he wants to go by the rules, I suppose I'll have to play along. And who mentioned love? I hardly know him, let alone love him! Still, I could do worse than ending up with someone like him." Off once more in her own dream world, Brenda wandered out of the room, sipping slowly at the hot beverage and returned to her bedroom to fight anew with her wayward tresses.

"Bloody hell! I never thought I'd see the day when that one got dewy eyed over a bloke she's only met once. Please God, he treats her right and doesn't ride rough shod over her. The last thing she needs is another knock to her confidence. Still, time will tell." Muttering to herself, Ruby resumed ironing her daughter's best dress, shaking her head every so often.

When Gary returned home, he found his mother in this perplexing state. He always assumed his mother was sure of everything and nothing would daunt her. Somewhat alarmed at her manner, he spoke from the doorway, reluctant to venture too far into the room.

"What's up? Has something happened? Who's died?"

"And you can shut up and all! Where the hell have you been? It's not as if I haven't got enough to do with Christmas just around the corner, but then your sister decides to fall for some mystery man and to cap it all, you vanish off the face of the earth!" Banging down the iron, hands now on her hips, Ruby glared at her son.

"I haven't vanished. I was only in the square with Billy Treist. We were helping Mr. Carmichael tidy up the fountain. You only had to look out the window and you would have seen me. I'm here now, anyway. What do you want me to do?" Trying to make amends, Gary was contrite.

"Don't take any notice of me, I must have got out of bed the wrong side. Besides, I've done it all now, except for the tree. While madam's out tonight, you and me will get down and decorate it together, OK? We'll make a party of it, just us two, eh?" Knowing how Gary liked to help with this particular task, Ruby held out the olive branch in an effort to cover her previous bad temper. "Here, just run this up to your sister. Be careful of it, I've just pressed it and she'll go mad if you crease it up again." Taking the dress from Ruby's outstretched hands, Gary sprinted up the stairs and barged into Brenda's bedroom, unannounced.

"If I've told you once, I've told you a thousand times to knock before you come in. I could have been stood here in my all together. You've got to learn to respect other people's privacy, Gary, right?"

"You don't want this, then?" Holding the dress aloft, Gary made to turn and leave the room.

"Give it here, you little sod! Don't bunch it up like that, you'll make it all creased. Come on, come in, just remember to knock in future. Here hold this mirror, while I try and do something with the back of this bloody hair. It's like bleeding rats tails."

After Brenda had finished struggling with her hair, Gary sat on the bed and watched as she applied her make-up, put on her new nylons, stepped into high heels and lastly, slipped on the blue dress.

"You look lovely, Brenda. If you weren't my sister, I'd quite fancy you myself."

"Cheeky bugger! Go on, get out of here, I'll be late if I don't get a move on."

Brother and sister descended the stairs together and went in search of their mother in order that she could give a last inspection before Brenda left for her all important date.

The weather had abated enough for Brenda to leave the Mews without the worry of snow falling on her precarious hair arrangement and although a brisk wind blew, the moon was full and the sky alight with sparkling star formation. Glancing up, she smiled to herself, thinking of the romance section in the library. In true romantic fiction, this night had a fairy tale beginning. She could only hope that it would have a happy ending and they would all live happily ever after.

CHAPTER 11

As Brenda left Mermaid Mews the time was 7.45pm and Seb Ridley was into his fifth pint at the Rising Sun.

The bar was packed with early Christmas revellers, but Seb sat alone. Elbows propped on the counter, his bar stool tipped forward on its two front legs, he stared long and hard into the amber liquid before him. The last month had been a test of his endurance and he was fast coming to the end of his tether. He was nearly out of control. In the past, he had only to raise his voice to see fear leap into the eyes of his wife. And just a couple of slaps would achieve wonders. These days he had to keep a tight reign on his temper and the mental games he had enjoyed playing with Angela, had all but ceased. As far as he was concerned though, this was only a temporary lull. Everything was in cold storage and when the time was right, all concerned would rue the day they had even thought of curbing him.

Some innocent bystander, pushed from behind by the crowd milling about, stumbled into the hunched figure at the bar. Seb swung round and let forth a stream of abuse.

"Now, now, Seb. There's no call for that. What's the matter with you these days? Your like a bear with a sore head. Cheer up, it'll soon be Christmas. Goodwill to men and all that, eh?" The Landlord tried, unsuccessfully, to jolly Seb along, but the latter was having none of it.

"Piss off! Who asked you anyway? Why can't you all mind your own bleeding business? I've bloody had it up to here," Seb raised his hand above his head to indicate the level he had reached, "and if one more fucker pokes his nose in my affairs, I'll bloody swing for them, right?"

"Oi! I've warned you before about your language. There's Ladies present and I won't have that sort of talk on my premises. So, either shut up and cheer up or drink up and get out. Is that clear?" Red faced with anger, the Landlord waved his finger in Seb's face, as he lent well over the counter.

Reaching forward, Seb's hand snaked out and grabbed the offending digit. Then, twisting his arm sideways, Seb bent the finger back viciously.

"Don't you sodding threaten me! I've been chucked out of better places than this flea pit. And as for the 'Ladies' in here, I've yet to see one. Who are you trying to bleeding kid? There might well be females in here, but they could probably teach me a thing or two where swearing is concerned. Tarts and Prossies, all of them - straight out the fucking gutter. It's not the likes of me that should worry you, you should be a bit more bleeding choosy about some of these so called 'Ladies' you let in." Giving one more brutal tug, Seb let go of the Landlord's hand, slipped off his stool and made to leave.

The silence that surrounded him was ominous. His steps faltered, then slowed and finally stopped as his passage was barred. Thirty pairs of eyes glared at him. The realisation that he had gone too far this time, was uppermost in his mind. More importantly, the need to escape the hostile people around him took precedence.

"And what are you buggers looking at? A bloke can't even come into his sodding local for a quiet drink these days, and the whole world's staring at him. Why don't you all fuck off and leave me be."

Not a sound could be heard and it was several heart stopping seconds before the booming voice of the Landlord, shattered the silence.

"Right, that's it. You're barred. Don't let me see your face around here again. Go and find some other pub to do your drinking in. That's if anyone will let you in after tonight's little show. And be warned. It's only because of the time of year that I haven't set my dogs on you. But I won't put up with any more of your dirty, rotten tricks in future. I've only to say the word and the dog's will be fighting their way to get to you through the crowds of folk who'd like to give you a good hiding. You might frighten women and children, but you don't scare decent folk. So, clear off and let this be the last time I have to set eyes on your vicious little face again."

An opening appeared in the throng of bodies gathered round Seb and he made a dash for the door. Once his hand was safely on the handle, he turned and made one more attempt at bravado.

"I was going anyway. This place is just right for you and your stinking kind. It's gone to the dogs in any case. I wouldn't drink in here if it was the last fucking pub on earth. And I'll put the word about. Before I've finished, you won't need glasses for serving drinks in, only bowls on the bleeding floor, because that's the only things this bloody lot will need!"

Whipping open the door, Seb swung out onto the pavement, letting the slamming sound behind him muffle the roar of anger that erupted from within the pub.

Running down the street, Seb cast fearful glances behind him, certain that he would be pursued. Apparently, the Landlord had been true to his word and had managed to calm down and subdue his customers and Seb achieved his get away without further trouble.

Slowing down, hands in pockets, he ambled along, kicking now and then at stray stones in his path. it was too early to go home and besides, he did not think he could stomach playing 'happy families' yet again. He racked his alcohol fogged brain for an alternative watering hole. Because of his surly manner and bad temper, there were few options left open to him, locally. His hands dug deep into his trouser pockets and jiggling the loose change there, he gauged how much money he had left. Two shillings and a few coppers would not allow him to take the bus up West and buy enough drink to satisfy his thirst. Mentally, he listed the public houses within walking distance and staggering distance home again. Finally, after running through the list, he decided that the Worlds End would suffice. This was a small public house on the borders of Chelsea and Fulham and a short cut through the new Wandon Road council estate would take him virtually to the doorstep.

Veering off to the right, Seb quickened his pace and entered a pedestrian walkway which linked the Chelsea and Fulham roads. Head down, he descended a small incline which led to a basin where blocks of maisonettes and flats had been erected in an effort to house the growing population of the area. Although the estate was barely six months old, graffiti was already in abundant evidence. The slogans of 'KILROY WAS HERE' and 'BAN THE BOMB' were the more popular written phrases. liberally interspersed with declarations of love. The tiled lower walls of the flats were the most abused and the garish colours of spray paint shone luminous in the light of an occasional street lamp. Seb was immune to these shows of defiance and defacement. Still walking at a brisk pace, he began the assent out of the estate which would lead him to his proposed destination.

As he continued his journey, Seb became aware of hushed voices ahead. Thinking of the commotion he had caused earlier in the Rising Sun, the small, spry man ducked down behind the cover of a parked car and waited with bated breath. He had been wary, of late, of night time encounters, not wishing for an undignified and painful repeat performance of before.

Two shadowy figures were approaching. At first, Seb could not determine their gender from the tones of their voices or the outline of their bodies. Only as the couple came abreast of his hiding place was he able to discern their identity as two male youths.

"Here, turn your back. The wind's coming from the front, so cup your hands, like this." Both boys stopped and turning, braced themselves against the oncoming blast of wind.

As Seb watched, the flare of a flickering flame illuminated the two faces as they dipped their heads to light the cigarettes hanging from their lips.

The youth nearest to the sheltering car could have been placed anywhere between fourteen and sixteen and was a stranger to Seb. But the second boy was well known to the hiding man. It was Frankie Carmichael, Eileen and Frank's eldest son.

"Here, where did you get that?" The taller of the two boys took hold of Frankie's wrist and snatched at the gold coloured lighter which had lit their now smouldering cigarettes.

Frankie closed his fist over the lighter in a protective manner.

"It's mine! And don't snatch, else I won't show it to you." He opened his hand and there, lying in his palm, was the article in question. It was small, shiny and expensive.

"You can't afford things like that. Come on, where did you get it? And don't tell me you found it. This sort of thing don't fall off trees."

"Alright, don't go on. I'd have told you later anyway. I nicked it tonight, out of old man Fosby's place when we were in there earlier."

Ron, the as yet unidentified youth, looked at Frankie in amazement.

"How did you manage that? This isn't one of his cheap lighters and he keeps the good ones locked up in the glass case so's people like us can't get our grubby mitts on them."

"Well he didn't have his eyes open tonight, did he? Remember when that old geezer came in and asked for one of the fancy cigars? Old Fosby came round the front and opened the glass top and handed the other bloke a bloody great big cigar. Then you asked him for a pack of Woodbines and while Fosby turned to get them for you and the other bloke was examining his cigar, I just put my hand in the case and swiped the lighter. I was so quick, no one even saw me move. They were still talking about the bleeding merits of different cigars, when we left the shop." Boasting of his prowess, Frankie flicked the lighter open then shut and turning it over noticed for the first time the engraved name on the back. The word DUNHILL, was clearly printed there.

"Bloody hell, Frankie! He's bound to miss it. This must cost a bomb, I've seen one of these before when I was helping my Dad at the Hotel. This posh geezer was leaving and my Dad had to go up to the rooms to get his bags. I went with him and when we were just about to come out of the bedroom, my Dad saw this lighter laying on the side. He picked it up and said how the bloke must have more money than sense to leave a thing like that lying around. When we went back downstairs, my Dad gave the posh bloke the lighter and he didn't even bat an eyelid. My old man was a bit miffed about it all as he said the bloke should have given him a tip for finding and returning it. Said it was worth more than a months wages. So, old Fosby's going to have a purple fit when he finds out this one's gone. He's bound to report it to the Police and sooner or later, someone's going to remember we were in there. They'll put two and two together and before we know where we are, we'll be down the nick charged with theft. You'll have to take it back or get rid of it, Frankie."

With growing dread, Frankie had listened to his friend. Other than the odd apple from an open fruit stall, the boy had not stolen before and now he was badly frightened.

"What'll I do? The shop's shut now so we can't take it back and anyway Fosby's probably already told the Police. I didn't know it was anything special, I just thought it was old Fosby being his usual mean self. You know how he's started locking up everything in sight and I thought this was just another lighter. How was I to know?"

The two boys stood in the light of a street lamp staring at the object of their concern. It was Ron who came up with a solution.

"Look. No one'll be able to prove it was you. After all, you said you were quick and if Fosby had missed it straight away, he would have come after us. Just chuck it away. Get shot of it. Throw it down the drain and then no one will ever be any the wiser."

Frankie searched about him and then his eyes found the ideal place in which to discard the unwanted item.

"Here, look! See where the gutter slopes down? There's a gap and if I put my hand in, I can put the lighter in there out of sight." Bending down, the boy pushed his hand into the small space at the edge of the pavement that was part of the drainage system and dropped the lighter there.

Straightening up, he looked around him to ensure he was unobserved and failed to see the bobbing head of Seb Ridley behind the parked car.

"Come on, let's get out of here before someone comes along." Throwing down their forgotten cigarettes, the two youths scampered away from the scene of the crime and were soon out of sight.

Rising up from behind the car, Seb slunk to the pavement's edge and dropping down in a crouching position, and dipping into the hole, his hand grasped the lighter and retrieved it in one fluid movement.

"Well, well and what have we here?" Seb spoke aloud, chuckling in the dark night. "Now, what can I do with this? How can I use this little thing for my own good? I think I'll just take it along with me while I decide what I'm going to do."

There were no signs of his earlier consumption of beer as Seb strode up the hill, whistling softly to himself and continued on his way to the public house of his previous choice.

CHAPTER 12

Matthew Goldberg pushed his way through the swing doors of the lounge bar, struggling with his umbrella which, as yet tonight, was unused. The high evening wind had blown his collar up around his ears and as he straightened himself and his clothing he glanced about the interior of the small dockside hostelry. Low oak beams hung over a small and cosy bar. To his left, a roaring wood burning open fire beckoned. Round topped tables with similar upright chairs were littered haphazardly in the centre of the floor space, whilst along the outer walls, couches sat soft and comfortable. The decor, although heavily coated in cigar and cigarette smoke, consisted of deep reds and golds and radiated a warm and welcoming atmosphere.

Pleased with his choice of rendezvous, Matthew made his way to the bar. As yet, there were only a handful of people present but Matthew knew that this would be rectified shortly. The Ship Inn was extremely popular, but not as a 'first drink of the evening pub'. Rather, this was where one finished, where people liked to spend the evening's end. He ordered himself a large scotch on the rocks, the barman smiling at his turn of phrase, then found a small couch in the far corner, near the fire.

Leaning back in his seat, Matthew saw in his minds eye a picture of a tall, solid, rosy-cheeked girl. He saw the long lashes that hid soft blue eyes, the full-lipped mouth, a shy smile lingering at its corners. He liked the way small tendrils of hair had escaped from the confines of her hat and lay in damp curls across her forehead and framed her face. In time, perhaps he would earn the right to brush those baby soft, blonde locks to their rightful place as he had longed to do last night. Brenda O'Shea, he thought, has a homely ring to it, but Brenda Goldberg sounded so much more pleasant to him. Shaking his head, Matthew brought himself out of his revelry. He must remember to take things slowly. Time and again he had been reminded that the British took their time in all matters. They were not a nation to be hurried and came to their decisions slowly. Unlike his own people. Americans were apt to rush in where wise men feared to tread and although this trait was strong in Matthew, he had learned to curb it during his stay in London.

Picking up his glass, he took a long, deep swallow and with eyes closed, savoured the taste of the fiery liquid as it trickled slowly down his throat. When next he opened his eyes, the image he had viewed behind closed lids, stood in reality before him. The hat had been replaced by a brightly patterned scarf and under her coat, Matthew glimpsed a deep midnight blue dress that set off her eyes and gave her hair a honey glow.

"Hello. Not late am I? The wind's so strong out there, it was all I could do to keep my pins upright and my feet on the ground. Still, like a bad penny, here I am." Brenda reached up and untied her scarf, slipping it neatly into her coat pocket.

Matthew rose quickly, stepped forward and helped to remove her coat. "Hi, Brenda. No, you're not late, I'm over eager and got here early. You look real nice - how do you say - a sight for sore eyes?"

"Oh! I'm not used to compliments, but thanks anyway. You look sort of good yourself and all." Brenda sat down nervously, not sure of her actions.

"What would you like to drink?"

"I'm not sure. What are you drinking?" She glanced at his now empty glass.

"Well, I don't know that you'll like my poison. It's scotch. Do you usually drink whisky?" Leaning forward, he looked down into her upturned face and felt his stomach start to do cartwheels.

"I don't usually drink at all. Leastways, only at Christmas and special occasions. Then I have a port and lemon or a sweet sherry. But I'd like to try what you're having, if that's alright?"

"Sure. You can have what you want. Just sit tight and I'll be back in a flash." Matthew winked at her then went to the bar.

Brenda sat back and surveyed the scene. She liked this place. It was quiet and intimate not like the pubs she had been to in the past. Those places had been rowdy and impersonal and she had spent her evenings in them propped up at the bar being pushed and shoved from all sides. Here she could relax. She would not have to shout to make herself heard above a babble of voices and neither would she have to strain to hear his conversation.

Wracking her brains, she tried to think of some interesting things to say. She so wanted to impress him with witty remarks and intelligent comments. Being prone to bluntness, she must remember to try to be beguiling and not blurt out her thoughts in her normal fashion. How she wished she was more worldly wise but all her knowledge had been gleaned from books, her limited awareness of current affairs she had gained from newspapers and Pathe News clips seen at the cinema. The radio was also a source of information and until now, she had regarded herself as adequately well versed. Especially among her peers. Of the few friends that Brenda had, she was somewhat of an oddity. They were only interested in latest clothes fashions and the music hits of that time and considered Brenda's interests to be boring and of no consequence. In truth, Brenda was equally disinterested in their pursuits and pastimes, but out of loneliness she still sought their company. Her mother also played a large role in forcing her to socialise with these so called 'friends'. Ruby could not comprehend her daughter's involvement with the written word and continually encouraged her to 'get out and about'. There were times when Brenda would have been quite content to curl up with a good book or listen to a play on the wireless, but Ruby would have none of it and would plague her until she gave in and went to one or another of the parties or dances that her mother urged her to attend. More often than not, Brenda would return home after one of these outings, vowing never to be persuaded to go the next time. Invariably she would find herself in the same situation during the following week end.

With Matthew, however, Brenda sensed that he would expect her to be a lively and intelligent conversationalist as he indeed, appeared to be. In theory, she could more than meet his expectations. However, she had never had the opportunity to exercise in full her self acquired education and was unsure of herself.

"Please God, don't let me make a fool of myself. Just for once, let me sit back and listen without putting my foot in it." She muttered under her breath.

"Penny for them? You were miles away. Anywhere interesting, or am I not supposed to ask?" Matthew put down on the table two glasses containing healthy measures of whisky and slid into the seat next to her.

"Sorry. I was just thinking how I hoped I didn't bore you to death tonight," Brenda put her hand over her mouth, giggling to herself, "and then I was giving myself a lecture on keeping my big mouth shut and not to blurt out everything that crosses my mind. But here I go again - I just can't keep my thoughts in my head, where they belong."

"Don't apologise. I meet so many people who act so cagey and won't let you know what they're really thinking, it's nice to speak to someone so open. You carry on. Say whatever you like, whatever pops into your mind, just let it all out. I'd be really interested in your opinions. I want to know all there is to know about you, so don't hold back - give!" Sitting back, his arm resting casually on the rest behind her, Matthew stared intently at her and waited for her to begin.

"I can't just sit here all night spouting on about myself. Anyway, as soon as someone says, 'Speak' I dry up and can't think of anything to say. You start. Tell me all about America and your family."

Once Matthew began, there was no stopping him. He talked of his home town, the school house and church. He spoke of his family whom he missed so much. There were five children in his family; two older brothers and two younger sisters, all married except him. He had been too busy travelling and seeing the world to settle down. And although his parents had both retired and were getting on in years, they still regularly entertained their rapidly expanding family (there were twelve grandchildren to date). Matthew described in such clear detail the large rambling house that had been his home since birth, that Brenda felt as if she had been shown a photograph of it, so vivid was the picture in her mind. He recalled amusing anecdotes of his childhood and Brenda laughed aloud at the picture he painted of the small boy caught with his hand in the cookie jar. Long lazy summers, warm balmy autumns, short sharp winters and bright breezy springs were the seasons of his birthplace. At this point, he compared British weather to American and made her laugh once more with his dry humour.

"How do you get used to this weather? How do you know what clothes to put on every day? And why do I still look like a tourist after all these years. I don't think I'll ever be able to pass myself off as an Englishman, except of course at home where most of the folks have never set foot out of their own state, let alone on foreign soil. Just what is it that I'm doing wrong?" Laughing at himself, Matthew went on to explain his extended stay in London. After being demobbed, the U.S. government had decided his services could be well used in the American embassy. It had suited him at that time to stay overseas. There was a depression at home and he did not want to burden his family with an extra mouth to feed. The years had slid one into another and he had been content to let time pass by. Lately however, as his parents grew older, he had begun to yearn to return home and he had already enquired after a post near to his home town. He would hear of the outcome in the New Year.

"Well, that's it. You now know me better than I know myself. So, it's your turn, take the floor, Brenda and tell all."

Laughing, Brenda related her own history. She recalled her early childhood with both her parents, the late arrival of her much beloved brother and the desertion of her father. She spoke of her mother's bitterness and of her cynical attitude towards those of the opposite sex. Feeling more relaxed, Brenda described her own home, not withholding it's true identity and the shabbiness of Mermaid Mews. Unfolding her dreams, she timidly showed Matthew her hopes and aspirations, telling of her retreat into the world of books and of her life in full.

On and on they chattered. The pub filled, then began to empty as closing time drew nigh. When next they paused for breath, the bar was practically deserted and the landlord was pointedly glancing at the clock then back to them.

"I think he may be trying to tell us something. Come on, I'll walk you home slowly and we can carry on with our talks." Matthew held out her coat and as she slid her arms into it, she felt his hands, warm and caressing at her neck and his soft breath in her ear as he leant towards her. She felt her face flame and hoped he had not noticed her blush with pleasure.

They were out in the street. Matthew pulled her arm through his, curling his fingers around her own in the warm confines of his coat pocket. Strolling through the late night streets, Brenda could not remember feeling so at ease with a male, other than her brother. But the feelings that awakened in her were not those of a brotherly ilk. She had never been so strongly attracted to a man before and being inexperienced in these matters, did not know how to react. Fortunately, Matthew kept up a steady stream of conversation and before she knew it, they were standing in the archway that was the entrance to the Mews.

"This is it. This is where I live. I can't invite you in as Mum and Gary will have long gone to bed. It was a lovely evening Matt, I've had a smashing time, I'm only sorry it ended so quick." She looked into his face, smiling openly.

"Hey, don't make it sound like it's the last time we'll see each other. Listen, this is only the beginning. If I'm reading you right, this could be the start of something good. I can't recall a time when

I was so relaxed in female company, nor a time when I was fortunate enough to have such a pretty girl as my partner for a whole evening, all to myself. Brenda, you just stop me if I'm going too fast, but I want to see you again. I want to see you everyday, all day. Is that OK?" Frowning, sure he had rushed like a bull at a gate, Matthew gently placed his hand under her chin and raised her downcast head up to meet his. What he saw in her eyes made his stomach again begin to do the acrobatics of before. Glistening with unshed tears, her eyes smiled back at him. Brenda raised her hand and softly stroked his cheek. "No one has ever said anything as nice as that to me before. You're a lovely man, Matthew Goldberg, Junior. I'm only surprised that some scheming female hasn't snatched you up years ago."

Slowly, Matthew bent his head and tentatively kissed her open mouth. Drawing back he looked at her, the question in his eyes. In answer, Brenda reached up, wrapped her arms around his neck and returned his kiss but this time with more fervour. His arms clasped her body to his own and they stood in the lamplight, the kiss becoming deeper and deeper until, out of modesty, Brenda pulled away.

"Sorry, sorry. I should learn to control myself around you. You certainly bring out the beast in me, I'll have to watch myself in future." Both hands holding her face, Matthew stared hard into her eyes, trying to convince himself of what he saw there. "You will see me again, won't you? I haven't scared you, have I?"

"No, Matt. You haven't scared me, I can do that on my own. I told my Mum earlier that I didn't believe in stupid games so I'll be honest with you, as I've always wanted to be. If you want to see me again, I'll be waiting. I just can't believe that you really want to be with me as much as I want to be with you. But please, just do one thing, will you? Be truthful with me. If you don't want to see me any more, just say so. Don't play with me, because I don't know the rules. Just don't hurt me, Matt, not any more than you have to."

Hugging her close, arms tight around her, Matthew whispered, "I promise. Should a time come, and it won't, when I don't want to be with you, I'll tell you straight and you do the same for me, agreed?" He waited as she nodded her assent into his shoulder, then continued, "I'll pick you up, from your house, tomorrow at 7.00pm sharp. We'll spend Christmas Eve together and as many other nights as you'll allow. Is it a deal?"

"Oh, Matt! Pinch me, I must be dreaming! How did I get this lucky? Perhaps someone up there likes me after all." Brenda felt so jubilant, she wanted to shout out, let everyone know of her new found happiness.

"Till tomorrow then, my love. Remember, 7.00pm on the dot. Goodnight, Brenda, I'll be counting the hours." With one last lingering kiss, Matthew turned from her and strode jauntily up the Brompton Road, whistling a tune softly to himself. He glanced back once and waved at the figure staring after him, her face in shadow, but knowing that she still held the smile he had left her with.

Brenda slowly walked into the square and once in the centre, looked up at the Mermaid sat upon her rocky throne. "Looks like you and me came into our own tonight. You with your new clothes and me with a dream that might, just might, come true. Night, Fish Lady, keep your fingers crossed for me." Fairly skipping across the square, Brenda unlocked her front door and slipped quietly inside.

*

Matthew, also on cloud nine, wandered along the road, deep in thought. He was in no particular hurry and the tune he now hummed was 'I Have Often Walked Down This Street Before'. "How corny can you get?" He chuckled to himself. Still walking on he glanced into shop windows, long since darkened and as he came to the corner, a movement in the shadows caught his eye. Peering into the darkness, he made out the form of a slight figure, its back turned away from the street. Matthew was able to determine that it was a man lurking there, fumbling with some object in his hands. Calling out, "Hey, what you doing, fella?" Matthew was surprised when the object in the man's hands suddenly flared and at the same time the stranger turned his head and spoke in a low, threatening voice. "Clear off, Yank! Mind your own bleeding business. Go on, bugger off!"

Shrugging his shoulders, Matthew walked on by the Rising Sun. His mood was too happy and he could not stir himself to retaliate. He had only meant to offer help in any case, if it had been needed.

Not giving the incident another thought, Matthew carried on his journey, still smiling with his recollections of the evening he had spent with Brenda.

CHAPTER 13

Ellie lay in her bed unable to sleep. It was after ten o'clock and even though she had tried counting sheep, she was still wide awake. She lay there thinking of all the things she wanted for Christmas and had hinted at to her parents.

Her mind drifted and she recalled her family's astonishment when she and Brenda had recounted the events leading up to and including the incident on the ice of the evening before. Her mother had wanted to rush out and find the man who had rescued her daughter, but Brenda had said she would thank him when she saw him next. They had fussed and worried over her, fetching her a hot cup of milk and two whole chocolate biscuits. She had sat in front of the fire wrapped in a blanket and had been allowed to stay up late with the adults. Her grandmother had, of course, pointed out that she should have been more closely watched and that the child would not have been in any danger if the adults who were with her had been more diligent in their duties. Her father had looked sheepish, taking the responsibility fully on his shoulders and had agreed with Sal. In future more care would be taken over her safety and she would be supervised at all times. Ellie was none too pleased with the outcome of it all. After all, she had not been hurt, just a little shaken up and she did not relish the idea of being constantly watched. She considered herself to be old enough to be allowed some freedom. Still, if she kept out of trouble for a few weeks everyone would probably forget all about it and she would be able to continue as she had.

Eyes wide open, Ellie listened as her grandmother mounted the stairs and heard the click of the bedroom door as Sal entered her room. Not long afterwards, she heard her parents also come up, their voices hushed as they passed her room. She heard the deep tones of her father's voice and the giggle in return of her mother. She smiled to herself in the darkness. All was right in her little world. Gradually, her eyes became heavy and she fell into a light sleep.

The insistent sound of an approaching fire engine awoke the small girl with a start. At first, she was disorientated and did not immediately realise what had startled her. Only when the light appeared at the bottom of her door and she heard her father go downstairs, did she become fully aware of the sounds around her.

The first fire engine had sped along the Brompton Road and was closely followed by another. The wail of a police siren in the distance brought the child sitting bolt upright, her ears straining towards the alien noises from the nearby road. Climbing out of bed, Ellie slid her feet into her slippers and pushed her arms into her dressing gown. Feeling her way across the room, she opened the door and peered out onto the landing. Simultaneously, the bedroom doors of Fay and Sal swung open.

"What's all the commotion? What the hell's going on?" Sal rubbed the sleep from her eyes. She was a formidable sight when dressed in her night attire. Her hair was caught in a brown net which stretched over her head, squashing her permed waves flat to her skull. And from neck to ankle a pale pink winceyette night gown made sure that not the merest hint of bare flesh would be seen. Over this she wore a candlewick dressing gown of a washed worn blue. On her feet were the carpet slippers that she favoured and were worn at all times except when she was going to church or left the square for any other reason.

"I heard a fire engine, Nan. Dad's already gone downstairs. Where's Mum?" Ellie stepped back as Sal brushed past her, calling over her shoulder that the two girls should stay where they were and keep out of the way.

At this point, Cathy emerged from the back bedroom. "And what are you two doing hanging around here? Go back to bed, there's nothing to see. Go on." She followed Sal down the stairs without a backward glance.

"Come on, Ellie. We'll go in my room. We can see up the road from my window. I suppose there's no point in trying to wake Billy, he'll be dead to the world as usual. Even if a bomb dropped on the place, he wouldn't wake up!" Re-entering her room, Fay pulled Ellie in behind her and the two sisters sat on the windowsill and watched the spectacle from this vantage point.

Below, the Mews was alive with people. Light spilled from open doorways and lit the small statue in the centre. Adorned in her festive garlands, the Mermaid stared with glassy eyes towards the entrance of her namesake. Most of the residents were milling about there.

"What's on fire? Can anyone see?"

"It's the pub. Christ, what a blaze!"

"It's taken hold, there's no way they'll save that, not now."

"Well, say goodbye to the Rising Sun, she'll never see another day."

"Anyone know how it started?"

"Silly bleeder probably left one of his paraffin heaters on. All those wood beams and panelling, it would have gone up like a match box."

"Well he'll get short shift from the insurance blokes. He was told not to have paraffin stoves in there, silly sod."

"Is everyone alright? Did they all get out?"

"There's no sign of an ambulance, so they must have, mustn't they?"

Jack, Cathy and Sal stood amid the chatter and speculation. neither one had uttered a word as they stared at the flames leaping high into the night sky. Thick black smoke billowed from the ground floor windows of the Rising Sun and the fire threatened to spread to the small confectioner's shop adjoining.

Firemen were frantically unreeling hoses and connecting them to the water mains in the road. Soon, like giant snakes, the hoses wriggled into life as streams of spluttering water were trained first on the neighbouring shop in an effort to contain the fire, then into the heart of the blaze. They sky above the building glowed a dull red and highlighted the scene below.

Slowly, the blaze was brought under control and by 3.00am it was all over bar the shouting. The Rising Sun, Public House built in 1886, was no more than a smouldering pile of rubble. The Landlord and his family stood in the street and gaped in shock at the remains of their livelihood and their home. No lives were lost that night and no injuries were reported, but a hard working, honest man and his family were left homeless and destitute. When questioned, the landlord was emphatic in his denial of leaving any heaters lit after he had retired to bed. He maintained that he was extra diligent in this matter and took great pains each and every night to ensure that all stoves were completely extinguished before he let the bar staff go home. "It's one of my little foibles," he insisted, "I always make sure the heaters are off as I knew what a fire could do to the place. To be honest, one of the only things in this life that really frightens me, is getting caught in a fire. You ask anyone, they'll tell you. Big strapping bloke like me and I'm frightened to death of fire. It couldn't have been because of one of my stoves, it just couldn't have."

The police made careful notes and took the landlord's statement. An investigation would have to be held by the Fire Brigade and if the paraffin heaters were not responsible and an electrical fault was not found, then arson would have to be considered as the only other option.

Jack and Frank had approached the publican and offered him and his family overnight accommodation at their respective homes. Although the offer was refused, it had been gratefully received. "Thanks Jack and you too Frank, but we'll be OK. I've got a brother lives just over the water in Battersea. I've sent my son over there and no doubt he'll be back shortly with the cavalry!"

People had begun to drift away back to the warmth of their houses. Sal and Cathy had said their goodbyes and were already tucked up in their beds as Frank and Jack stood by the fountain discussing the evening's events.

"Seems to be a bit of a mystery, doesn't it? I reckon Ernie's right about the stoves. He wouldn't have left one of them burning. I've heard people say he's almost fanatical about putting them out at night." Jack drew deeply on his cigarette and gazed up at the sky.

"Yeah, it's all a bit odd, isn't it? But I can't see as anyone would want to torch his place. He's as good as gold, old Ernie. You couldn't wish to meet a nicer bloke. I can't understand it." Hands in pockets, Frank leaned against the base of the fountain, his feet shuffling at the snow sludge that lay there.

Suddenly, Jack turned his head towards the archway. "Shush a minute, Frank! Listen. Who's that coming in here at this late hour?" The two men peered into the darkness as a slight figure ambled into the Mews.

Head down and whistling under his breath, Seb meandered into the square. So intent on his own thoughts was he, that he did not notice the two men stood staring at him. He was brought up short as Jack spoke, his voice echoing round the empty square.

"Bit late, even for you, isn't it, Seb? Your wife will be waiting behind the door with a rolling pin, I shouldn't wonder."

Frank immediately took up the theme. "What you been up to till this hour then, Seb? I wouldn't want to be in your shoes when I got indoors. Christ, she'll have your guts for garters, what with her being such a tyrant and all. You'll be black and blue all over tomorrow and it being Christmas Eve as well. What a shame!"

Seb stood eyeing them warily, poised at the entrance, ready to run back the way he had come if needs be.

"You missed all the fun tonight and all. Mind you, I'd hate to see a grown man cry and you would have been real upset to see your local go up in flames. Don't seem to be many more pubs left that'll let you in now, does there Seb? At this rate, you'll be doing your drinking out in the sticks. What do you reckon, Frank?"

Jack and Frank laughed at the little man before them, their wide grins splitting their faces, white teeth gleaming in the moonlight.

"Oh, yeah, ha, ha! You go on and have your little joke. You're like two old women, snooping about and meddling in other people's lives. What's the matter? Got nothing bleeding better to do? Haven't you got any homes to go to, or have your wives kicked you out. I expect they could do with a couple of real men in their beds instead of you two nancy boys. Well, after tonight you'll have something else to think about, you mark my words."

Taking a wide berth around the fountain, Seb sidled into his own house and before the two men realised it, he had banged his front door shut.

Frank turned to his neighbour, "What was all that about then? What's he on about?"

"Search me. Did you notice, though? He wasn't drunk. Sober as a judge, wasn't he? And where would he have been until now? The pubs closed more than four hours ago."

"Unless he's got a bit on the side, though God knows who'd have him. Must be some old tart, someone real desperate. Well, I'm off to my bed, can't stand here chatting to you all bloody night. See you in the morning, Jack. Cheerio."

Jack raised his hand absently in farewell. Making his own way home, he pondered Seb's last words. What could he have meant? What sort of trouble lay in store for them all now? Closing the door softly behind him, Jack ascended the stairs and entered his bedroom quietly.

"That you, Jack? You took your time, didn't you? I was just going to come and have a look for you. You must be freezing." Cathy pulled back the bedclothes as her husband climbed into bed and the two lay down, close together, hands clasped.

"Me and Frank was nattering outside and guess who walks in, Cool as a cucumber and not a smell of drink on him? Bloody Seb Ridley! Anyway, we had a little dig at him and he had a go back, but it was what he said at the end that's got me worried. Sort of like a warning, like something nasty was going to happen. And soon, real soon."

"Don't worry about it, Jack. You know what the little weasel's like. He probably wanted to get you all stirred up, so you wouldn't be able to get any sleep tonight. Just forget about it. It's Christmas Eve tomorrow, no, today. It's Christmas Eve now. We've got enough on our plate without worrying about petty little threats from scum like Seb Ridley."

Leaning over, Jack kissed his wife's brow. "You're right. Goodnight, love. See you in the morning."

*

Even as Jack and Cathy settled down for the night, Seb sat in his living room in the darkness, smiling to himself. When the overhead light was suddenly switched on, he sat up sharply, blinking in the brightness. "Turn that light off, you stupid bitch!"

"I thought we had burglars, Seb. What are you doing sitting here in the dark? And where have you been? I've been worried to death. I thought you were in the Rising Sun tonight? Have you heard? It went up like a powder keg, there's nothing left and Ernie and his family have had to go to his brother's house." Vera stood in the doorway, her hand still on the light switch.

Seb shot out of his chair and in two strides, he crossed the room and was before his wife. Hands clenched by his sides, he spoke quietly and menacingly, "I did go to the Rising Sun earlier, then I went to the World's End, not that I have to answer to the likes of you." Both his hands now grasped Vera's neck as he continued, "And after the pubs closed I went for a walk round the shops looking in the windows, then I went down the embankment for a stroll and bumped into some mates of mine and we went back to their place for a while, OK? But remember to keep your big mouth shut. I don't want my business bandied round the bleeding neighbourhood, understand? Else I'll have you. And I don't care how many fucking body guards you get, I'll see you get yours, right?"

Eyes bulging as Seb's hands squeezed tighter, Vera struggled to free herself. Gasping for breath she replied, "Yes, Seb, yes. Let go, I can't breathe!" Seb loosened his hands abruptly and Vera collapsed in a small heap at his feet.

"Just remember, Vera. This was just a warning. If I have to remind you again, you'll wish you were dead when I've bloody finished with you, hear?"

"I won't say anything, Seb. I never do. Honest, I always stand by you. Why do you have to do this to me? I don't deserve it, you've no need to act like this with me." Openly crying now, Vera huddled on the floor, knees bent under her chin, arms clasped around her upper body.

Sneering at her, Seb pulled open the door and went to bed.

Slowly, her sobs subsiding, Vera stood up. She looked about her in a confused manner. What had brought this attack on? Everything had been going so well and now suddenly they were back to square one. What had changed to give Seb the courage to turn on her again? And the strange thing about it all was that Seb did not appear to be at all drunk. In fact, when his face had been close to hers, there had not been even a hint of alcohol fumes. Surely, she thought, if he had been with any of his friends before returning home, he would have smelt of some sort of alcohol? After all, the people Seb was acquainted with, liked to drink. It was unthinkable that he had returned to one of their homes and come back to her sober. What was going on? These questions spun in her head as Vera turned from the room, switched off the light and reluctantly returned to her bed.

CHAPTER 14

Christmas Eve found each and every household in Mermaid Mews abustle with activity. Delicious aromas of slowly cooking turkey mingled with the smell of chestnut stuffing, sausage rolls and mince pies, wafting from open kitchen windows. Children played close to home in the square under a threatening sky, heavy with the promise of more snow. The women toiled in their kitchens; rolling pastry, basting birds and generally overseeing the men.

"Jack? Have you brought in the coal? And what are those kids up to? I told them to tidy their rooms and put the hoover round. Go and see if you can find them, will you?" Cathy wiped a floury hand across her brow. She had been up since six o'clock and although she had been working steadily for four hours, there was still so much to be done. Glancing across at her mother-in-law, she said, "I'll skin them kids alive if they've gone off. We've got enough to do without chasing after them all day." Putting down the rolling pin, Cathy placed her hands on her lower back and stretched, a soft weary sigh escaping from her. "You ready for a cuppa, Mother? I think you and I deserve a break."

"Sit yourself down, Cathy. I'll do it. I could do with stretching my legs. I feel as if I've sat at that table for a fortnight and if I never see another brussel sprout or carrot again, it'll be too soon." Lumbering up from the table, Sal rose and filled the kettle. Idly, she glanced up and through the kitchen window and in that instance the nose of a black Wolsley inched into the archway and came to a stop within the shadow of the fountain.

"Eye, eye. What's up, now? Quick, come here, Cathy. A police car's just turned up."

The two women stood at the kitchen sink and watched as two plain clothed policemen climbed out of the parked car and made their way up the path of No. 3. Knocking sharply on the door, they stood and waited. Answering, Frank Carmichael exchanged a few brief words with the two men then ushered them into his home.

"What's all that about then? I hope it isn't bad news. Eileen's people live out Windsor way and she said her Mum had been ill lately. Please God, it's not something to do with that. Not today of all days."

Now that there was nothing to see, Cathy turned from the window and returned to her chair.

"No, it won't be that. They don't send out plain clothed detectives to tell you if someone's died. Just an ordinary Bobbie would do that. No, it must be something else and something really bad for that lot to turn out. I wonder what they've been up to?" Sal stayed by the window, hoping for some clues when the policemen left.

It was over an hour before the door of No. 3 opened once more and the two detectives stepped out onto the path. Only this time they were not alone. Between them, Frankie Carmichael, head bowed, also left the house. He shuffled awkwardly to the gate, sandwiched between the two adults and slid into the back of the waiting car. The first policeman walked around the car and opening the door got in and sat behind the wheel, whilst the other detective climbed into the rear with Frankie.

Sal watched in astonishment as the black shiny car circled the square and disappeared back through the Mew's entrance. The playing children had stopped and now stood in huddles, staring after the retreating vehicle, glancing from time to time at the door of the Carmichael's house.

Cathy had rejoined Sal at the window when Sal had muttered, "Well, I'll be buggered! Look at that!" as Frankie had been escorted from his home. They both stood there staring into the square until the sound of the front door opening then slamming shut made the two women jump, guilty at the thought of being caught acting like peeping Toms.

Jack entered the kitchen, looking first at Cathy's questioning look, then at his mother's more inquisitive face.

"Don't stand there looking at me as if I know all the answers. I'm as much in the dark as you two. Cathy, get the kids in. I don't want them standing out there gawping at Frank's house. They're like bloody vultures waiting to swoop down and pick over the bones. If Frank and Eileen want us involved, they'll come over and tell us. Until then, I don't want to catch my family peering out of windows, spying on them."

Not uttering a word, Cathy left the kitchen and went in search of her children. As she opened the front door, she clearly heard the exchange between Sal and Jack.

"Give over, Jack. We weren't doing any harm. It's only natural that we would want to know what was going on. After all, it's not everyday that a police car rolls into here, is it?"

"I don't care if the whole of Scotland Yard comes here and starts crawling all over the place. Frank and Eileen are our friends and we shouldn't be snooping into their affairs. As I've said, if they want to tell us anything then they will, but not one person in this house is going to go poking their nose into their business, right Mother?"

Softly, Cathy closed the front door. Jack was right. It was none of their business. Feeling ashamed of herself and annoyed with Sal for encouraging her, Cathy spoke sharply to the children still standing in the Mews.

"Fay? Get in doors. And you two. There's nothing to see and even if there was, it's got nothing to do with any of you. Go on, get in. You can get on with the jobs you were supposed to do this morning. And as for you other kids, get on into your own houses and stop mooning around out here." Turning abruptly, Cathy followed her children into the house and as she shut the door, she noticed with some satisfaction that the square was now empty, the only figure still remaining was one of marble and she would be unable to tell of the morning's happenings.

Half an hour passed without further event. As was their custom, the cockney inhabitants of Mermaid Mews stayed behind closed doors. Should the need arise, they would be more than willing to rally round and lend their support but until such time as this was called upon, it would appear to be unseemly to exhibit any show of curiosity.

As the first flurries of snow that day drifted down upon the shoulders of the Mermaid statue, the door of No. 3 opened and Frank Carmichael came out and hurried down his path and up that of the Treist's. He rapped loudly at the door, jigging up and down, from foot to foot as he impatiently waited for an answer. Jack did not keep his friend lingering there long. Almost as if he had been waiting in the hallway, the door opened quickly and Jack beckoned his neighbour into the warmth of his home.

"You OK, Frank?"

"Yeah, I'm alright, but Eileen's in a bit of a state. The police have been round and arrested Frankie. They say he's mixed up with the fire last night. Something to do with nicking a lighter from the tobacconist's over the other side of the new council estate. Of course, they haven't actually arrested him as he's a minor, but they've taken him down to the cop shop in Chelsea for further questioning. I'm just on my way down there to make sure they don't frighten the boy into saying something stupid and making a full confession to something that I'm sure he had nothing to do with."

"Bloody hell! Why do the coppers think Frankie's mixed up with that business last night? Just because they think he pinched a lighter, doesn't mean he had anything to do with a fire half a mile away. Anyway, your Frankie might be a bit rash at times, but he's no arsonist. Why would he want to do a thing like that in any case? He's got no reason to torch the pub." Indignant for his friend, Jack's voice had risen.

"I know, I know. It doesn't make sense. The thing is though, this lighter that Frankie's supposed to have nicked was worth a few bob, gold plated I think, and the bloody thing only goes and turns up in the ashes of the Rising Sun. Apparently, the police did a search through the rubble with the fire brigade, trying to find out what caused the fire in the first place and somehow they can tell where it all started. And right at that spot, round the side of the building, is this lighter. The old geezer from the shop went down the station this morning and reported the theft, even said he had an idea who had filched it. Frankie and his mate go in there a lot it seems and the old bloke knows who they are. Well, when the police find the sodding stolen lighter at the scene of the crime, they put two and two together and then come a calling." Standing in the dim hallway light, Frank's troubled face looked drawn and pale and Jack could only listen with sympathy as the tale continued.

"You can imagine how scared Frankie is. When they started questioning him, at first he said he had nothing to do with any of it, but after about twenty minutes, the boy really got the wind up and admits that he did steal the lighter, but that was all. He says his mate Ron told him to get rid of it because it was too hot to handle and Frankie's supposed to have chucked it down a drain on the Wandon Road estate. He swears that's the last he saw of it and he hasn't a bloody clue how it ended up at the Rising Sun. Like you, I know Frankie acts before he thinks and that's probably how he came to swipe the bloody thing in the first place. But, honestly Jack, I don't believe he would set fire to a pub. He would have known there was people in the building. He might be a little sod at times, but there's no harm in him. There's no way he'd have deliberately put people's lives at risk."

Jack squeezed his friend's shoulder reassuringly. "Of course not. I know Frankie and he wouldn't have done something like that.

Don't worry, there's no way they'll be able to pin this on him. Christ, once they start really questioning him, they'll be able to tell right off that he's not guilty. Listen, do you want me to come down the cop shop with you? You might need a bit of morale support and I know one or two of the Bobbies down there, they might be able to keep us in the picture."

"Thanks, Jack. I'd appreciate any help I can get. One last favour. Do you think your Cathy would go over and sit with Eileen until we get back? I don't want her worrying on her own. She wanted to come with me but I thought it best if she stayed put. The last thing Frankie needs is his mother crying all over the place and making a scene."

"Hang on a minute, I'll go and ask her." Jack hurried down the hallway and shortly reappeared with Cathy in tow. Donning coats and hats as it was now snowing heavily, husband and wife followed Frank back to his house.

Not two minutes after the three had entered No. 3, than the door swung open again and Jack and Frank emerged and walking at a brisk pace, crossed the square and left Mermaid Mews. Neither man looked right nor left, too intent were they in their own conversation so the twitching of the curtain at No. 1 went unnoticed.

As the two men rounded the corner, Seb Ridley watched their departure with mean and hateful eyes. The smile on his face was not one of innocent joy but rather the grimace of malignant pleasure. Any onlooker seeing that face framed in the window through swirling snow flakes would know instantly that a foul deed was afoot. His image beyond the glass conjured thoughts of evil men and the atrocities that man can perform. Slowly, he turned from the window, muttering slyly under his breath, "Now we'll see what happens to bleeding trouble makers and do gooders. Let's see how they get out of this one because no amount of smooth talking is going to put that lot in the clear. I only wish I could find a way to get at the Treist's and all. Still, mustn't be greedy. Getting one of them's better than none at all." Rubbing his hands together, Seb could hardly contain his glee and even the appearance of Vera did not quell his spiteful pleasure. Pushing past his wife saying, "I'm off up the Worlds End", Seb pulled on his outdoor clothes and left the house, a snigger on his lips as the door closed behind him.

Puzzled, Vera stood in the space by the window that her husband had vacated and watched Seb's retreating back. She remained there long after he was out of view still trying to fathom his buoyant spirits and when some time later Angela entered the room, this was how she found her.

The young girl crossed the room and placed her arms about her mother. "Everything alright, Mum?"

Vera shook herself and smiling she replied, "Yes, love. I'm just wondering what your father's up to now. He was standing in here looking really pleased with himself, like the cat who's got the cream. I don't like it when he's like that, it usually means trouble for someone. And knowing my luck that someone's probably me."

"Oh, Mum. You must be imagining it. He's been behaving himself for ages now. There hasn't been any sign of the usual trouble, has there?" When Vera shook her head, Angela continued, "Well, there you go. Come on, there's still lots to do before tomorrow. This is going to be the best Christmas we've ever had." Pulling Vera behind her, Angela led her from the room.

Outside, heavy snow clouds gathered over London and they shed their load in a continual downpour of large, white flakes. By that evening all traffic would be at a standstill and the city would be a locked frozen world. The normal hustle and bustle of England's capital would gradually come to a halt, with only the bravest of souls willing to venture out and face the elements.

The exception to this rule were those who sought spiritual comfort and the promise of a better life in the hereafter.

"I don't care if it snows until hell freezes over, nothing and no-one's going to keep me from going to Mass tonight. And in case anyone in this family thinks they can use the weather as an excuse not to go to Midnight Mass, they've got another think coming. As far back as I can remember, the Treist's have always been present at the Oratory on Christmas Eve and Christmas Day. Even through the wars, someone from this family was there. So don't anyone try telling me that it's too cold or slippery for us to go tonight, right?" Sal glared at her grandchildren.

Billy and Ellie, eyes downcast, stood in the kitchen doorway whilst Fay, who had dared to make the suggestion of missing the evening service, sullenly stared back at her grandmother.

"Well, I was only thinking of you Nan. By tonight the roads and pavements are going to be like an ice rink and anyway, no-one else will bother, so perhaps there won't even be a Mass. Father O'Connell's hardly likely to have Mass on his own, is he?"

"There are times, my girl, when I could really slap you. Don't you go pretending you were thinking of my welfare, the only person you're thinking of is you. And if Father O'Connell can open the church and perform Mass when there's bombs falling round his head, don't you think he might laugh at a little snow? I don't want to hear another word about it and when your Mum and Dad gets back, I'll tell them the same thing. Now go and make yourself useful, there's plenty of things to be done before anyone goes anywhere tonight. And you two," Sal nodded her head at Billy and Ellie who had not uttered a word since following their sister, curious as to the outcome of her suggestion, "you can both fetch in the coal. Your Dad didn't have time to do it before he had to go off with Frank. God knows we've got enough to do today, but then this has to happen. When either of them'll be back, is anyone's guess, so until they do, I'll give the orders round here and we'll get on with it without them."

The three trailed out, Fay hissing under her breath about 'the old dragon' and the other two obediently going about the business of bringing in the coal.

Thus, the Treist household occupied themselves, awaiting the return of Jack and Cathy. Some good three hours would pass and the time would be almost three o'clock before they heard further news of the plight of Frankie Carmichael.

And still the snow fell. Large flakes settled on the head of the statuette, covering her in an icy mantle and blinding her eyes to the events which would follow.

CHAPTER 15

By the time Jack and Frank returned to the square, large snow drifts were banked up all around the fountain. The snow had fallen thick and fast and now it was not possible to discern where the pavement finished and the road started. Even the tracks of the odd car that could still be found on the roads, were soon covered, thus giving the streets of London and eerie, deserted look. Add to this a strong north-easterly wind causing the snow to fall at a spiral slant, then the scene is set.

Shoulders hunched forward, their bodies leaning into the wind, the two men almost stumbled into the Mews. Not speaking and with Frank leading, they made their way up the path of No. 3 and pushed their way into the house. As Jack entered the hallway of his friend's home, he turned quickly and with both hands, shoved hard at the door and closed it against the bitter cold and insistent icy snow flakes.

Unwinding his scarf from around his lower face and neck, Frank shook himself as a dog might do, leaving fast melting piles of ice at his feet.

"Get yourself out of them clothes, Jack, before you catch your death of cold. I'll go on in and get Eileen to put the kettle on. I'm not going to start reciting word for word what happened, because that's what she'll want, until I've had a cuppa."

Soon, both men were sat at the kitchen table, their hands clasping steaming cups of tea. Eileen and Cathy sat at one end, waiting patiently for their men to thaw out, glancing apprehensively at one another. By the looks on Frank's and Jack's faces, the news did not bode well.

Eileen fidgeted in her chair, her eyes darting from one man to the other until she could wait no longer.

"Frank, you'd better start talking, or I'm going to go crazy. It can't be that bad and even if it is, I have to know. So, out with it, what happened?"

Looking first at Jack, then raising his head, Frank spoke directly to his wife.

"Now, Eileen, don't go off the deep end, try and stay calm and let me tell it in my own way. You can ask questions after I've finished, OK?" Pale faced and eyes wide, the plump redhead nodded in acquiescence.

"Right." Frank placed both hands on the table, putting together in his mind the pieces of the events that had taken place at the police station.

"When me and Jack got to the cop shop, Frankie was being interviewed by one of them detectives. The desk sergeant told us that a social worker had been called and the three of them were all together in a little room down a corridor. He told us that it was nearly over and that we should take a seat and someone would come and fetch me when they'd finished. Well, we must have waited about an hour before the door opens and a bloke comes out. He was the taller one of the two cops that came here. Anyway, he sort of beckons to me and when I goes over he says that they've finished questioning Frankie for now and that I can go in." Fiddling with his empty cup, Frank looked to Jack for confirmation. The other man gave a quick nod of agreement and Frank continued.

"I went into the room and saw Frankie sitting on one side of a table and this woman sat the other side. She looks up and when she sees me, she gets up and holds out her hand, saying, "Good afternoon. You must be Frankie's father, Mr. Carmichael. I'm Miss Ansell. The police have asked me to act as Frankie's Welfare Officer, as he's a minor. This is quite normal in these circumstances, unless you have any objections and would like to appoint another officer in my stead." Well, I thought, we wouldn't know one Welfare Officer from another, so we might just as well stick with this one. Anyway, I sits down with Frankie and puts my arm round him. He was shaking all over and sort of buried his head in my shoulder."

At this point, Eileen could no longer contain herself. Raising her hand to her mouth, she whispered, "They hadn't hit him or anything, had they Frank?"

"No, love, no. He was just scared. So this Miss Ansell, who was only a kid herself, she couldn't have been more than twenty five, starts telling me what's happened. She said that Frankie had been charged - with theft and suspicion of arson and because of the time of year and because Frankie is a minor, he would have to go to a house of detention until he could go to court. Of course, I started ranting and raving and said that we'd take him home and keep an eye on him until the case came up, but she said that arrangements had already been made and a car was coming for them soon. I argued until I was blue in the face, saying this was his first offence and everything and Frankie starts crying and holding on to me. But the mean faced bitch said that the authorities were taking a much harder stand as there'd been too much of this sort of thing going on with the youngsters these days."

Eileen was openly crying now, her fists bunched into her mouth, whilst Cathy hugged her, making small soothing sounds. Still Frank, did not go to his wife. He knew he would have to finish the story before comforting Eileen, otherwise he might not be able to continue.

"Well, they brought us in a cup of tea and I made Frank drink his. I put lots of sugar in it, because that's supposed to be good if you've had a shock and I kept telling him it would be alright and that he'd only have to go to this detention place for a few days, just until the courts opened up again. I didn't like to tell him that I thought they were closed until the New Year, because I thought he might go hysterical on me."

Frank stopped for a moment and almost to himself, he muttered, "What really worries me is: Frankie's never been away from home before and this place he's going to is probably full of yobs and bloody hooligans. The poor little sod won't know what's hit him being thrown in with a crowd like that. It shouldn't be allowed. First timers shouldn't be put with hard nuts. Frankie's only fourteen and although he likes to act the big man, inside he's still a kid. Besides, kids of that age should be with their families at Christmas, not shut up in some bleeding kids prison."

Jack looked across at his wife, who was near to tears herself. When Frank had come out of the interviewing room and told Jack what the authorities were planning to do, Jack had spoken to the desk sergeant. And even though he had pleaded with the man, the sergeant had shook his head, saying that the matter was out of their hands now and that they would just have to go along with it all.

"Whereabouts have they taken him then? We must be allowed to go and visit him. You did find out where this place is, didn't you, Frank?" Asked Eileen, her eyes seeking those of her husband's.

"There's no way, love. They've taken him right out of London, somewhere in Sussex, we'd never be able to get there. Have you seen the roads? There's no cars around and the buses have stopped, which means there'll be no trains either. I've got an address and a phone number. We'll go down the road in a minute and try and call him, alright? They told me as we were leaving that the case'll be up on 3rd January and someone'll let us know what time and which court."

Frank rose from his chair and went to his wife. Kneeling by the side of her chair, he took both her hands into his own, saying, "Come on, love, don't take on so. He'll be alright. You know what Frankie's like, nothing gets him down for long. Look, we've got to keep our chins up for the sake of the other kids. We can't go spoiling their Christmas and all, can we?"

Slowly Eileen stopped crying and, sniffing loudly, she looked down into her husband's face. "You're right, Frank. We've got to keep our spirits up. It's just that I can't believe it. One minute we're all getting ready for Christmas, laughing and joking together, then the next thing I know, someone comes along and takes one of my kids off to a police station, then shoves him into the back of beyond where I can't get to him. What a bloody mess, Frank. How can they think that Frankie would do something so awful? I know he took that lighter, but I also know he wouldn't have done a terrible thing like setting fire to the pub. They won't be able to pin that on him, will they Frank? He'll never be able to hold his head up round here again, if they do."

"Of course they won't. We'll get him a good Solicitor and he'll get off with a telling off and a fine for pinching the lighter, that's all. Now come on, give us a smile, eh?" Reaching up, Frank hugged his wife and she put her arms around his neck and leant her head on his shoulder.

Clearing her throat, Cathy caught Jack's attention and indicated with a small shake of her head towards the door, that they should leave. They both rose and left the couple still holding on to each other. Taking their coats from the stand in the hallway, Cathy and Jack went quietly out into the snow filled square, closing the door softly behind them.

Cathy linked arms with Jack, saying in an undertone, "Poor old Eileen. She thinks the sun shines out of Frankie and even though he's not the saint she'd like to think he is, Frankie's not the thug the police are making him out to be. Jesus Christ, it could happen to anyone, not least of all, us. Kids will be kids. They do stupid things at that age and it's only luck that most of them don't get caught. It could just have easily been one of ours down the station now."

Picking his way carefully down the path, Frank replied, "I know what you mean. Still, what puzzles me is; how did that lighter come to be in the rubble at the pub? Young Frankie swears he threw it away long before the pub caught fire. Apparently, the police are off round Ron's house this afternoon, that's the boy that was with Frankie last night. Frankie insists that Ron had nothing to do with stealing the lighter, but the police are going round to check out his story. I only hope Ron backs up Frankie and doesn't make up a different tale to make himself look good."

Entering their own house, Jack and Cathy went directly to the kitchen. The children heard their parents arrive and all three came tearing down the stairs, not wanting to miss out on one single word of explanation. Tumbling into the room, Fay first, they bumped one after the other into the backs of their parents.

"Oi, you lot! What's your hurry? Stop pushing and shoving and let me and your mother get our coats off and sit down. Now stop your chattering else we'll make you go back upstairs and then you'll not find out a thing." Glancing over at Sal, Jack asked, "Everything alright, Mother? Sorry we've been so long. It couldn't be helped."

Sal looked first at her son's worried face, then at Cathy's red rimmed eyes. "Not good news, then? I saw you and Frank come back and gathered they'd kept Frankie at the station. How's Eileen taking it? Is she alright?"

Piece by piece, Jack and Cathy retold the sorry tale, with Sal tutting and making small 'Humph' sounds. When, finally, they had finished, Sal looked at both of them and said quietly, "Well, there, but for the grace of God, go we."

Silence reigned for several minutes as each member of the Treist family inwardly digested the meaning behind Sal's words. Then, Cathy rose abruptly and going to the oven spoke loudly to her family.

"We can just thank our lucky star that it's not this family that's going to have a rotten Christmas. And you kids, just think about it and let it be a lesson to all of us." Bending down, she opened the oven door and peering inside said, "When was the last time someone had a look at this bird? It'll be cremated if it's left in for much longer."

Smiling, Frank ushered the children out of the room, saying, "Right then, you lot. Who's going to give me a hand with the tree? If we don't get a move on, it won't be decorated before Father Christmas comes tonight."

Skipping backwards before her father, Ellie shouted, "Me, me! I'll help you, Dad. Can I put the fairy on the top? Can I, dad, can I?" Whilst Fay, winking knowingly at her brother, whispered, "Father Christmas, eh? Looks like we'll have to play along for another year, else we'll get it in the neck for spoiling it for Ellie."

Billy giggled and winked back, but secretly he was disappointed. He wished he had not found out that Santa Claus was a myth and that he could still be blissfully happy in his ignorance. Some of the sparkle had gone out of this Christmas for Billy, as is want to happen when children discover that the red and white clothed gentleman exists only in fairy tales.

At the afternoon drew to a close and darkness cloaked Mermaid Mews, fairy lights twinkled from behind closed curtains and winked at the dainty, frozen figure sat atop of the fountain.

Christmas Eve had truly arrived. For some, such as Brenda, this night held a dizzy anticipation, the like she had never known before. And the same could be said for Fay, who still harboured plans for her secret rendezvous at the youth club. And for others, this Christmas was marred. Eileen and Frank would celebrate as normal for the benefit of their other children, but Frankie would be sorely missed by his absence.

Other than Vera and Angela, who looked forward for the first time to a happy Christmas, the other residents expected this year to be no different to many other merry Christmases: A time of sharing and forging the bonds between family and neighbours. And a time to squirrel away memories ready to be taken out in later years to be perused with pleasure.

Not so. Events of that day and the incidents leading up to them, were coming to a head. Soon, very soon, the Mermaid would witness a tragedy that although inevitable, would compromise the beliefs and opinions of all her residents.

CHAPTER 16

Lottie and Sal sat in the cosy warmth of the kitchen. They were seated at Charlotte's table, two full glasses and a half empty bottle of port between them. Having excused herself from the Treist household on the pretext of offering her services to the lone woman, Sal had rushed over at the earliest opportunity. She loved to be the bearer of the latest gossip, whether this be good or bad news.

For the past hour, Sal had relayed every last piece of information pertaining to the day's happenings and they had picked over each morsel with a morbid relish.

"Of course, I always knew that boy would come to no good. Too much freedom, that's what I say. You have to keep your kids on a short leash, else they get themselves into all sorts of trouble. I remember my old Mum saying, 'Children should be seen, but not heard' and I think that still holds today. All this freedom of speech, what a load of old codswallop. How can kids of fourteen and fifteen know their own minds? They haven't even lived yet. So, it's up to us grown-ups to tell them how to behave and what to think. I'm not wrong, am I Lottie?" Not waiting for a reply, Sal continued with her favourite tirade, more than confident of her own opinions.

"The times I've said to Jack that he's making a rod for his own back, but will he listen to me? No, will he hell as like. But there you have it - the kids of today think they know it all and we know nothing. How the bleeding hell do they think we've lived this long and through two wars? But if I so much as open my mouth to give them the benefit of my advice, which I had to learn the hard way, then I get my head bitten off." Sal paused for breath and Lottie seized her chance.

"I couldn't agree with you more, Sal. The trouble with the kids today is, they just won't listen. They're in such a bloody hurry, rushing through life, always wanting to get onto the next thing, that they don't stop and think. Well, when they get to our age, they'll have more than enough time to look back on their mistakes. And you know what? At the end of the day it'll all be our fault. It'll be our generation that'll get all the blame for repressing them when they were young. No respect that's where the problems lie. No respect for their elders. They want to stick them all in the army for a spell, that's what they should do with the louts hanging round street corners. Give them a bit of discipline and burn off some of their energy. I always say if

Churchill was still in power, none of this trouble with kids would have happened. He wouldn't have stood for no nonsense. You wouldn't have the bullying and stealing that goes on today. He'd have come down on them like a ton of bricks, squashed all the trouble before it had time to take a hold."

Sal nodded her head, sagely, her iron grey, permed waves bobbing as she sympathised with Lottie.

"Where's it all going to end, that's what I'd like to know? They all just want, want, want and when all's said and done, sooner or later they're going to have to give something back. You can't keep taking from the pot, because one day you'll go to it and it'll be empty. All these new fangled gadgets the women want today. Cathy's been on to Jack for a washing machine! I ask you! Who does she think Jack is? Bloody royalty or something? Why can't she make do with a sink and scrubbing board? She's got a boiler and a wringer, which is more than I had. You wait, if he gives in to her, she'll be after a car next! I'll have to start practising my royal wave else they'll leave me at home!"

More than a little tipsy, the two women bent their heads together and laughed, giggling and spluttering until gasping for breath, Lottie managed, "Oh give over, Sal! My face aches and my stomach hurts from laughing so much. No, stop, stop!" Sal was waving her hand in an imitation of what she thought was a queenly wave, "I'll wet myself in a minute, I will, I will!"

"How do you do? Queen Sal here. What an exceptionally nice house you have, Mrs. Goodbody. And is this room for preparing food? Where are all your servants? Given them the day off, have you? Jolly good show, what?"

Pushing at her friend, Lottie's eyes streamed with tears of merriment. "Oh, you are a one, Sal. I haven't had a good laugh like this in years. You should be on the stage." Simultaneously, the two said, "Yeah, sweeping it!"

Outside, Matthew Goldberg had just entered the Mews and was walking at a brisk pace towards Ruby's house. As he passed Lottie's house he could hear loud, raucous laughter coming from within. He stopped and listened for a while, smiling at the sound. "Someone sounds as if they're having a good time. A little Christmas spirit, perhaps? More like a double, if the truth were known!" He carried on and soon found himself standing in the small hallway of No. 2, hat in hand, looking into the face of Ruby O'Shea.

"She won't be a minute. Come on into the lounge." As with most working class families, this room was reserved for special occasions. Rarely used, the curtains drawn part way shut at all times to preserve the furniture against sunlight, Ruby came in here only to clean. She glanced quickly about the room, checking it's tidiness and, once satisfied, ushered Matthew in.

"Have a seat and I'll give her a shout. Would you like a drink, while your waiting? Tea, coffee or something stronger. We don't normally keep booze in the house, but I've got some in for Christmas." Turning to a small, glass fronted cabinet, Ruby swung open the doors to reveal several green and brown unopened bottles. "What would you like? Brenda tells me you like whisky. I can offer you a glass of this, but I don't know if it's the one you like." Indicating a half bottle of Scotch whisky, Ruby looked with enquiry at the American.

"Fine, that'd be just fine, Mrs. O'Shea." Matthew sat on the very edge of the small brown sofa, hat dangling in his hands, between his knees.

"Now, I know you like ice with it, but we can't stretch to that here. I can put some ginger in it or just water?"

"No, really. It's fine as it is." Leaning back Matthew surveyed the room whilst Ruby was busy with his drink. The dominating colours of this reception room were brown and green. Full length sage green curtains hung at the only window. They had obviously seen better days as the colour was pale where the natural folds were exposed to sunlight. Other than the sofa and two matching easy chars, there was a wooden coffee table in the centre of the room, the drinks cabinet that Ruby stood by, just inside the door, and on the adjacent wall stood a small bookcase. This held numerous sized books and, judging by their covers and the titles that Matthew could just make out, they covered a wide variety of subjects.

The floor was bare except for a small rug placed before the hearth, but the floor boards gleamed with wax polish and were obviously well cared for. In the small grate, a newly laid fire glowed. Ruby had been prepared. She had purposefully lit the fire in this room, anticipating her daughter's tardiness.

Looking up, Matthew noticed several framed photographs of smiling children, set proudly on the tiled mantlepiece. Predominantly these family snaps were mostly of a young, cheeky faced boy, taken at various angles and at different stages of his life. This must be the younger brother, Gary, that Brenda had described in glowing terms the night before. There were also several photographs of other children that Matthew could not identify, but the one that caught his eye was that of a shy blonde girl, smiling demurely into the camera. He recognised a Brenda of some years ago, probably in her early teens. Even at that tender age, Brenda's smile was open and honest. If only he had known her then, but perhaps she would not have looked twice at a man so much her senior at that time of her life.

Sighing, Matthew's eyes continued in their exploration. Hanging on the walls were several pictures, mainly of landscapes and country scenes. Here was a woman who yearned for wide open spaces and clean fresh air. She might not readily admit to flights of fancy, but in these framed water colours, were Ruby's dreams.

And all around the room, cluttered on every available surface were ornaments and brick-a-brack. Small china houses and animals, figures made from sea shells, brightly coloured glass objects and painted stones were littered everywhere. These were a life times accumulation of mementoes either brought back from the children's school trips or purchased during summer holidays. Some of these pieces dated back to Ruby's childhood and others beyond to her own mother. Not one would ever see the inside of Sotheby's but to Ruby they were worth more than their weight in gold.

In the far corner, fairy lights blinking, stood a gaily decorated Christmas tree. Barely five feet tall, it sat majestically, the pride of what would otherwise be a drab room. At it's base, bright red crepe paper covered the bucket that it stood in and scattered on the floor around it were several gift wrapped presents. On all the branches hung both home made and shop bought decorations of many shapes, sizes, colour and designs. And as Matthew lifted his gaze, a fairy princess, wand in hand, winked at him in the glow of the many glittering bulbs surrounding her.

Swinging his eyes back towards the door, Matthew caught Ruby's gaze upon him. His now prepared drink in her hand, she had taken the opportunity to scrutinise him whilst his attention was elsewhere. She had already decided that she liked what she saw and thoroughly approved of her daughter's choice. First impressions were important to Ruby and she judged most people on the first instant of meeting. Matthew had passed the test and now, smiling at him, she offered the glass, saying, "Like what you see, eh? It's not much, but it's home to us. We might not have any money, but we're rich in other things, if you know what I mean?"

Taking the whisky from our outstretched hand, Matthew smiled back at Ruby.

"This room speaks of a happy family. It holds objects that have been collected through a lifetime and although it'll never feature in any of the glossy magazines, it's been well cared for and looked after. Expensive furniture and works of art are OK in themselves, but you can't buy the atmosphere that I can feel here. You can tell a lot about a person by the way they keep their homes and I can see you're a house proud lady, who runs a tight ship. Am I right?"

Ruby blushed. Like her daughter, compliments did not sit easily on her shoulders, but all the same she enjoyed his praise.

"I've heard you Americans have got silver tongues, but I reckon yours must be made of solid gold! No wonder my Brenda's fallen for you, hook, line and sinker!"

"Who's fallen for who?" Neither Ruby nor Matthew had seen Brenda slip silently into the room and she stood now looking from one to the other, the question still on her lips. Somewhat amazed, Brenda caught her mother's secret wink to Matthew and his chuckle back. She had never known Ruby to take to someone so quickly, especially a person of the male gender. It would appear that even her cynical mother was not immune to Matthew's charms.

Matthew had risen from the sofa and uttering a small, "Hi, Brenda." he gazed at her with smiling eyes. What he saw before him, was definitely pleasing to the eye. Brenda wore a soft wool red dress, the hem resting on her knees. The material clung to her curvaceous form and emphasised her full breasts and flaring hips. He had never liked 'skinny women' and was a man who could appreciate a more Venus like figure. She wore the black shoes of the night before and the same coat was now draped over her arm. But it was her hair that really caught his attention. She had twisted the blonde locks into an elegant roll and this was swept up and secured by a silver coloured clip. A small droplet of silver hung from each ear, thus completing the picture.

Whilst Matthew appraised Brenda with his eyes, she returned the compliment. A dark grey suit, white shirt, red and black striped tie and black polished brogues gave him the appearance of a debonair, man about town. What he lacked in stature, he certainly gained in good taste and a natural flair in dress sense.

"Are you two just going to stand here all night, or are you going out?"

Tearing his gaze from Brenda, a silly grin still fixed upon his face, Matthew stuttered, "What? Oh, right, yeah. Are you ready Brenda? I know this nice little place in the West End, where they serve steaks that actually look as if they came from a cow. Not the small slivers of meat that you English pass off as steaks. How does that sound? Do you like steak, Brenda? Because we can go where you want, just name it."

"No, Matt, that sounds great. I like steak, not that I've had a lot of it in my time." Turning to Ruby, Brenda kissed her softly on the cheek and as Matthew helped her with her coat, she said, "Well, we'd better make tracks. God knows if we'll get a bus in this weather and on Christmas Eve, but we'll just have to try, won't we?" Smiling, she linked arms with Matthew and as they left the room, Ruby heard the American say, "We won't have to bother with buses, I've borrowed a friend's car. He's gone back to the states for Christmas and I've got the use of it until after the New Year. I've left it out in the street as I wasn't sure if I could get it into the square, what with all this white stuff floating about!"

As the front door closed, Ruby went to the window and watched as the pair stepped gingerly over the cobblestones, the sound of their laughter reaching into the room and bringing an answering smile to her face.

"A bloody car, no less! My Brenda's being taken out in a bleeding car, up the West End to be wined and dined! Looks like she's fallen on her feet for a change and not before time. Lucky moo! If I was only fifteen years younger, she'd have to watch out, that's for sure!"

Chuckling quietly to herself, Ruby returned to the kitchen, back to her preparations for the following day.

Other eyes had also watched Brenda and Matthew's gay departure. Not from the warm confines of a house making ready for Christmas, but from a marble stone, set upon a snow filled fountain bowl.

CHAPTER 17

Fay stood at her mother's side, a tea towel in her hand. For once, the girl had volunteered to help with the housework. This was a ruse. She had bided her time and now she calculated that the time was right. Carefully drying a tea cup, she said, with what she hoped was a nonchalant air, "I promised Father O'Connell that I'd go up the church later and help set out extra chairs and make the place look nice and tidy, ready for the service tonight. Is that alright, Mum?"

Astounded, Cathy looked into her daughter's face, searching for a hint of deception. But all she saw was an innocent, open expression.

"I can't see any reason why not. What time is Father expecting you?"

"Oh, anytime after eight o'clock. There's lots of kids going up there and he said we could do the work, then he'd give us all a hot drink and some minced pies and we could sit in the hall next door and wait for our parents to come to the service. It starts at half past eleven and Father reckons we won't have finished getting everything ready before ten." Fay turned her face from her mother as she spoke, afraid that a guilty blush might give her away.

"Well, in that case, I can't see your father raising any objections. Even your Nan won't be able to find fault. As far as I'm concerned, I think it's good for you kids to help out at the church. It'll keep you out of mischief and out of my hair." Putting her arm around Fay, in a rare show of affection, Cathy hugged the girl to her.

"You growing up at last, Fay? Seems like you're beginning to show a bit of concern for others. See? It's not difficult to be helpful, is it?"

Hiding her face under her mother's arm, Fay felt a twinge of guilty conscience. Some of what she had told her mother was true. Father O'Connell had made arrangements with some of the local children to lend a hand with the preparations of the church and he had also promised to supply drinks and a snack afterwards in the adjoining church hall, where the children could wait for their parents arrival. What she had omitted to tell her mother, was that Fay would not be there until the latter part of the evening. She was banking on the Father displaying his normal absentmindedness. As long as Fay was in the church hall with the other children before the service began, then the priest would assume she had been present all evening. With a little luck and no unforeseen complications, Fay would be able to attend the youth club disco with the boy of her present dreams and still make it back to the Oratory in plenty of time.

"Go on, go and make yourself beautiful. I expect they'll be boys around, so you will want to look your usual devastating self." Giving her daughter a slight push, Cathy turned back to the sink and continued washing the dishes from the evening meal.

Faltering on the threshold of the kitchen, Fay looked back at her mother. For one crazy moment, she wanted to run back into the safety of her mother's embrace and admit her lie. The feeling passed. Instead, Fay muttered, "Thanks, Mum." and left the room, darting up the staircase to her bedroom, already planning in her mind the outfit she would wear for the evening.

Sal caught sight of her granddaughter's running feet as the old woman came in the front door. Huffing slightly from her short but arduous walk across the square, she removed her coat and scarf and went in search of Cathy.

Cheeks glowing, the cold weather not being wholly responsible, Sal sank gratefully onto a kitchen chair.

"I'm back. Everything alright? Fay looks like she's in a good mood, skipping up the stairs, she was. What's she got her own way with now?"

"Oh, Mother! Why do you always have to see the worst in everyone? Why does Fay have to be up to something to be happy? Just to put the record straight, Fay is doing something tonight that even you would approve of." Wiping her hands on her apron, Cathy looked over to her mother-in-law, a cross look upon her face.

"She's off to help Father O'Connell up the church, along with some other kids. They're going to get everything ready so the likes of you and me won't have to stand up through the whole service tonight. You know how packed it can be up at the Oratory for Midnight Mass. So she's going to put out extra chairs and generally tidy round. Just for once, your suspicions were wrong, Mother."

"Alright, alright, don't blow a gasket." Sal flapped her hand at Cathy, "I didn't mean to sound so grumpy. Mind you, it must be a first. Fay don't usually offer to help people and normally I have to drag her to church. Still, praise where praise is due, that's what I always say. She's a good girl to lend a hand and I shall tell her so when she comes down, alright?"

Relenting, and being slightly ashamed of her outburst, Cathy smiled at Sal and nodded her head.

"Now then. What about a little tipple? Just you and me. It is Christmas Eve after all and we have worked like slaves all day." Her eyes sliding from Cathy to the small cupboard by the window, Sal waited expectantly.

Taking in Sal's bright eyes and rosy cheeks, the younger woman laughed softly and reaching up, opened the cupboard door and took down a small bottle of brandy.

"Just a small one then. It looks like you and Lottie might have started before the rest of us and if Jack comes in and finds you swaying about the place, he'll blame me for not keeping an eye on you."

With what little indignation Sal could muster, she crossed her arms under her ample chest and raising her shoulders, blustered, "I don't know what you mean. What a thing to say! I only went over to Lottie's to see if she needed anything and when I come back, my only daughter-in-law accuses me of being drunk. I don't know what the world's coming to." Giving a small wink, she continued, "Can I help it if my best friend insists I have a little drink with her whilst we're wishing each other a merry Christmas? So come on girl, get pouring then I can wish you one as well."

Good feeling restored once more between the two, Cathy poured generous measures of the golden liquid into two tea cups. Raising these, both women clinked the cups together, saying, "Merry Christmas and a Happy New Year!"

Heads back, Sal and Cathy drained the cups in one swallow and this was how Jack found them when he entered the kitchen at that moment.

"Oh yeah? And what's going on here, eh?" Taking the cup from his wife's hand, he sniffed at the few remaining drops in it's base.

"I thought as much. You two don't usually drink your tea in one big mouthful, then smack your lips together after. Whatever should I do? I come into this kitchen and what do I find? My wife and my mother guzzling down bottles of brandy. And to make matters worse, they're drinking it out of tea cups, hoping that I won't realise what it is. There's only one thing for me to do. I'll have to go and fetch Father O'Connell. Perhaps he'll come round and say a few prayers to stop you both from rotting in eternal hell." Striding towards the door, Jack made to leave and carry out his mission.

"Jack!" Sal had swivelled round in her chair, her voice shrill with anxiety. "Don't you dare! Come back here and stop mucking about."

Leaning against the sink, her hand covering her mouth to stifle her giggles, Cathy watched Sal in her growing panic.

"It's my duty, Mother. Father O'Connell always told us to beware the demon drink and to watch our for others. I ought to go and get him," Jack's poker straight face suddenly split with a huge grin as he added, "Mind you, if I'm going to bring the good father back here, you'd better open another bottle. They'll never be enough in that one for three of you!"

"You little sod! Get back in here and stop acting the bloody fool. And you should be more careful, Jack Treist, saying terrible things like that about Father O'Connell." Raising her eyes to the ceiling, Sal whispered, "Someone might hear you!"

At this last comment, Cathy could no longer restrain herself. Choking with laughter, she clasped her middle and spluttered, "You should have seen your face, Mother. He really had you going. Especially when he said he was off to get the father. I though you were going to have a heart attack! Your face went even redder than it was and you looked like you were about to jump up and grab Jack and beg him not to tell."

Still grinning widely, Jack sat down opposite his mother and taking her hands in his own, spoke affectionately to her.

"Did I really get you worried, Mother? Did you think the game was up and that Father O'Connell would come here and bring down the wrath of God on you? Silly old moo! Still, I got you good and proper this time, didn't I?"

Pulling her hands sharply out of Jack's grasp, Sal spoke gruffly to them both. "Don't be so bloody stupid! Of course I wasn't worried. Father O'Connell would never have believed you, anyway. He knows which of us are his good sheep and the nearest he gets to thinking of sheep where you two are concerned, is black! Not that I fell for your tricks in any case. It'll be a cold day in hell when anyone in this family pulls the wool over my eyes, I can tell you. Now, have you finished? Get another cup, Cathy and give this cocky bugger a drink. Perhaps that'll shut him up for five minutes."

"Oh, I don't think I should. I don't want to end up like you two, writhing in the flames of hell for evermore."

Sal's hand shot out and reaching over the table, she cuffed her son smartly on his ear.

"And don't think you're too old for me to give you a good hiding, you aggravating bleeder! Just stop fooling around and get that drink down you. It might bring you back to your senses, if we're lucky enough."

The three sat on, drinking and laughing together. It had been a long time since any of them had felt this close and it was with reluctance and only after they had consumed the contents of the bottle, that Sal rose and went to make herself ready for Midnight Mass.

Jack watched his mother's slightly unsteady departure and turned to Cathy, saying in an undertone, "She'll be snoring through most of the service tonight, but God help anyone who mentions it!"

As husband and wife cleared the table, Fay came and said her farewells, promising to be careful of the roads.

"See you all later." Was her parting shot as she left the house and head down, hurried across the square, dodging past the fountain, unmindful of the figure perched there.

All was quiet once more in Mermaid Mews, only the soft strains of some late Carol Singers, drifting into the square from the main road.

CHAPTER 18

The world had turned white, or so it seemed to Ellie as she gazed out into the square. No one had ventured out since Fay had left the Mews and the steady snowfall had quickly covered all evidence of her departure. Now, at last, when the clock struck ten o'clock, almost as if some invisible hand had flicked a switch, the snow shower stopped. Not gradually, but in an instant. One minute large flakes had been falling in a white, steady curtain and in the next, all was silent and still.

Standing at the window, elbows resting on the sill and chin propped in her hands, the small girl wondered at the scene before her. Shafts of light shone into the centre of the square from each of the six houses, their beams merging one into the other. And caught in the vortex was the fountain. It stood, gleaming in the moonlight, the eternal passenger riding atop. No chips or cracks were visible, hidden under a dusting of snow. The mermaid had recaptured her lost youth. Now clothed from head to fin in a brilliant white veil, sprigs of pine peeping out from under a snowy blanket in the fountain bowl at her base, her radiant smile had returned. The smooth, lithe figure of the past was hers once more and she positively revelled in her regained splendour.

As Ellie watched, transfixed with the glorious picture beyond the glass, Sal entered the room behind her and she was brought back down to earth with a bump. The bubble of her dreams burst, as Sal demanded, "What are you doing, mooning around in here?"

Sighing, Ellie turned and faced reality with a certain reluctance.

"Nothing, Nan. I was just looking out of the window." Wanting to share the moment with her grandmother, she urged, "Come and have a look, Nan. It's lovely out there. And look at the mermaid, doesn't she look beautiful?"

Sal joined her granddaughter at the window. Seeing the scene through the young girl's eyes, she murmured, "She does, doesn't she? I never really looked at her before, but now I do, I can see she's a pretty little thing, just like you."

They stood together, their faces wreathed in smiles, the youngest and the oldest member of the Treist family. Ellie snuggled into Sal's side and, self consciously, Sal slipped her arm about the girl and hugged her in an almost rough fashion.

"Well, we can't stand here all night. Come on, let's go and find your mother. I'm sure if we try hard, we'll be able to persuade her to let us have a couple of mince pies and a hot drink before we have to leave for church, eh?"

Giggling at the thought of her grandmother having to cajole anyone, Ellie clasped Sal's hand and they left the room and went in search of bodily sustenance.

*

At the time when Sal and Ellie were indulging themselves in a little girl's fantasy, Fay was twisting and jiving to her favourite pop record. She could hardly believe that she was actually dancing at a real disco and with the boy of her dreams.

All had gone to plan, with only one exception. The faithful Caroline had backed out at the last minute and refused to accompany Fay to the forbidden dance. Threatened with dire consequences, the plain girl had sworn she would not reveal Fay's whereabouts and the two had agreed to meet up later in the evening at the Church Hall. In retrospect, Fay realised that this could be an advantage for if Caroline were present all evening at the Oratory, it would naturally be assumed that she herself would also be there somewhere.

Glancing about her, Fay noticed with some pride that she was the youngest person in the hall. Not that this was evident. At the moment, even Cathy would not have recognised her eldest child. On arrival, Fay had ducked into the 'Ladies' and applied her make-up with the expertise of a working model. She had spent many an hour practising the application of false eyelashes, blusher and lipstick and could now transform her young face to that of a late teenager in a matter of minutes. The school girl sensible hair style had been quickly replaced by a bouffant arrangement. This was attained by rapid, all over back combing and finally smoothing the surface hair over the matted whole to produce a fuller, more fashionable look. Next, she had turned her attentions to her attire. The dress she wore would suffice with just one or two changes. First, Fay had unzipped the garment and delving into her bulging handbag, had produced large wads of cotton wool. These she had pushed into the cups of her bra and once her dress was refastened her adolescent figure had miraculously changed into a mature and fully developed shape. Pushing off her sturdy lace up shoes and discarding her knee high socks, Fay dipped again into the bulky bag and produced sheer nylons and a tiny, black suspender belt. But her most prized possessions were the shiny, black patent, stiletto shoes that she had slipped on her feet with an audible sigh of pleasure. Four months it had taken her to save enough money to purchase these much desired shoes and although they had been hers for two whole weeks, this was the first time she had had occasion to wear them in public. Secretly during the past fortnight, she had tottered back and forth across her bedroom floor until she had mastered the art of walking in them without stumbling. And now as she twisted and turned on the dance floor, she was rewarded for her hard work and determination as her feet slid gracefully and without effort into each dance step. If Fay would only apply herself as diligently in her school work and studies as she had with the task of looking older, then she would have soared far and above many of the pupils in her class. Unfortunately, this realisation would only surface much later in her life, when the appreciation of a good education becomes evident to most people.

"Fay? Did you hear me? I asked you if you wanted a drink?"

Bringing her attention sharply back to the present, Fay nodded her head and linking arms with her date, they made their way to a makeshift bar at the far end of the room. Officially, only non-alcoholic drinks were permitted at the Youth Club dance, but some of the more enterprising youths had smuggled in a variety of other 'beverages'.

The rim of the plastic cup between her teeth, Fay took a deep draught of the black liquid within. As she swallowed, her eyes widened then watered as she spluttered, "That's not Coke! What the hell's in it?" Only a wink and a sly smile were her answer. She shrugged her slim shoulders, shaking off the feeling of being out of her depth and laughed back at the handsome face close to her own.

They returned once more to the dance floor and continued in their frenzied rhythms. Fay was in her element. If only her friends could see her now! Here she was dancing the night away with a boy most girls would kill for and this same, adult guy was heaping praise upon praise on her. Telling her how good she looked and saying that they were alike, that they were soul-mates and kindred spirits. In her naivety, Fay lapped up his compliments and as the evening wore on, she accepted other cups of unfamiliar taste. She knew her drinks were spiked as she had smelt a similar odour on her father's lips on the rare occasions that Jack had indulged in a celebratory drink, but she threw caution to the wind. The warm feeling in her stomach and her growing confidence as her inhibitions melted away, spurred her on. With each drink she discovered a hidden mine within herself of witty remarks and light banter. And even more surprising, every returned conversation was hilariously funny! Each and every word that fell from her partner's mouth was hysterical and highly amusing. As she looked around the hall, Fay's giggles rose in pitch as she pointed at several couples swaying together in time to the blaring music.

"Come on. Let's get you out of here. What you need is some nice fresh air. I know a place just round the corner where we can be on our own." Fay found herself being pulled through the crowd of youngsters and out of the building via a back entrance. Suddenly, the cold, icy blast of the winter's night was slicing through her thin dress. She drew in deep gulps of frosty air and the effect was immediate. Her stomach churned and her body doubled over as the speedily consumed alcohol made just as hasty an exit.

When the heaving had finally abated, Fay wiped the last of the vomit from her mouth with the back of a quivering hand. She leaned weakly against a brick wall, her legs shaking and shivers running up and down her spine. Opening her eyes, she searched around her until she found the object of her misery.

He leant nonchalantly against a street lamp, cigarette dangling from his lips, arms folded over his broad chest and one leg crossed, his foot tapping with impatience. As the light from the lamp shone down on him, Fay saw him with eyes no longer veiled by rose coloured spectacles. His face did not hold a debonair and worldly wise look but rather one of a cynical and sarcastic nature. The lips were not smiling in a caring way at her but were drawn up at each corner in an open sneer and the once friendly eyes now appraised her coldly. His whole appearance was unkempt, not trendy and casual as she had been made to believe and as she glared at him she wondered whatever had possessed her to think he was worth lying and scheming for.

"Finished have you?" Pushing himself away from the post, he advanced on her. "Now we can have some fun, eh?" His arms were fast around her and as she struggled, shaking her head from side to side, he spoke harshly in her ear. "Just a little kiss, eh? It'll get you in the mood then we can get down to some serious business." His lips burned against her neck and one hand pulled at the buttons on the front of her dress, whilst his lower body pinned her against the wall behind her. Frantically, she kicked out and was pleasantly rewarded when her sharp heels made contact with his instep. Taken unawares, the youth howled and hopped in surprised pain on one foot, the other raised to his administering hands. Fay saw her chance. Quick as a flash she ducked down and swerved past him. But just as she believed she had made her get away, his hand shot out and caught at her knotted hair. Her head jerked back and looking up with fear filled eyes at the grim face hanging over her she heard him whisper, low and menacingly, "You don't think I've spent all my money on booze and the rest of the night buttering you up not to get anything in return, do you? Oh no, you don't get away that easy. It's pay up time, little girl and after this little show, I'm going to really get my money's worth." Once more, his hand snatched at her dress front and a scream tore from Fay's throat as she heard the material rip and felt icy air on her exposed skin. Just as she reached up with claw like fingers aimed at his eyes, a shaft of light pierced the inky darkness of the shadowed wall and a voice called out.

"What's going on? Who's out there? Is someone hurt?" A tall figure approached and suddenly Fay was free. Her hair was no longer held in a vice like grip and throwing herself forward, her feet stumbling in the high heeled shoes on the icy surface beneath her, she ran from the small back yard and away from the terror that lay there.

Vaguely, she heard raised voices behind her and someone calling out for her to stop, but her feet took wing and she flew down the dark side road, not daring to look back and not noticing that both her precious shoes lay forlorn and abandoned in the gutter.

On and on her feet pounded the pavement, some inner instinct leading her to the safety of the church hall. Her lungs burned with the freezing air within them and her heart beat faster and faster as she sped through the narrow back roads. Her one and only thought was to reach her mother.

Still running, she rounded a corner and there, stood in the light spilling from the open doors of the Oratory, was Cathy and the rest of her family. The last thing she remembered as she slid gasping to her knees, was the look of shock on her mother's face and the sound of her father's feet as he ran towards her.

CHAPTER 19

Brenda and Matt sat close together, hands clasped and heads bent, whispering softly in the darkness and sharing their dreams.

They had returned from the restaurant replete and content at 11.30pm. Matt had parked the borrowed car in the street adjacent to the Mews' entrance and now he glanced at his watch and leaning forward kissed Brenda lovingly at the corner of her mouth.

"Merry Christmas, Brenda and here's hoping this will be the first of many."

"Is it Christmas Day already, Matt? I've had such a lovely evening and now it's over. How come, when you're enjoying yourself, time goes so quickly. But when you're doing something really boring, it drags on and on? It seems to me that since the night we met, the days have just flown by and yet I feel as if I've known you all my life." Brenda reached up and tenderly touched his lean cheek. "I read somewhere an article about reincarnation. It said that when two people become really close in a short space of time, it means they recognise each other from a past life. If that's true, then you must have been very special to me, because I've never felt this way about anyone before. I suppose you think I'm stark, staring mad, don't you?"

Matt did not have a chance to respond, as at that moment a running figure raced past the motionless car. The couple watched with some alarm as the person skidded at the corner and disappeared into Mermaid Mews. Their surprise was multiplied as some seconds later, it reappeared and stood looking first up, then down the road in a frantic manner.

Matt opened the door and leaning his arms on the roof of the car, called across the street, "Anything wrong? Can we help at all?"

Winding down the window, Brenda asked, a note of puzzlement in her voice, "What's up, Frank?"

Peering into the darkness, Frank Carmichael crossed the street, asking, "That you, Brenda?" As he reached the car and identified it's passenger, he said with some relief, "Can you give us a hand Brenda? Young Fay's had an accident and we need some help to get her home. Jack's carrying her at the moment, but Cathy and Sal are in a bit of a state and Ellie's crying her eyes out. We couldn't get a taxi and the buses aren't running now, so we've had to walk back from the

Oratory. I came on ahead and left the missus looking after all the kids - my lot and Ellie and Billy. I was going to knock at your house, but all the lights are out. I thought Ruby might come back with me and take charge whilst I helped Jack with Fay."

Brenda looked up at Matt, the question in her eyes. To his credit, the American did not hesitate as he leaped back into the car, shouting, "Get in, buddy. I'll turn this bus around and you can show me where they are."

With a squeal of tyres, Matt turned the car in one expert move and sped down the Brompton Road in the direction Frank had come from.

Some minutes later, the car's headlights picked up the straggling line of people picking their way through the slush. As the car came to an abrupt halt at the curbside, all three passengers jumped out.

Frank was the first to reach the head of the line and speaking to Jack, he said, "I've managed to get us a lift, Jack. Brenda was out with her young man and he's got a car. If you, Fay, Sal and Cathy get in the back, they'll take you home, OK?"

Shifting his daughter's weight in his arms, Jack gratefully replied, "Thanks, Frank. She might only be thirteen, but Fay weighs a ton when she's a dead weight." Looking back over his shoulder, he called, "Come on, Mother and you too, Cathy. Get in the car and then we can get Fay home and sort her out." Turning to his friend, Jack enquired, "Will you see that Ellie and Billy get back safe and sound? I'll have to go on with Cathy and Mother because I don't think they can cope right now."

"Don't you worry about them, I'll see to them. Just get yourselves home and we'll catch up in no time." Taking the limp figure from Jack's arms, Frank waited until Jack, Sal and Cathy were seated on the back seat, then passed the still form of Fay into the car. He watched as the car once more spun about in the road, it's red tail lights glowing in the night as it sped swiftly back towards Mermaid Mews.

He turned and led his, and what was left of Jack's, family along the road and home.

*

"Well, what the hell was she doing out at that time of night? Why wasn't she with the other kids at the Oratory? I knew this day would come. If I've told you once, I've told you a thousand times to be more strict with the kids, but would you listen? Oh no, not you lot. And now look what's happened!" Sal stood over the huddled form of her granddaughter, who sat shivering at the kitchen table.

The young girl had come round rapidly after Cathy had administered smelling salts and now she waited in silence, a spectator at her own trial.

For the first time Fay, who was studying the black and white kitchen tiles at her feet, realised that her shoes were missing. She opened her mouth to protest at their loss, then closed it sharply, thinking better of such a remark at a time like this. Still in shock, her body trembling with intermittent spasms, she marvelled at her close escape. If they had been uninterrupted, then that boy would surely have completed his mission. She would not now be safe and warm in her own house, but possibly still laying undetected in the back yard of the Youth Club. How long would it have been before someone missed her? And for how long would Caroline have held her silence before they had enough information to come looking for her? She was adult enough to know exactly what the boy would have subjected her to, but the child in her did not understand how the situation could have arisen. Now, as Sal's voice ranted and raved above her, the full realisation of her reckless actions dawned upon her. Shaking convulsively, the young girl laid her head on the table and sobbed, crying our her fright and bringing a momentary hush to the room.

Matt and Brenda stood in the doorway and watched as the people present became stock still at the sound of Fay's wails. Then, suddenly, all were galvanised into action, fluttering around the distressed girl.

"It's the shock, that what it is. Someone slap her face before she gets hysterical." Sal reached down and pulled at Fay's shoulder, but was stopped short as Jack bellowed. "That's enough, Mother. Leave her alone and get out of the way. I'm warning you, don't say another word, do you hear? Now shut up, you interfering, meddling old cow or the only person round here who'll get a slap, is you."

Cathy knelt by her daughter's chair, her arm about the heaving shoulders.

"It's alright, love. You're alright now. We've got you and no-one can harm you here. Have a good cry, you'll feel better after, then you can tell me all about it. And don't worry, I won't let anyone tell you off," Cathy looked meaningfully up at Sal, now stood at the far side of the room, "It's all over and you're home, safe with us."

"That's right, Fay. Everything's alright now. Nothing's going to get you now." Whispering in an aside to his wife, Jack asked, "Is she hurt? We've got to find out how far the bastard got. I'll kill the bloody sod when I find out who he is!" Hands clenched and teeth gritted together, Jack stood helplessly by as his daughter cried as if her heart would break.

Then, in a rush, out poured the words of explanation and conveying her terror to her family, Fay stuttered, "Oh Mum, it was horrible! I thought he was going to kill me and there was nobody there to help me. And I'd been so sick, Mum, I could hardly stand up. But he went for me, ever after I stamped on his foot. I thought I'd got away, but he grabbed my hair and pulled it so hard I thought it would all come out at the roots." Gingerly, she reached up and felt her scalp, then drawing a deep breath, she continued, "I was really scared and it was so dark and cold. I don't know what I'd have done if someone hadn't come out after I screamed. He let go of me then and I just ran. I had to get away from there and I knew you were all going to be at the church, so I just kept going until I got to you." Her voice had risen and her hands clutched at Cathy as she relived the nightmare.

"Shh, shh, it's OK, you found us and everything's alright now. Come on now, calm down. Take deep breaths and hold onto me." Cathy fought with her daughter's blind panic, holding her arms tightly and soothing the child with comforting words.

"I'm so sorry, Mum. Really I am. You trusted me and I lied to you. It's all my fault, all my own stupid fault. I should have listened to you, especially Nan. If I hadn't been such a know-all, none of this would have happened. And how could I have ever thought that bloke was nice? He was horrible, really nasty and he would have hurt me badly if he had the chance. What a silly cow I've been! Say you'll forgive me, Mum? And all of you. Give me another chance and I won't ever do anything so stupid again, honest I won't."

"Oh, love! Of course we forgive you." Taking her daughter's face in her hands, Cathy looked searchingly into the girl's tear filled eyes. "We were only worried that you were hurt and people say harsh things to each other when they're worried. Now Fay, you've got to be brave. I have to know if he did anything to you, if he touched you in your private places?"

Standing to one side, Jack screwed up his face and shut tight his eyes, fearful of the answer to his wife's question.

Sal also wore a horror-stricken expression and waited apprehensively for Fay's reply, whilst the couple still hovering in the doorway looked to each other. This moment was so intimately private that outsiders should not be present to witness such a scene. However, all eyes were on Fay and no attention was spared for anyone else.

Not a sound could be heard. The drop of a pin would easily have been detected during those seconds. Then, Fay raised her eyes and looking directly into her Mother's, whispered, "No, Mum. He didn't get a chance. Someone came out and scared him off before he could do anything to me."

The sound of breath escaping in a rush as several people expelled the air from their lungs in relief, was quite audible in the room. Cathy hugged Fay close to her, tears streaming from her closed eyes as she murmured, "Thank God!"

Jack had opened his eyes and looked around him distractedly. He watched as his mother's shoulders slumped and saw her rub her face with a large white handkerchief and as their eyes met, he smiled at her and she in return nodded her head in understanding. No reference of his harsh remarks to her would ever be mentioned. It was understood that these were just words spoken in the heat of the moment.

Crouching down before his daughter, Jack spoke softly, "What was his name, love? Tell me who he was and then we'll let the police deal with him."

"No, Jack!" Sal pushed herself away from the wall and looking into her daughter-in-law's distressed face, spoke with more concern than she had shown for her family in a long time.

"You can't involve the police. Do you know what they put young girls through in these sort of cases? Let me tell you, it's not pleasant. They'll question her for hours and make her go over and over it all. They'll get their own doctor in who'll examine her all over, then if they believe her story they'll bring in the sod who did this to her. No doubt, he'll say she led him on and he thought she was older than she is. And because most of them down the station are men, they'll sympathise with the bloke. Jack, even if you get that far, the next bit will be awful for Fay. She'll have to go to court and stand up in front of a load of strangers and tell them everything. And I mean everything. They'll want to know why she was at this dance and why she was dressed like she is. They'll ask her why she was wearing all that make-up and why she was trying to look older. They they'll want to know why she went outside with this bloke in the first place. She'll be painted as a right little tart because they'll make out she's done this sort of thing before, with other blokes."

Cathy had risen from Fay's side and nodding her head, she clutched her husband's arm, forcing him to look up at her as she continued where Sal had left off.

"She's right, Jack. I've heard of this happening before with other girls. It'll be plastered all over the newspapers and you know what folk will say: 'There's no smoke without fire'. Everyone will blame Fay and she'll get a reputation that she'll never be able to live down. And for what? That bastard will get a couple of months, if they find him guilty. And even then, he'll probably not serve time in the nick. They'll more than likely smack his wrist and give him probation. No, Jack, we can't let Fay go through all that. We'll have to hush it all up. If anyone asks, we'll say she had a little accident and leave it at that."

Jack too, was standing upright now and Fay sat between her parents, her face raised to theirs, her eyes darting from one to the other in fright. After what her grandmother and mother had said, there was no way she wanted to go to the police, but her father's next words made the tears spring once more to her eyes.

"What, and let that bleeder get away with it? You must be joking! No one interferes with any of my kids, no-one. If you say Fay'll get such a bad time at the cop shop, then I'll deal with it myself. I'd rather swing for it that let filth like that roam the streets. He could go out and do this again, to some other young girl. No, Cathy, someone's got to put him right, someone's got to stop him or else he'll think he got away with it and do it again." Ignoring his wife's please, Jack said with determination, "Now, young lady. You tell me who he is. You tell me where I can find this cow son who did this to you."

"And what do you think that'll achieve?" Grabbing her son's arms, Sal pulled at the distraught man, making him turn away from Fay and face her. "So, you'll go off and find the bloke and beat the living daylights out of him. He's probably only a kid himself. The police will throw the book at you and then where will this family be with no bread winner? Ho long do you think we could survive without a wage coming in? Just think about it, Jack. Stop being the big man, out to get revenge. This is the real world, not some stupid cowboy picture."

Jack's head had dropped lower and lower with every word his mother spoke and now she had to strain to hear his next words.

"What can I do then, Mother? I can't just stand by and do nothing. Everything in me tells me it's all wrong. There must be something I can do."

Emotion choking her, the old woman shut tight her eyes against the sight of her only son standing before her, defeat written all across his face.

"There's more ways to kill a cat than skinning it. You have to bide your time, wait a while. Let all this blow over, then when all the commotion dies down and he thinks nothing's going to come of it all, you can find him and put the fear of God up him. But you'll do it when you're not in a blind rage, when you've got a hold on your temper. That way, you'll not kill the swine, just rough him up a little so's he'll never look at another girl again, never mind what he's done tonight. Listen to me, Jack. I know you and I don't always see eye to eye, but I'm your mother and I know what's best for you. This way, you'll be able to plan it, choose the right time. Then there will be no come back, no-one will be able to prove it was you." Still clutching the big man, Sal willed him to see sense.

The soft voice of Cathy as she said, "Listen to her, Jack. She's right and you know it." brought Jack back to his senses, the red curtain of rage falling from his mind. He nodded his head once, then pushing past the couple at the door, left the room.

The sound of the front door slamming, brought Cathy's head swinging round in alarm, but Sal's restraining arms stopped short her pursuit.

"Leave him be. There's nothing you can do now. He needs to be on his own for a while. Don't worry, he won't do anything stupid, he just needs to get away from all of us for a minute. You must understand Cathy. He thinks he looks little in our eyes. After all, he's the man of the house and he feels he should protect us all. In his own mind, he thinks he's failed. But when he's calmed down, he'll realise that he had no choice. And we'll all make sure he knows we don't think no less of him." Turning from the younger woman, Sal now addressed Fay.

"And you, young lady, are you all right? Do you understand what's been going on here tonight? It's important that you realise exactly why we've come to this decision. You won't understand all of it, but I hope you'll come to know that we've all acted in your best interests. What you did tonight was a very silly thing to do, but nothing that we all haven't done, or wanted to do when we were your age. All the same, it doesn't matter what a woman does or how she acts, it doesn't give a man the right to force himself on her and that's one of the reasons that your Dad is so upset. You just remember, Fay. Tonight, if we hadn't stopped him, your Dad would have gone out and killed a bloke for what he did to you. He's a good man and he loves all of you so much that he wouldn't have cared what happens to him, as long as he made that bloke pay." Reaching down, she brought the young girl to her feet and pulled her into soothing arms.

Stroking Fay's hair, Sal continued, "I know you're frightened, but you mustn't let this put you off men. There are more men out there like your Dad, then there are like that rotten pig you were with tonight. All you've got to do is wait. Grow up slowly, enjoy being young. You've got all the rest of your life to be an adult and you only get a really short time to be a child. So don't be in such a rush, it'll all happen in it's own good time and soon enough." Placing her hand gently under her granddaughter's chin, Sal raised the tearful face to her own.

"Just one more thing, before we close the whole matter. Don't ever think that this was your fault. Alright, you might have disobeyed your Mum and Dad and you might have dressed yourself up to look like a grown-up, but that's all part of growing up. It wasn't your fault that some bloke, who doesn't know right from wrong, took it upon himself to take by force something that should only be given to your husband on your wedding night. And when that time comes, it's not frightening like it was tonight. It's right and proper, because you'll be giving it to someone you love and who loves you. Do you understand, girl?"

There was not a dry eye in the room, as Fay stifled a sob and putting her arms around the old woman, hugged her fiercely, burrowing her face deeply into Sal's soft and comforting bosom.

Sal had truly shown the wisdom of her years that night. She had never been so right in all her life as she was then. The situation was under control and she had averted what could have been a disastrous incident in the Treist family's history. Her granddaughter would see her with different eyes in the future and Cathy had been given an insight of her husband's mother that she had never dreamed existed.

As for Jack, he too would view Sal with more respect in the future. At a time when he had almost lost all self-control and could have brought his family to sure destruction, she had stepped in and shown him the way.

Head tilted upwards, his back against the fountain with the blind eyes of the Mermaid upon him, Jack gazed up into the night sky. His temper now firmly under control, he was able to approach the problem calmly.

Although the full details would never be disclosed to his family, Jack did regain his status within the household, albeit, a fall from grace only in his own eyes.

Mysteriously, some weeks after the unsuccessful rape of Fay, the youth who perpetrated the act, met with a nasty 'accident'. He suffered only minor cuts and bruises to his face but would carry with him for the rest of his days a three inch scar to his groin. This would not rob him of fatherhood, but he was made to see how precious certain parts of his anatomy were to him.

No charges were brought against anyone over the attack on the youth and when questioned, he denied all knowledge of his attackers or their reasons for so doing. This, however, was only for the benefit of the authorities. For Fay's would-be rapist, was left in no doubt.

As he had slipped into unconsciousness, his attacker had whispered, "This was for Fay and for any other girl you might have touched without permission. Learn this lesson well, because the next time you won't be around to tell your side of the story."

CHAPTER 20

As the folk of Mermaid Mews awoke on Christmas Day 1959, each household reflected the mood of their own particular moment.

The Treists were a happy crowd, although not untouched by past events, and it was a somewhat subdued Fay who joined her family for breakfast that morning. The dark rings framing her eyes and pale countenance spoke of the sleepless night she had endured. However, she appeared relaxed and at peace. During the small hours, the hapless girl had come to terms with her foolhardy actions and as she watched and listened to the people gathered at the meal table, she smiled in appreciation of her good fortune.

"Hurry up Billy, I've finished mine."

"Give over Ellie! You haven't stopped rushing me since we woke up. Let me eat my breakfast in my own time."

Jack looked on and raising his eyebrows addressed his youngest daughter.

"No-one's going to come in and steal your presents, Ellie. Just calm down a minute. You've managed to wait 365 days, so half an hour more isn't going to kill you, is it?"

"But Dad......?"

No but's. Sit quietly and wait for everyone to finish, then we can clear up and go into the sitting room to open everything."

Sal offered her opinion, as usual, without prompting.

"Blooming kids today! It's just what I always say: They're in such a hurry to get through life, and that one's the worst of them all. One of these days she'll turn round and bump into herself coming the other way!"

Ellie started to protest but Jack was already one jump ahead.

"Oh and I suppose you're so old you can't remember how excited you were when you were a kid at Christmas, eh Mother?"

Bustling back and forth from sink to table, Cathy nudged her husband, a twinkle in her eye.

"No-one can remember *that* far back, Jack. It must have been in the dark ages then, wasn't it?"

"And what have you been drinking?" Sal threw Cathy a sidelong look. "You've been living with this cheeky sod too long, Cathy and now his clever talk has rubbed off on you. Let me tell you, I've got a memory as clear as a bell and when *I* was a child......."

She stopped in mid sentence as the room erupted with laughter. Staring hard at the five beaming faces about her she struggled to maintain an air of offence. This was impossible. Knowing that their merriment was not malicious, Sal grudgingly smiled back.

"Alright, alright. I know you all think I'm a stupid old woman, but if you were to stop and listen to me sometimes, you might all learn a thing or two."

The chuckles and giggles grew louder.

Wearing a lop-sided grin, Billy leaned across the table and goaded.

"You always say that, Nan. It doesn't matter what's going on, you always tell us to listen to you so that we can learn a thing or two!"

Not to be outdone, Jack continued.

"And how many times a day does your Nan say: "When *I* was a child...."?" Addressing his family, he finished, "You should all think yourselves lucky! I've had to put up with it for much longer. I think it must have been the first words your Nan ever said to me and she's been repeating them since day one!"

"I don't know how you can say that, Jack Treist! I hardly ever mention my childhood and as for telling you lot to listen to me...well! I might as well save my breath for all the good that's ever done." Finger wagging, Sal went on: "You wait and see. When I'm dead and buried, you'll look back and realise that I was right and then you'll all be sorry that you treated me so badly."

More laughter resounded within the kitchen as yet another of Sal's much used phrases tripped off her tongue.

This time, even Sal joined in. Face wide and grinning, she flapped her hands at them all, unable to deny this, her most favourite of remarks.

Thus, with familiar and easy banter, the Treist family finished their first meal of the day, cleared away the dishes and departed to the sitting room to begin unwrapping their gifts.

This was the normal custom. Cathy insisted that everyone have a good breakfast before the presents were opened, en masse. The gaily wrapped parcels would be handed to each recipient from beneath the Christmas tree, then in this way, Jack and Cathy could enjoy their children's pleasure and also keep 'tabs' on which gift had been received from whom.

On awakening, the children had found stocking bulging with small delights; a treasure trove for youngsters. There would be playing cards, a game of five stones, a set of 'Jacks' together with a tiny coloured rubber ball, a whip and spinning top, a hand-made embroidered handkerchief (initialled), a variety of festive confectionery and always, at the bottom, snuggled into the toe of the stocking, an orange and a handful of whole nuts. Jack would deliver these woollen receptacles in the early hours of the morning, tip-toeing into darkened bedrooms and quietly hanging them on bedposts. Sal also received her 'Christmas Sock' in this manner, although hers would contain gifts more in keeping with her age and needs, whilst Jack and Cathy exchanged theirs on rising. In this manner, the children would be appeased and held at bay until the main presents were given later in the morning.

Sitting on the floor, bouncing with impatience, Ellie and Billy waited expectantly. Sal, Cathy and Fay sat in easy chairs, or on the sofa and watched Jack, paper hat balanced precariously atop his head and cigar dangling from smiling lips, as he knelt beside the tree and began to hand out the gifts. This ritual would be drawn out for as long as possible, all the better to savour their enjoyment, and would be timed to allow an hour before Cathy would announce that dinner was ready.

*

A similar scene could be seen at No. 3. Frank and Eileen wore cheerful expressions for the benefit of Toby and Jacob, but the undercurrent of anxiety was unmistakeable.

Throughout the morning the two adults had exchanged worried glances and it was with some relief on their part when the boys took their new roller skates out into the square for 'trials'. As soon as the door banged shut on their coat-clad figures, all pretence at festive frivolity was dropped.

"Thank God they've gone out for a few minutes. I thought they'd never go and I wanted to have a quiet word with you." Eileen spoke urgently, her tone agitated. "Frank, let's go up the road and try and phone that place and speak to Frankie."

Shaking his head, Frank turned to his wife and trying to temper his words he replied, "Look love, when I phoned yesterday, they told me that the boys weren't allowed to come to the phone. They said they'd pass on a message, but who's to say that Frankie will get it? It sounded like Bedlam in that place - there was a God-awful racket going on in the background and the woman who answered the phone kept breaking off to try and get them to keep quiet. I think they've got their hands full without having to answer the phone every five minutes."

Eileen glanced down into her lap at her hands, twisting her wedding ring nervously.

"He'll think we've forgotten him. And he won't have any presents. What a lovely Christmas he's going to have."

Putting his arms around his wife's shoulders, Frank offered what small comfort he could give. "He'll be alright. He's tougher than you think. And we'll make it all up to him when he comes home. Now, you go and tidy yourself up. Jack and Cathy will be expecting us. They said to come round about half eleven and it's twenty past now. It'll do us good to get out of here and have a drink with friends."

"Oh I don't know Frank. I don't feel much like socialising today. Besides, I've got to keep an eye on the dinner. Why don't you go round for an hour?"

"Come on, love. I won't go without you and it'll take your mind off everything. Put the dinner on low and we'll just pop round for a little while, eh?"

Reluctantly, Eileen left the room and went to apply fresh make-up. Within a few minutes the two were standing at the Treist's doorway, having checked first that Toby and Jacob knew of their whereabouts.

As Jack answered the knock at his door, Matt Goldberg swung into the square, his steps light and jaunty. He raised a hand to the three stood at No. 4 and deftly side-stepped as a small boy careered towards him on runaway roller skates.

"Sorry, Mister."

The American tousled the child's hair, saying: "That's OK. Just mind you don't hurt yourself."

Considering the packages that Matt carried, not so much their weight as the bulkiness of them, he did not falter and soon was ushered into the warmth of Ruby's home. A large whisky was thrust into his hand before he had time to remove his outer clothes.

"Merry Christmas, Matt. It's nice to have a man about the place, especially today. Now, sit yourself down and make yourself at home. Don't be frightened to ask if you want anything - we don't stand on ceremony here." With a wink and a nod, Ruby left the room, leaving Brenda and Matt alone.

Sitting on the low couch, elbows resting on his knees, Matt kept his eyes averted from the girl stood in the centre of the room. She looked down at his bowed head and formed her own conclusions. Not able to keep her own counsel, Brenda blurted, "Is something the matter, Matt? You've hardly looked at me since you came in."

Guiltily, Matt's hand stole to the inside pocket of his jacket. His fingers touched the envelope hidden there and taking a deep breath, he raised his head and looked directly into Brenda's questioning eyes.

"I wasn't going to mention this before we'd eaten, but there is something really important that I've got to talk to you about." Rising from the sofa, he took her hands and continued.

"First let me ask you something. Brenda, do you love me? Or, do you think in time you could come to love me?"

Her eyes wide with surprise at his forward question, Brenda scanned his face. What she saw was a man who had come to mean more to her than she had ever thought possible. She took in the broad forehead, the nose that did not quite fit his face, the mouth that curved gently when he looked at her, and last of all, his eyes. Their colour seemed to be black at close range, deeper in tone because of the anxiety they held. As the seconds ticked by, she felt the muscles tense in his arms and a deep frown appeared on his brow.

Slowly, she took her hands from his and stepping forward, hugged him to her.

"You shouldn't have to ask me that, Matt. Can't you tell? Can't you see that I think the world of you? I only come alive when you're around. Time won't make any difference to the way I feel about you because I couldn't love you any more than I do now and that's more than I can put words to."

His breath left his body in a rush of relief as Matt crushed her to him. Then placing his hands on her shoulders, he pushed her to arms length and very softly whispered, "Do you really mean it, Brenda? Can I have got so lucky that you feel exactly about me as I feel for you? Do you understand what you've got yourself in to? I'm not the sort of fellow that falls in love easily - how else have I reached my ripe old years and never been married? And you should also know that once I see something I want, I never let it go. Brenda, what I mean is, this isn't just 'I love you for now', this is 'I'm always going to love you'. Do you know what I'm saying? This is for keeps, forever, always. Because if you do, the next question I'm going to ask and the answer you give me, will depend on you fully understanding everything I've said here today."

Speechless, Brenda nodded her head, her mind soaring with what she hoped that question would be.

Tenderly, Matt took her face between his hands and smiling into her wide open eyes, he spoke slowly but clearly.

"In my pocket there's a letter I received today. It came in the late night dispatch at the Embassy and I was given it this morning. You remember how I said I missed my folks and felt that time was running out? Well, I applied for a post in Washington D.C. which is only a couple of hours by plane from my home. And this letter," he touched his breast pocket, "accepts my application and offers me the job. It's a step up for me Brenda. One I couldn't take here and it offers a house, a car and promotion in the near future. The only snag is; they want me to give them an answer by return as the position becomes vacant on the first of February. That'll only just give me enough time to clear up everything here and ship out my belongings. What I'm trying to say is: Brenda, will you marry me and come home with me as my wife?"

Tears sprang to Brenda's eyes and unable to reply for the large lump lodged in her throat, she once more bobbed her head.

"Is that yes? Brenda, say something and put me out of my misery!"

Clearing her throat and flinging her arms around his neck, she replied breathlessly, "Yes, yes, yes! Oh, Matt! The answer's yes a million times!" Each word was punctuated by tiny kisses showered on his neck and throat and as her words sunk in, Matt drew back his head and kissed her deeply and with such passion that she would feel his lips on hers long after he left that evening.

So it was that Ruby and Gary found them when they entered the room.

"Now, now. That's enough of that in front of the children. Put him down Brenda, you don't know where he's been! And you, young man, kindly keep your wayward hands off my daughter! At least, in public and in broad daylight!"

Laughing, the couple disengaged themselves and with eyes shining, Brenda turned to her mother.

"Mum, we've got something to tell you. You'd better sit down, because this could come as a bit of a shock."

Eyes darting from one to the other, Ruby waited, her expression already showing that she knew what was coming next.

Matt coughed and straightened his tie. Then facing his future mother-in-law, his voice strong and confident, he said, "Mrs. O'Shea. Brenda has made me the happiest man alive. She has agreed to become my wife and now all we need is your blessing."

Ruby sat down sharply and raising her apron, covered her face.

Both Brenda and Gary rushed to her side, all solicitous and concern.

"Mum, are you alright? Get her a glass of water, Gary." Rubbing her mother's back vigorously, Brenda went on, more to herself than anyone else present, "I should have broken it to her more gently, I knew it would be a shock. After all, she thought I'd never leave home and that I'd still be here even after Gary has grown up and got his own family. And I can see why. Neither of us ever dreamed that someone would take me off her hands."

Brenda never got any further with her tirade. Ruby's hand shot out and grabbed her daughter's wrist and her head whipped up, anger glinting in her eyes.

"Don't you ever say that, Brenda. I always knew your worth, it wasn't me who had a problem with that. It was you who always brought yourself down, not me. And I was right, wasn't I? I told you someone would come along and see the real you, see that you're worth your weight in gold." Then more gently, her face soft and smiling, Ruby looked over to Matt, still standing in the same place, more unsure of himself now.

"I admit it is a shock, but only because it's all happened so fast. But I can see how happy you've both been lately, Brenda and that's good enough for me. I hope you'll both be very happy together and you've got my blessing, not that you really need it."

Looking over at Matt, Brenda sought frantically for the right words to soften the next blow.

"Stay where you are, Mum. That's not all. This next bit is probably going to be the biggest shock. Mum, when Matt asked me to marry him, he also asked me to go back to America with him. You see, he's got the offer of a better job over there and we'd have to go in January so's we'd be all set up by the beginning of February, when the job starts."

"What? How are you going to get everything done in that time? There's the bans to be read, the church to organise, and God knows what else! We'd never be ready, Brenda."

Matt broke in at this point, telling Ruby of the special licence he could obtain and how certain privileges were available to him as an overseas diplomat. "Just leave everything to me. I can get things rolling as soon as the new year's in. The final say will be down to you and Brenda, so if you tell me what you want, I'll see to it."

Beaming, the two women agreed and after a toast had been made and Ruby had shed a few tears, the matter was settled. After the wedding, Brenda and Matt would leave for America and embark upon a new and exciting life together. But not before events came to a head. And not before Matt would be inextricably drawn into the tragedy to come.

CHAPTER 21

Lottie leant heavily on Jack's arm as he escorted her over the cobblestones and, keeping pace with her, they made their slow way to the door of No. 4.

Although it had not snowed since the night before, the temperature had dropped over night and now the square was slippery and treacherous underfoot. Thin, stubby icicles hung from the archway roof where snow had begun to melt before the 'big freeze' had set in. Each house in the Mews was coated in brilliant white as if freshly painted, reflecting every movement within the square as sure as any mirror.

Catching sight of himself as he passed the fountain, Jack grimaced at the image he portrayed. Within a few months he would be forty four years old and until recently, the passage of time had been good to him. Of late, however, the appearance of a thickening waist line and more than one or two grey hairs, had heralded middle age and he found himself wandering where the years had gone. Old age loomed on the horizon and the thought of his children growing up and leaving the nest was something he tried not to dwell on. True, Jack loved Cathy. Not with the passion they had shared in the early years, this had been replaced with a deep tenderness and an enduring contentment. Still, after so many years of children constantly demanding their attention, he wondered now if they shared any other common interest. Of course, there were spells when they were alone but never for more than two or three hours and always there was Sal, hovering in the background and to ignore her presence was a feat beyond anyone's capabilities. Still, time was running out for the 'old girl' and Jack was becoming increasingly aware that once the children had gone, inevitably, Sal would also have moved on to whatever other world she believed awaited her.

Looking down at the aged, bird-like woman clinging to his arm, Jack voiced his thoughts.

"Another year nearly over, Lottie. Soon be 1960. I wonder what that'll bring. That saying about 'time flies' is bloody right. God, it only seems like yesterday when Fay was born and here she is, nearly a grown woman. I was thinking how I'd like to stop the clock and keep everything as it is today."

Lottie stopped and raising her eyes, spoke quietly to the tall man by her side.

"Don't you go thinking like that, Jack. You've got lots of good things in store for you yet. And besides, you're only a young man. Time enough when you get old like me and your Mum to harp back on the past and wish for extra time." Nodding her head at the fountain, Lottie laughed, "Course, me and her have been here from the beginning, but she looks better on it than me!"

Smiling, Jack glanced up at the Mermaid. Not only frozen in time but also in reality, the petite figure gleamed in the weak sunlight, her ice covered form white and smooth. Her normally ebony surface was surprising to her residents in its transformation. Only a glimmer of black could be seen shimmering at her core and her outer skin was now pale and glistening. As if by magic, she appeared to be a negative of her former self. Whereas she had always sat, dark, mysterious and somewhat forlorn, now she perched on her throne, light, shining and young, wearing nature's camouflage as easily as a new coat.

"It's good of you to let me join in with you all today. Sometimes, it's not good to be alone. And Christmas always makes me think of the past. My Albert and me had some lovely times together when Cyril was a boy. We might have been poor, but there're some things that money just can't buy. Being among people you love and who love you at times like this, is one of them. Memories can be a comfort but sometimes it hurts to remember. And even when you try to forget, the dead have a way of coming back. They sort of creep up on you when you least expect it. When you're asleep, or when you're just doing something you do everyday. It's like being haunted, but not in a frightening way, it just makes you sad." Lottie wiped a tear from the corner of her eye. She found she was prone to sudden weepy spells as her life drew nearer to its close. Nowadays, she hardly noticed when her wrinkled cheeks became damp with the presence of tears.

Jack pulled her arm tightly through his own and gently patted her hand.

"Now, now. Don't go thanking me - you're doing me a favour. Cathy and Sal'll be so busy fussing over you, they won't notice if I nod off this afternoon. Anyway, we like having our friends with us at Christmas, the more the merrier, that's what we say. Besides, we'll all be over at your place tomorrow and I for one am really looking forward to it. Boxing day's usually a bit flat after all the excitement of Christmas day. We normally just sit around, eating the left overs and making pigs of ourselves. It'll be nice to have somewhere to go and something special to do."

The old woman nodded her head and squeezed Jack's arm. Then, once more, the unlikely couple continued on their way.

*

As usual, any movement within the Mews would not go unnoticed by at least one member of the square.

The eyes that watched Lottie and Jack were malevolent and bitter, full of self righteous indignation and tinged with an evil and spiteful presence that spoke of the man within.

Stepping back from the window, Seb turned and strode towards the sideboard. Pulling open the door in an angry gesture, he reached in and grabbed at the half empty bottle of whisky inside. The glass tumbler in his hand was brimful before he slammed the bottle down again.

Vera and Angela exchanged glances. Until this moment, events in the Ridley household had run smoothly. Presents had been exchanged in the normal fashion and even Seb had managed a mumbled "thanks" when Angela had presented him with a new flat cap and Vera had shyly handed him a gaily wrapped parcel containing a blue wool scarf and real leather, black gloves. The only blight so far had been when Vera insisted that Angela go upstairs and put on her new red dress. Without a thought, the young girl had returned to her parents, twirling in front of them to show the full skirt. Vera had beamed at her daughter, remarking on its good fit and suitable colour, whilst Seb had looked on, behind hooded lids. A slow grin had spread over his face as first his eyes took in the tight bodice stretched tautly across her young breasts, then the grin had turned to a leer as he spied her shapely legs as she spun about. Cheeks aflame, Angela had sat down abruptly, tucking the offending limbs beneath her and folding her arms tightly across her chest. Vera had noticed her daughter's embarrassment but did not realise its source. She assumed that Angela's flushed cheeks were due to pleasure and an inability to express her delight.

Now, as Seb took a large mouthful of his drink, Vera glanced over at him, unmindful of his mood and innocent of the undercurrent that flowed from her husband to her daughter.

"You'll spoil your dinner if you have too much to drink, Seb. It won't be long and I've got you a bottle of beer to have with your turkey." Unaware of the sudden stillness in the room, she continued, "Anyway, if you drink all that whisky, there'll be none left for tonight and tomorrow. Shall I put it away? You know what they say, 'out of sight, out of mind'." With a small laugh, she rose from her chair and crossed the floor. Not until her hand reached out for the neck of the bottle did full realisation dawn. In the spilt second before the situation exploded, her mind registered the horrified look on her daughter's face and the ominous silence and stillness of her husband.

Like a beast of prey, Seb pounced. A low, deep growl erupting from his throat. Vera stepped back, her hand still outstretched before her, but she was too late. She saw the glass leave Seb's hand and jerked her head sideways. She felt the rush of air pass her face as the tumbler hurtled past her, then screamed as its contents hit her wide, terrified eyes. The alcohol streamed into every open orifice, blinding her and making her choke and splutter as it flew into her mouth. The force with which Seb had thrown it was so great that the liquid bounced off her chin and entered her nose, causing her to gag and, for a moment, fight for breath. Coughing noisily, Vera raised her hands in an effort to wipe her face free of alcohol just as Seb dealt his first blow. His hand came crashing down on her head, glancing off her defending forearms. This only caused him to become more incensed. He rained blow after blow upon the falling woman, his breath laboured as he bellowed at her.

"Take my drink, would you? Who the fucking hell do you think you are? Don't you bleeding tell me what to do! I've just about had enough of your sodding interference. This is my house and I'll do what I bloody like in it. If I want to get rolling drunk before dinner, then I fucking will! Do you hear? And as for your bottle of beer, you can poke it! What do you think I am, some little snot nosed schoolboy who has to be doled out his drink so's he don't have too much? I'm the one who knows if I've had enough or not, not you, you silly, bloody cow!"

Angela had jumped up and hung on her father's arm, trying to stem the attack.

"Don't, Dad, don't! Stop it, you'll kill her! Please, Dad, stop, stop!"

Seb flung his arm outwards but was unable to loosen the girl's grip. He resorted to kicking out at the crouched form beneath him. With a grunt of satisfaction as he heard his wife whimper, he aimed one last vicious shot, then stood back, his arms now free, and leant heavily on the sideboard behind him.

Angela fell to her mother's side, turning her body away from the monster still lurking above them and shielding the battered woman from any further onslaught. Gently, she raised Vera's head onto her lap and rocking back and forth, cradled the bleeding, torn face, her own tears mingling with those of her mother's. The sound of their weeping filled the room and only the loud, staccato bang of the door slamming announced Seb's departure.

"Oh Mum! Look what he's done to you. Your poor face, it's all cut and bleeding! Wait there, I'll go and get a cloth, just lie still, Mum, don't move, OK?"

Angela flew from the room and Vera lay stock still, listening to the sound of running water and her daughter's loud sobs. Struggling, she raised herself to a sitting position and dropped her head low until the blackness receded. She winced as a wet flannel was applied to her forehead and took the cloth from her daughter's hands, dabbing softly at her eyes and mouth.

Slowly, Vera raised her eyes and looked to her daughter. The girl was kneeling by her side, both hands jammed into her mouth, tears streaming down her face.

"It's alright, love. Honest, it wasn't that bad. Look, I'm fine now, there's only a few little cuts and a couple of bruises. it was the blood that frightened you, that's all. There's always more blood than there should be even if you have a tiny little cut. Come on now, stop crying and give me a hug, alright?"

Angela crawled across to her mother, and threw herself into the safe shelter of her arms.

"How do you stand it, Mum? He's worse than an animal! It shouldn't be allowed. No-one should do what he's done to you." Looking fearfully at Vera, she asked, "Are you sure you're alright? Perhaps I should go for a doctor?"

"No, no. There's no need. Crumbs, I've had worse than that, falling off my bike! I'll just go upstairs and clean myself up properly then we'll sit down and have our dinner. You go out to the kitchen and put the plates in to warm, I won't be a minute." Carefully, Vera pulled herself to a standing position and smiling brightly at Angela, she left the room and went upstairs.

Once in the privacy of the bathroom, Vera let go of her self imposed grip on calmness and composure. Turning on the tap fully, she filled the bowl with cold water, her left hand covering her mouth to stifle her gasps of pain. Then, she immersed a hand towel in the ice cold water and lifting it, placed it whole across her face, patting it gently all over her burning skin. After several minutes, she removed the towel and stared at the face reflected in the mirror before her. One eye was half closed and already showing signs of blue-black markings. Along her left cheek ran an angry welt, presumably caused by Seb's wedding ring. Her nose was red, but not bleeding. It was her mouth that made her eyes well again with unshed tears. Her upper lip was twice its normal size, shapeless and swollen, whilst her lower lip protruded from her teeth, showing a deep cut running from one corner of her mouth to the other. When, gingerly, she ran her tongue over her front teeth, she was horrified to find several of them wobbled in her gums. At last, something snapped inside her. Some inner voice finally broke through the fear and she saw herself as she truly must appear to others. A weak-willed, coward of a woman, allowing a mean, nasty, little man to beat her until she feared for her life. Suddenly, all the years of pent-up emotion rushed to the surface.

"You bastard, Seb! You rotten son of a pig! How could you do this, today of all days and in front of Angela? How could you make me look so weak in front of our daughter? All these years I've put up with your bullying, hiding it from everyone and sticking up for you. Well, you've gone too far this time! This time I'm not going to make out I fell down the stairs, or tripped on the carpet. I'll get you back for this Seb, if it's the last thing I do!"

Angela was in the kitchen, making gravy when she heard a sound behind her. Turning swiftly, she gasped at the spectacle before her. Vera stood in the doorway, the cuts and bruises vivid on her face, staring at her from one open eye. The girl ran to her mother and placing both arms around her waist, hugged Vera to her, not speaking.

Stroking Angela's hair, Vera spoke softly in a sing-song voice.

"Shh,shh! It's alright, don't be frightened, everything's going to be alright. Don't worry, I won't let him touch you, I'll keep you safe, we'll be alright. He'll not lay a hand on you, not as long as I can draw breath. You do believe me, don't you, love? You do know

I wouldn't let anything like this ever happen to you, don't you?" Stopping shortly, Vera pushed Angela away from her and looking determinedly into her daughter's face she spoke with more confidence than Angela had ever heard her use.

"Now, this is what we'll do. We're going to get our coats and a few bits and pieces, then we're going to go over the road to Ruby's and for once in our lives, we're going to ask someone for help, right? Then, we're going to call the police and get them to come over and deal with it. Is that okay with you? Will you do as I say, Angela?"

Nodding her head, Angela looked back at her mother, a small smile on her lips.

"We should have done this years ago, Mum. I know you thought I didn't know everything that was going on, but I've always known. You shouldn't have covered this up for so long. I've been scared to death, wondering when he was going to come after you again. And every time, I wondered when it would be my turn. He looks at me funny, Mum. You know what I mean. He looks at me like he wants to do horrible things to me, things only a husband does with his wife. I wanted to tell you Mum, but I thought you wouldn't believe me. I thought you'd try to push it under the carpet and tell me I was imagining it. But I'm not, honest Mum. One of these days he'll get me and if you try and stop him, he'll kill you. There's something really evil about him, he's not right and, just lately, he's been bottling it all up and soon he'll really explode. And when he does, that'll be the end for you and me, because if we're not both dead, then our lives wouldn't be worth living anyway."

Vera hugged her daughter tightly to her, her chin resting on tope of Angela's head, the tears flowing in a torrent, running unchecked over her battered face.

"Jesus, Mary and Joseph! How long have you kept this all to yourself? I thought I was doing the right thing, trying to smooth things over, trying to protect you from knowing the whole truth. What kind of mother am I that lets her daughter carry a burden like that? I'm so sorry, love, so sorry. I'll make it up to you, really I will. I'll put things right, you see if I don't."

Quickly, now the decision was made, the couple gathered their belongings together and left the house, relieved to face their problems and at last admit them to the outside world.

CHAPTER 22

"Who the bloody hell is that? You'd think that anyone with a bit of common sense would know not to knock on someone's door at this time. Still, that'd be right. Go and disturb folk just as they're about to hear the Queen's speech." Grumbling loudly, Ruby heaved her large frame out of the comfortable chair and stepping over her son's stretched out form went to answer the knock at the door. "Don't you move, Gary. After all, it's easier for me to climb all over you."

Grinning, Brenda looked at Matt's expression. Being a newcomer, the American was unaccustomed to Ruby's ways. Her gruff and blunt manner hid a warm heart and only those close to her knew that secretly she was a 'soft touch'. Since arriving that morning, Matt had been shown a hospitality that is common among the cockney classes. He had been made to feel welcome and at home and had felt relaxed and at ease in Ruby's home. Nothing was too much trouble for Brenda's mother. She had insisted that he take on the role of 'man of the house' especially as he would soon be Brenda's husband. As such, he had been granted the privilege of carving the turkey and saying grace before the meal.

"Don't look so worried, Matt. She's not really angry, just a bit put out. Any other time she wouldn't mind. Mind you, I don't see why she has to listen to the Queen on Christmas Day. It's more or less the same speech every year. Still, there it is. She must have the radio on and hear every word."

Brenda leant forward and patted Matt's arm in reassurance. He smiled back, his face clearing of the frown and covered her hand with his own. Gary observed them from the floor. The young boy had never seen his sister courted before and although a large part of him was glad for her, another darker side was jealous of their closeness. He did not like the way Matt had become the centre of her attention. Nor did he like the way Matt looked at Brenda, with a glimmer in his eye and the air of an unspoken secret between them. Gary had always enjoyed his sister's undivided attention and had basked in the affection she lavished on him. Suddenly, he was no longer in the main spotlight and even though, he reasoned, Brenda must live her own life and take any happiness that might come her way, the child in him resented Matt's intrusion.

He sighed now and rolled over, his head resting between his arms as he sprawled upon the rug before the fire. His life would certainly change drastically now that Brenda and Matt were to be married. There would just be him and his mother left here once Brenda went to America and although he knew Ruby would not stand in his way, he would feel obliged to spend more time with her and less out and about. Who would he confide in then? There were only limited subjects that could be discussed with his mother. Some topics are strictly taboo where parents and their children are concerned and Brenda had always been his best friend as well as his sister.

"That was a deep sigh, Gary. Something troubling you?" Matt left the couch and joined the boy on the rug. "You know, I think the two of you are going to miss each other a great deal once Brenda and I are back in the States. All I ever hear is what a wonderful brother you are. Clever, witty, brave, the list is never ending. And from what I know of you, I think your sister has extremely good taste. But to tell you the truth, I feel real guilty about coming between you two so I've got a big favour to ask of you. Gary, as soon as we're settled in, will you come out and stay with us for a while? Perhaps for the summer vacation? If you'll say yes, I'll send you a ticket as soon as I get back. Otherwise, she'll pine away for you and then where will I be? Stuck with a woman whose heart still lives here. Fine mess I'll be in then, eh?"

Gary raised his head and looked at the man waiting in earnest for a reply. Glancing over at Brenda he saw her soft smile and realised with a jolt that he need not feel threatened or isolated by Matt. For Brenda had enough affection for the two of them and he would still be her little brother, no matter what the circumstances.

"Just try keeping me away." A man to man note of conspiracy had entered the boy's voice. "I know what these women can be like, Matt. They don't really know what they want. She might have you to boss around over there, but she'll still want to run my life and all. Don't you worry about it, I'll come over and keep her in line for you."

Ruffling Gary's hair, Matt grinned at Gary and with a wink murmured, "That's fine, just fine."

"Alright, that's enough of that. I can't have the two men in my life ganging up on me and right under my nose and all......" Brenda's words were cut short as from the hallway came the sound of Ruby's voice.

"My God! What the bleeding hell's been going on? Come in, come in. Don't stand out there you two. Get yourselves in here."

Soft voices could be heard along with several pairs of footsteps coming down the passageway. Then, the door was flung wide and Vera and Angela Ridley entered the room, followed closely by Ruby.

"Oh, Vera! Who's done that to you? Here, sit here and I'll go and put the kettle on. Come on Gary. Don't just lay there with your mouth hanging open. Get up and see to Angela." Brenda helped the battered woman to the couch, then bustled out to the kitchen, tutting all the while.

Matt had risen from the settee and stood now with his back to the fire. He had heard Brenda talk of a Vera Ridley and her abusive husband, Seb, but until today had not set eyes on either one. Hands clenched behind his back, Matt silently fumed. It was obvious even to himself, a stranger, that the poor woman had taken a severe beating and there would be no prizes for guessing who had meted out the punishment. As Matt watched the scene before him, he became increasingly more angry at the unjust treatment of the frail woman. He could not understand how a man could inflict such blatant cruelty on a defenceless woman. What made a man behave in this fashion? And how did that man manage to sleep nights? Biting his tongue, Matt kept his counsel, all the while watching and waiting should his help be needed.

Ruby sat by Vera's side, her arm around the trembling woman's shoulders and her voice loud with indignation.

"So. It was him again, I suppose. The bloody coward! Are you alright, love? Do you want me to fetch a doctor? That's a nasty cut on your lip and that eye doesn't look too good either. I think we should get you up to casualty, because it looks like you'll need some stitches."

Vera shook her head, fighting to keep back the tears. It had been so long since someone had spoken a sympathetic word to her and the kindness she was now receiving brought a lump to her throat.

"Mrs. O'Shea's right, Mum. You should let someone have a look at you." Angela knelt before her mother, her hands clasping Vera's upper arms.

"No, no. That's not the way to play this." Raising her head, Vera looked into Ruby's face, her expression determined. "Don't worry. I'm not about to let him get away with this, not this time. I want to call in the Police. Let them handle it all. Then, if they think

I need to see a doctor, I'll go to the hospital. But first of all, I want it on record and I want them to see me at my worst, before I get cleaned and patched up. Do you think you could arrange it for me? I don't want Angela out of my sight and I don't think I could manage to get down to the station. Will someone here go for them?"

"No sooner said, than done." Turning in her seat, Ruby instructed Gary to go to the Police Station and bring an officer back with him.

Already halfway to the door, Matt pulled Gary along with him, saying over his shoulder, "Leave it to us, Mrs. O'Shea. We'll deal with it, won't we Gary? You all just sit tight and don't answer the door to anyone until we get back."

A tea tray in her hand, Brenda met Matt and Gary at the door and quickly grasped the situation. Reaching up she kissed Matt's cheek as he donned his coat before leaving the house with Gary close on his heels. She stood in the hallway staring at the closed door for several seconds before making an about turn and re-entering the lounge.

"They won't be long. Matt's taken his car, so it shouldn't take more than fifteen minutes. Now then, Vera, can you manage a cup of tea? I'll make it milky so's it's not too hot and put lots of sugar in it just in case you're suffering with shock as well as everything else."

These last kind words from Brenda were all too much for Vera. Bursting into tears, she fumbled for her handkerchief, muttering, "Sorry, I'm sorry for being such a nuisance." Also in tears, Angela hugged her mother, whispering, "It's alright now, Mum. It's alright. Don't cry, please don't, Mum."

At last, Vera brought her sobs under control and wiping her face carefully she pulled her daughter up from her knees and brought her close to her side. Then, turning her bruised and tear streaked face to Ruby and Brenda, she spoke softly.

"You've all been so kind to us and we'll never be able to thank you enough. I'm sorry to put all this on you, especially today. But I didn't know who else to go to. Me and Angela have tried to keep our troubles to ourselves. Well, we've ignored them really and today was the last straw. He just went for me and all over a bottle of whisky. Like a madman he was and in front of Angela as well. I always thought I was doing the right thing - keeping it from everyone. But I was only fooling myself. Here was my own daughter, too frightened to speak out and knowing what was going on all the time.

I should have realised that I was being a bloody fool after that trouble back in the autumn. Not me. I kept on burying my head in the sand even though everyone in the square must have known. Why else would you all have warned him off? And it worked for a while. He didn't raise a hand to me again, until just recently and that was only mild, more a threat than anything else. But today was different. I've taken some hidings off him in my time, but this lot beats them all. He wasn't even drunk either. He'd only had a couple, not enough to touch the sides really. It was like a dam rushing out. Well, I've had enough. I can't go on putting Angela through this and I can't live with myself acting like a stupid, down trodden idiot. If I've got nothing else, then I should at least have my pride. I've got to be able to hold my head up and be able to look folk in the eye."

Throughout this long speech, Ruby and Brenda had nodded their heads in encouragement. On their faces, beaming smiles reflected their pleasure in seeing a brave, new Vera emerge with each word she had uttered.

"That's telling them, Mum. Go for it. We'll start again, just you and me. No more hiding behind closed doors and being terrified of what he's going to do next." Angela smiled widely at Ruby, her eyes shining with respect and admiration.

"There's enough people round here to back you, Vera. You're right you know. We all knew what his game was, but we couldn't do anything about it, not in the long term, until you were willing to help yourself. Well, now you have. This is the first step and we'll all be behind you. You won't be alone, Vera. Once everyone finds out that you're fighting back, they'll fall over themselves to lend a hand." Ruby turned to Brenda and finished, "That's right, isn't it Brenda?"

"Course it is. Everyone's always been on your side, Vera. All you ever had to do was say the word and we'd have all rallied round, because you're one of us and we always take care of our own. He won't stand a chance now. Just wait until the men find out what he's done, never mind what the Police will do to him, the rotten sod." Handing Vera a full cup, Brenda continued, "Now, you drink that up, it'll make you feel better. Then, when the Police get here we'll do a vanishing act and you and Angela can tell them everything. If you need us to bear you out, just shout and we'll put them straight. After all, we're none of us deaf and we could hear what he was doing to you all these years. OK?"

Eyes welling once more, Vera shook her head. "I should have done this years ago, then I could have saved Angela from all this trouble. Thanks, Ruby and you too, Brenda. I'll never forget how you've helped me today, I really won't."

Vera was stopped from expressing her gratitude any further when the sound of the front door opening echoed down the hallway, followed by Gary's voice calling, "We're back, Mum and we've got a copper with us." His turn of phrase made all three females smile and shake their heads.

"Trust Gary to put it so bluntly. There's never a dull moment when he's about." Rising from her seat, Ruby ushered the uniformed Policeman into the room then gathered her family, including Matt, into the kitchen. "We'll wait in here until she's finished. Here, Matt. Get that bottle of sherry down from the cupboard and pour me a large glass. I need something a bit stronger than tea just now."

Talking quietly among themselves, Matt and his soon to be in-laws waited patiently. The kitchen clock read three o'clock, just one hour since Vera had sought sanctuary and help from that household, when the Policeman poked his head around the door frame and announced that he had finished taking a statement from Vera and Angela.

"Bit of a nasty business, all this, eh? Still, now we know all the facts, we'll be able to put a stop to it all. Mrs. Ridley seems determined to press charges and I can only hope her resolve is strong. Normally, we find in these sort of cases, once the drama is over, the women weaken and retract. But if she's got enough friends to see her through all this, then we'll be able to protect her from any further assaults."

"We'll see she goes through with it, officer. And if you need any witnesses, we'll come forward, no trouble. In fact, you could ask just about anyone in the Mews. We've all seen it and heard it. Like you, our hands were tied until she decided to do something about it." Ruby had stood, her face set as she confronted the officer.

"That's as maybe, but I hope you're not thinking of taking the law into your own hands. You leave this to the people who know how to deal with it. You'll do more damage if you take the matter upon yourselves. A good representative in court will easily be able to get him off the hook if he's been harassed by the neighbours." Opening his notebook, the Policeman changed tactics, "Now, would any of you know where we could start looking from Mr. Ridley? Any favourite haunts he might go to?"

Brenda shrugged her shoulders, "Not today, all the pubs are shut and that's the only places he ever goes to. He's probably hiding out at one of his cronies houses, but we don't know where."

Closing the black book, the officer sighed saying, "Right then. We'll have to put out a description and hope someone spots him. In the meantime, I think Mrs. Ridley should pay a visit to the hospital. It'd be better to have a medical report on her injuries and it would be as well to have her checked over. The daughter seems to be alright, but I'd rather someone saw her. She's had a nasty shock, they both have. Perhaps this gentleman wouldn't mind taking them both in his car while I go back and file the report? The sooner we get things moving, the better. It's not uncommon for an assailant to return and have another go. With any luck, Mr. Ridley should be safely in custody by this evening and Mrs. Ridley will sleep easy in her bed."

Matt was on his feet, nodding his head. "No problem, Officer. I'd be glad to help, if I can. I'll just go and bring the car into the square."

Thus, as the other residents enjoyed the remainder of Christmas Day, Brenda and Matt escorted Vera and Angela to the casualty department where Vera underwent stitching to her lip and treatment for multiple cuts and bruises. Both Angela and Vera were given mild sedatives and told to rest for the next twenty four hours.

Rest was something that would not come easy to the pair, as by the time darkness fell, Seb Ridley was still at large and both knew that his mood would not have improved with the passage of time.

CHAPTER 23

A weak and warmless sun struggled into Mermaid Mews on Boxing Day, 1959. The ice maiden still surveyed her kingdom, such as it was. To Ellie, she wore a faintly bored expression and in the child's opinion, this was only to be expected. The small girl stood, head pushed back as far as it would allow and scrutinised both fountain and occupant. In her mind, the Mermaid led a tedious existence. Never could she climb down and run, jump or play. Nor could she laugh, sing nor shout. And always, she must continue with a task that held no hope of ending. True, she could keep a secret for all time. Could watch and listen and be so still that her presence would be forgotten and so be privy to the many mysteries of life, as yet unravelled by Ellie. Not worried by old age, illness or despair, the child did not envy nor consider the fortunate position the statuette held, who also found these miseries incomprehensible. Others may have looked upon the Mermaid with sadness as time etched its mark on the marble of her form, but, like an ageing Child Starlet, she only saw herself as she had been in the beginning. This illusion was enhanced and shared by the people around her since nature had thrown an icy mantel about her shoulders, hiding her flaws and covering her wrinkled surface.

The crunching of packed ice underfoot, made the girl whirl about as strong, male arms looped around her waist and large hands caught under her armpits. She gasped with surprise as she was flung high, her head on a level with the Mermaid's swishing tail. Then, she was falling, hands spread wide, mouth open and hair chasing her descent. Down she plummeted, the grey speckled cobblestones rushing up to meet her. So sure was she that this union of flesh and stone was imminent, that she shut tight her eyes and waited for the inevitable as gravity would surely lay claim to yet another victim.

At the last instant and only then, she felt those same hands that had thrown her skyward pull her sideways and upwards once more until her nose nudged against bristled, day-old whiskers.

"Caught you!"

Air, caught in her throat, erupted in a torrent as Ellie opened wide her mouth and screamed.

"DAD!"

Small hands pummelled a broad chest, whilst legs so slender they looked to break under the weight of even this small child, kicked and flailed at a soft belly, made more so by the heaving and rolling of its owner. Loud, resounding laughter split the air as Jack unsuccessfully endeavoured to still the wild creature that was his daughter.

"You frightened me to death! Bully! Sneak! Rotten thing! I'm going to tell Mum, I will. Then I'm going to tell Nan. She'll get you for this, see if she don't!"

More laughter met these threats as Jack placed Ellie firmly on the ground and backed up, arms covering his head, until he bumped into the lip of the fountain. Hands on knees, he bent, trying to quell the merriment, lungs bursting for a deep breath.

"You should have seen your face! It was a picture. I've never seen anyone look so surprised. You must've been miles away for me to be able to creep up on you like that. I really got you, good and proper, Ellie!"

Ellie stood back, hands on hips, left foot tapping, an angry frown on her pretty face.

"It wasn't fair! I wasn't ready and I never heard you. You can't have that one, Dad because you didn't play by the rules."

"Oh no! All's fair in love and war and I reckon I should get two points for this one. Perhaps this'll teach you to be on the look-out all the time; sleep with one eye open, boots on and all that."

This was a game Jack and Ellie played constantly. The idea was to take the other completely off guard and scare themselves silly. No holds were barred and almost all situations were allowed (Jack drew the line to Ellie springing out of his wardrobe, so his and Cathy's bedroom were out of bounds). Points were awarded and allotted according to the originality of the surprise and a running total was kept by both parties.

Not able to stay mad at her father for long, Ellie's face broke into a huge grin.

"It was a good one, Dad. It really made me jump. But you'd better watch out, because I'm going to get you next time and I'll get you even betterer than you got me!"

Just then, Cathy called and father and daughter clasped hands and returned indoors, their repartee continuing until they reached the kitchen, where Cathy and Sal bustled back and forth, the endless battle between stove and sink under way.

"Where have you two been? Out making nuisances of yourselves, no doubt. In case you haven't noticed, Christmas is for everybody, not just you two and we need some help around here."

Jack winked at Ellie and the girl smiled in return. It was not unusual for either Cathy or Sal to reprimand them and it was commonplace for both to be missing simultaneously and later to be found together.

"Right then, what's to be done?"

Cathy looked to her mother-in-law and raised her eyebrows. "Can you believe him, Mother? We've only been going on and on all morning about how much work there is to do if we're all going to get to this party this afternoon."

The older woman wiped her hands on her ever-present apron and sighed. "I don't know how you put up with him sometimes, girl. He was the same when he was a boy. I thought at one stage he might be deaf but he can hear a dish rattle a mile off. We'll just have to put it down to only hearing what he wants to." Her eyes, now turned to her son, Sal continued, "For a start you can go and have a shave, you look worse than the Rag and Bone Man. Then, Frank will need a hand setting up tables, chairs and organising the drink." Sal swung her stare down onto the child stood at her father's side, "And you can start taking some of these trays of food over to Lottie's. Fay and Billy are already over there, buttering bread and getting plates and cups ready." Handing a full tray of sausage rolls to her granddaughter, she admonished, "Mind how you go and don't run. If you drop even one of these, you'll have me and your mother to answer to, right?"

Ellie took the tray carefully from Sal's grasp, the tip of her tongue protruding from one corner of her mouth as she concentrated on keeping every morsel on the platter. "Yes, Nan. I'll be careful. You can trust me."

With a snort, Sal turned from the child and, in an undertone, muttered "Of course I can. Just like I trust your father."

Cathy watched as her youngest child turned slowly, placing one foot after the other in an exaggerated fashion and left the room. "Ellie! You heard your Nan. Now don't act the fool and walk properly." A faint "Yes, Mum." could vaguely be heard as the girl disappeared down the hallway.

*

The Treist household was not unique that morning. All around the square, steam rose from hard working ovens and misted over window panes as the women prepared their own special offerings for the coming party. Like Ellie, the children from each house trotted back and forth across the Mews with dishes, plates and trays. As Ellie set foot on her path, she saw from the corner of her eye, Gary O'Shea also leave his house and head in the direction of Lottie's, both hands occupied with a huge glass bowl of trifle.

"Hey, Gary! Wait for me." In her rush, she slid on the slick path, tottered for a moment, then regaining her balance, hurried after the figure of her hero.

"Morning, squirt. What you got there? They look good enough to eat. Don't mothers make a lot of fuss about nothing? We'd be quite happy with a bowl of crisps and a bottle of lemonade. As long as someone plays the piano, that'd be good enough for me, eh?"

Trudging on, the petite girl and rangy youth crossed the square and entered the maelstrom that had become Lottie's house. Adults and children alike hustled about. The babble of voices rose as each person attempted to make themselves heard.

"Where shall I put this, Lottie?"

"Lottie, where do you want this table?"

"Don't leave that there. Someone will sit on it."

"Did anyone think to bring a tablecloth?"

Lottie stood among them all, appearing to be calm and collected, a thoughtful expression on her face. It had been a long time since her house had rung with the laughter of children and the comfort of adult voices and these served to drown the drone of her 'ghosts'. Her head to one side, she seemed to listen for a particular noise, then, visibly shaking herself, she returned to the present and began to issue orders.

"Put that on the table, Fay. Frank, the table's got to go in the living room. That's right, take that off the chair, Billy and it can go in the larder on the cold shelf. The bottle opener's in the left hand drawer of the dresser, along with the tablecloth, Brenda. Vera, can you give me a hand with these glasses? And you, Angela, grab a cloth and dry up some plates."

By two o'clock all was ready. The tables were laid and groaning under the weight of surplus, home made fare. In the far corner of the living room, a makeshift bar had been set up by Jack and Frank. They would supervise this table, making sure that no youngster helped themselves to alcohol, at the same time keeping a watchful eye on empty, adult glasses.

Vera and Angela were the last to return to their home in order wash and change into their party clothes. Arm in arm, they sauntered back, laughing at some of the antics that had occurred that morning. Although Seb had not been apprehended, they both felt reasonably safe within the confines of the Mews and, as Seb had not made an appearance the night before, they assumed he had fled the district. By now, word would have spread and he would be aware the Police had intervened. Vera felt that this threat alone would keep him from her door.

"Mum, what if he never comes back and the Police don't find him?"

Vera stopped and looked down at her daughter. "We'll cross that bridge when we come to it. I think you should know, Angela, that I'm not out to get him. As long as he keeps away from us and doesn't cause us any trouble, then I'd be quite happy."

"But we'd never know, would we, Mum? He could just turn up one day or even one night. You know what he's like, Mum. He doesn't forget. He could wait a while, then come back and get us. We'd never feel safe, at least I wouldn't." The fear in Angela's eyes tore at her mother's heart. Time would not erase the horrors that Angela had lived through, but the memories would dim if only mother and daughter could find a safe haven.

"Look, love. Let's get ourselves into the New Year. Then, we'll take a proper look at where we stand. If you still feel the same way, we'll ask the Council to rehouse us. I'm sure they would help, under the circumstances. Once we've moved, he'd give up because no-one round here's going to tell him where we are - they'd shop him first."

The girl nodded her head in agreement and seemed to be satisfied with Vera's assurances. Unknown to her mother, the girl had crept down into the kitchen the night before and taking a long bladed carving knife from the drawer, returned to her room.

Slipping the knife under the corner of her mattress, Angela lay back. A small sigh escaped her lips as she snuggled down, able to sleep now. She might never need to use the implement, but its presence relieved her anxiety and gave her a feeling of safety.

As sleep claimed her, Angela's last thought was: *Just in case. It's there, just in case.*

CHAPTER 24

He gazed out at the river, elbows resting on the parapet that ran along the embankment. Large, grey clouds gathered overhead, a warning of more snow to come and emphasised his black mood.

Since his brutal outburst of the day before, Seb had had a hard time of it. It was not his conscience that pricked but rather the lack of creature comforts. After leaving the Mews, he had headed, out of habit, towards the Rising Sun. Only as he had neared the site and looked into the distance at the charred remains that had once been his favourite haunt, did he remember. His steps had slowed, then faltered to a stop. "Stupid bugger!" he muttered. How could he have forgotten? A small voice questioned him on the rights to damage other people's property, but he shrugged this off. *It serves them right*, he thought. *They should never have crossed me. No-one messes with Seb Ridley and gets away with it and it's not over yet, not by a long chalk.* An evil grin had crossed his face when he recalled how one incident had set in motion a chain of events that would serve to even the score between himself and his neighbours. However, these thoughts of revenge did not solve his present problems. The realisation that today was Boxing Day and there would be no pubs open now until the next day, caused him further dilemma. He stood in the street and racked his brain on his next plan of action. *There's no point in going home. Those two bitches will just sit around staring at me for the rest of the day, jumping like cats on hot bricks, every time I move. No, that's no way to spend Boxing Day*, he pondered. After some deliberation, he decided to pay a visit to a drinking pal who lived just over the river. This particular friend lived alone in a bedsit and would probably welcome some company.

Seb's luck, however, had run out. On arriving at the old Victoria property that housed several bedsits, one of which was rented by Seb's friend, he had knocked loudly until a sleepy resident had answered. After a short exchange of words, Seb had discovered that his erstwhile pal had gone away to stay with relatives until the New Year.

Feeling let down and angry, Seb had returned across the river, having decided that he would have to go home after all. As he was strolling along the Chelsea embankment, a voice had hailed him.

"Oi! That you, Seb?"

"Alright then, Cyril?" Crossing the street, Seb joined the tubby man who had called out to him. "What you up to? Anything going on today?"

"Naw, everywhere's closed up tighter than a coffin. The only place open is the cop shop and I've already had the pleasure of their company this afternoon. I hear you've been livening things up a bit, though." Cyril leaned closer, his breath reeking of beer, and nudged Seb in the ribs.

"What do you mean? What are you on about?" The small man had stepped back, a scowl on his face.

Cyril leered at Seb, an exaggerated wink closing one eye. "You know, all that business with your missus. They're all buzzing about it down at the station. I heard one cop say you'd taken a few swings at her and she'd had to go to the hospital. You're not exactly flavour of the month down there, mate. On the hot list, you are, they've got an arrest out on you. Here, you alright?" Seb's face had become redder and redder as Cyril had passed on his news.

Without a word, Seb had turned on his heel and stalked off back in the direction from which he had come. He did not hear his friend's shout of, "Where are you going now? You'd better watch out, every cop in London's on the look-out for you." Walking blindly on, a red mist of fury before his eyes, Seb pieced together in his mind what had happened. *The Bitch!*, he thought, *she must have shopped me. What bloody lies has she told the Police? I hardly touched her. Christ! A few little slaps and she goes running off to the cops. I'll bet that little cow, Angela, backed her up and then they'll have gone all round the square, telling everyone. They'll all be laughing at me! Just waiting for an excuse, that's what they've been doing. Waiting to catch me out. Well, it'll be a cold day in hell before any of that mob gets the better of me. I'll lay low until things cool down a bit, then when the times right, I'll get even. If it's the last thing I ever do, I'll make them pay for this, all of them!*

Now, as he stood before the Thames, thinking of the cold night he had spent yesterday, shivering on a park bench, moving on every hour to keep his circulation working, the time had come. He knew that everyone would have been at the party that afternoon and the revelries would go on into the evening. This was yet another snub, in the man's eyes. An invitation had not been given to him, only to Vera and Angela and therefore, another debt was outstanding. But first things first. His hand crept into his jacket pocket, feeling the house keys there. A nasty sneer crossed his face as he pushed himself away from the wall and started in the direction of the Brompton Road. Darkness had fallen and in the distance, a clock chimed the half hour. It would not take him more than fifteen minutes to walk, at a leisurely pace, to Mermaid Mews. By eight forty-five p.m. he would be there.

I'm coming Vera and you too, my darling daughter. Have yourselves a nice time at the party, because it'll be the last time either of you ever smiles again. By the time anyone misses either of you, I'll be long gone, far away from here. And no-one will ever find me. I'll disappear off the face of the earth then, when I'm ready, I'll make my way south and start a new life with a different name. So, make sure you both enjoy today, because this is the last day you'll ever see.

CHAPTER 25

Eight o'clock, December 26th 1959. The party had been going full swing with no sign of abating. The merry making had begun promptly at four o'clock with the first arrivals.

Jack Treist and his family had all trooped across the square laughing and calling out for everyone to join them. Doors had swung open around the Mews as if the occupants had been waiting for a signal. Although Jack was the first to cross Lottie's threshold, it was only by seconds. Almost within the blink of an eye, the tranquillity of the house was shattered by giggling children and rowdy adults. This gathering had been planned for so long, that everyone was determined to enjoy it to the full. Even the Carmichael's, after the first hour and several drinks, had cast aside their troubles and entered into the spirit of celebration wholeheartedly.

"Frank! You can't get any more in that glass and what the hell's in it, anyway? I think you're trying to get me drunk."

Frank carefully passed the overfull tumbler to his wife, winking widely and with a comical leer replied.

"Go on, get it down you, girl. There's plenty more where that came from and it'll do you good. And as for me trying to get you drunk, I don't know how you could think such a thing!"

Pouring a refill for Cathy, Jack stood with his friend on one side of the 'bar' and snorted at Frank's wide-eyed innocence. "Oh yeah, and butter wouldn't melt in his mouth, either. You watch yourself, Eileen, I'd hate to see someone take advantage of you."

"I'd never have said that about you, Jack. Never knew you was in to watching. Tell me does Cathy know about this little preference you've got?" Then in a loud whisper, Frank leant towards Jack and continued, "Or shall we keep it to ourselves?"

Just having taken a large mouthful of her drink, Cathy spluttered and coughed, looking over her shoulder to where her mother-in-law was sat in a comfortable chair, her wrinkled face flushed and fading blue eyes twinkling.

"Shh! You don't say things like that when Mother's about. She only gets the wrong end of the stick and before we know it, it'll be all over the place that Jack's a peeping Tom and she'll be up the confessional, crying on Father O'Connell's shoulder, poor man."

Sal looked up as the two couples burst into loud, helpless laughter. Smiling, the old woman turned to Lottie who was perched on the arm of her chair. "It's good to see them having a nice time, isn't it Lottie? Frank and Eileen have had their fair share of troubles just lately and Cathy and Jack don't let their hair down enough. I'm glad they're all getting on so well with each other, perhaps they'll start going out together once the New Year's here and everything has been sorted."

The lady of the house, shifted her weight, juggling a glass and a plate piled high with food. "Yeah. It's nice to see the youngsters enjoying themselves. And I hope you're right, Sal. I hope young Frankie comes home soon and the Police get to the bottom of it all. There was definitely something fishy about the whole thing. Still, mustn't worry about that now. We're all here to have a good time and if Frank and Eileen hear us, it'll put a blight on it all."

Standing up, Lottie called for everyone to be quiet. "Now then, let's have a bit of hush." She waited until the chattering voices had diminished, then raising her glass she gazed about the room. "I'd just like to propose a toast. Here's to you all, I'm very glad you could all come and may 1960 bring you all what you wish for yourselves."

Every voice in the room joined hers as they raised their glasses high. "Here's to 1960!"

Jack's voice boomed over the others. "And I'd like to thank Lottie on behalf of us all for inviting us into her home and putting on such a good spread. Here's to you, Lottie and God bless you!"

Once more, glasses clinked and voices rang out in appreciation of their hostess. Lottie bowed her head in acceptance, then holding up her hands once more, ordered silence. "The only thing this party has lacked, is music and a good old sing-song. Now, I know that there's someone here tonight who is very useful with a Joanna and I'm sure if we all shout loud enough, that person could be persuaded to give us a few tunes."

Shouts of, "Come on Sal, play us something." and "Go on, give us a tune, Sal, show us what your made of!" reduced to "Sal, Sal, Sal!" accompanied by clapping hands and cat-calls.

When she had extracted as much from the situation as she could, Sal rose, regal and rosy-cheeked. "Alright, alright! Keep the noise down, it's enough to wake the dead. If you all insist," and she paused here to allow enough people to insist they insisted, "then I'll see what I can do. Don't expect too much though, it's been a long time since I played a piano and the old fingers aren't as nimble as they used to be." Going over to the far side of the room, Sal pulled out a small red velvet stool and sitting down, raised the piano lid and went straight into a lively rendition of 'Roll out the Barrow'. Soon the whole house was alive with the sound of people singing, in a variety of keys. Indeed, the noise travelled out into the square and it was as well that every resident, or almost every one, was present, otherwise there would surely have been a number of complaints.

Matt stood with Brenda at the head of the piano, a bemused expression on his face, singing along with the rest, even though he did not know the words and even if he had, their meaning would have escaped him. His arm around Brenda's waist, he looked down into her upturned face and unable to resist, bent and kissed her open mouth. This gesture did not go unnoticed. Nor was it missed that Ruby had also observed this open demonstration and that she was smiling widely at the couple. Not ignorant of her neighbours questioning glances, Ruby strode up to Matt and whispered in his ear. He smiled in reply, then shrugging his shoulders, bent over Sal and spoke quietly. The older woman, played on until the end of the song, then stopped, waited patiently and looking around, brought order to the room just by the stare of her piercing eyes.

The hubbub died down slowly and then when Matt was sure he had their full attention, he spoke distinctly and proudly.

"Good evening, folks. Now I know that some of you don't know me, so first I would like to introduce myself. The name's Matthew Goldberg, or Matt to my friends, which I hope you will all become. Most of you will have noticed that I've been paying particular attention to a young lady who lives not many miles from here." Jovial laughter met these words with calls of, "Go on? Who's that then?" and Brenda blushed scarlet and buried her head in Matt's shoulder.

"Anyhow, I am honoured to announce tonight, that the young lady in question has accepted my proposal of marriage and Brenda and I are to be married early in the New Year. Well, that's all I really wanted to say except it goes without saying that everyone is invited to the wedding."

There was a slight hush as everyone absorbed this announcement, then voices rose to a newer, higher pitch as Matt and Brenda were congratulated. The men slapped Matt on the back and the women kissed Brenda, their pleasure and approval evident. The sound of 'Here comes the Bride' rang forth from the piano, as Sal thumped the keys and encouraged people to join in. As the last cheering died away and the next song had begun, Matt pulled Brenda gently out into the hall.

"OK, honey? I know I should have asked you first, but your mother said I should say something as people were beginning to ask questions. It was my fault. I just couldn't keep my hands off you."

Brenda looked into his deep brown eyes. Sometimes, she felt that she would just drift away within those mirrors to Matt's soul and she smiled now and hugged him tightly. "Everything you do is alright, Matt. You could run naked round the place and I'd still think it was OK. You must be the most caring and loving man I've ever had the good fortune to meet and I'm going to try as hard as I can to make you happy."

Matt's eyes glistened. It was one of his most endearing features, to Brenda. She was extremely touched by Matt's ability to show his feelings, whether happy or sad. He was so open and trusting, and his emotions were displayed at all times, for all the world to see, on his rugged face. His kiss was fierce and full of promise as he pulled her closer still. Brenda clung to him, her teeth grazing his own as their tongues met and caressed. It was he that pulled away, his breath ragged and whispered, "When did you say was the earliest we could be married? I don't know if I can hold out much longer, you're driving me crazy!"

Playfully, Brenda pushed at him. "It's only a couple of weeks." Then her smile increased to a grin and fluttering her eyelashes at him, and her voice dipping to a husky drawl, she went on, "Then I'll make all this waiting worth your while."

"Oh, so that's how you limey's play it, is it? Get a man all hot and lead him on until he begs to be put out of his misery. Well, you teasing witch, I think you should know that it's definitely working. So, if I throw myself at your feet, will you run off with me to this Gretna Green place and marry me tonight?"

Not sure if he was joking, Brenda stood, half smiling, half serious, until Matt gave in and laughed at her expression. "Don't worry, I'm not going to carry you off in the dead of night and risk the wrath of Ruby. She'd never forgive us if we did her out of the 'Big Day'. I'm just going to have lots of cold showers and long runs in the park in the meantime."

Sighing with relief, Brenda leaned against him and was about to reply when a small voice at her side shrilled, "Your Mum's looking for you, Brenda. She says I'm to come and find you, because you've been out here long enough." Ellie's serious face looked up at the pair as she tugged on Brenda's skirt. Matt winked down at the child. "And she's quite right. This woman just won't leave me alone, Ellie and I just don't know how to tell her that I'm madly in love with another, but I've got to wait for her to grow up before I can do anything about it." He rolled his eyes dramatically, until Brenda pulled herself from his grasp and bending down conferred with the small girl. "Well, Ellie. I think you and me had better have a serious talk. Did you know he was two-timing us? Men! You just can't trust them. What do you think we should do with him?"

Ellie looked up at the American, a small frown on her face and her chin resting in one hand as she contemplated his fate. Matt held his hands up in surrender. "OK, OK I give in. I'm at your mercy. We men just haven't realised that we can never get the better of a woman. So while you two decide how I can ever make it up to you both, I'll just take a wander and check out the car."

Taking his jacket from the peg at the door, Matt walked out of the house, feet dragging in a dejected manner.

"He's alright, isn't he, Brenda? I was only joking. He doesn't think we meant it, does he?"

Brenda laughed and putting her arm around the girl's shoulders, replied, "No, love. He was playing. These Americans are a funny lot, but I suppose we'll just have to get used to him. Come on, let's go and see what my bossy mother wants."

As Matt left the square, Brenda rejoined her family and friends. Her eyes sparkled and her smile was warm as she was surrounded by them all, answering their questions and telling of the new life she would soon be beginning with a man who had stepped straight out of her dreams.

CHAPTER 26

Matt raised his arms high above his head and stretched. He looked around the Mews. One or two of the residents had left lights on to light their way back tonight, but mostly the square was in darkness. Deep shadows created dark hollows and bottomless pits and the entrance conjured up an image of a gaping, black mouth, waiting in readiness to swallow anything or anybody who dared to venture near. One solitary beam caught the Mermaid within its flight path. From Matt's view point, she rose up in profile, her perfect form outlined clearly under her clinging hair. Hands in pockets, Matt admired the clean sweeps of her curves; the flat stomach, rounded breasts and long sweeping line of her neck. When first he had entered the Mews, he had had eyes only for the living, breathing woman at his side. The female marble figure had only caught his eye on leaving. He had been surprised to find such an artistic and provocative figure living in what could only be termed as a slum area.

He turned his attention back to the matter in hand. Being as the car was not his own, he felt duty-bound to be more vigilant than if it had belonged to him. His footsteps were short and sharp as he strode over the cobblestones, through the archway and emerged, as if spat from the discerning mouth, into the street. Looking left then right, the road appeared at first glance to be empty. Then the glow from a cigarette caught his eye directly in front, on the opposite side of the road. Leaning on a lamppost, light filtering down from grime covered glass, was a motionless figure. Matt squinted out into the darkness, trying to distinguish the person's features. He stepped forward to the curb, his foot resting lightly on the bumper of the borrowed, parked car. The form opposite raised a hand, drawing deeply on the cigarette and with the glow of its lighted end and the umbrella of light from overhead, Matt could clearly see the face of the man. Two staring eyes looked back, their colour not visible and thus appearing deep black. The nose was straight and aquiline under which a thin line of a mouth cut from cheek to cheek. No lips were visible until, once more his hand lifted and he sucked at the glowing cigarette. His chin and cheeks were stubble marked and unshaven. His hair was greased back over which he wore a brown flat cap. Trousers, shoes and jacket were also brown, but of different shades and on his hands he wore black, shiny gloves. Around his neck and tucked into the front of his jacket was a startling blue wool scarf and appeared incorrigible with the rest of his attire.

"Hi. Turning cold now, isn't it?" Matt's breath hovered before him in white clouds as he spoke.

For several seconds there was no response. Then the man blinked his eyes and with a short, downward movement nodded his head and threw the stub of his cigarette into the gutter at his feet.

"Hey, don't I know you from somewhere? I think we must have met before?" Friendly as usual, Matt attempted to elicit a reply from the silent person.

Only a silent shrug of narrow shoulders acknowledged the question.

Giving up, Matt turned to attend to the car, muttering, "Sorry, fella. My mistake, I thought I knew you." After checking the car was locked, Matt returned to the Mews a puzzled frown on his face, sure he had seen the man somewhere before and recently - sometime within the last week or so. The memory was vague and dim and as it began to surface, a movement in the square caught his eye, pushing the identity of the lone figure back into the recesses of his mind.

"Hey, Ellie. Where are you off to?"

The little girl stopped in her tracks and watched as Matt strode over towards her.

"I'm just going home to get Nan's cardigan."

Matt smiled down at her and reaching out, put a friendly hand on her shoulder. "Shall I wait for you?"

"Naw. I'll only be a minute. Dad said he'd left a light on, so I won't be frightened. Anyway, I heard Brenda ask if you'd come back yet. She's looking for a dance, I think." Lightly, the girl ran on to her gate, calling back, "I won't be long, see you in a minute." Then she skipped up the path and disappeared into the house. Matt sauntered back to No. 6, all thoughts of the man in the street forgotten.

Meanwhile, Ellie took the stairs two at a time, ran into her grandmother's bedroom, found the woollen cardigan on the back of a chair and returned downstairs. As she passed the hallway clock she noticed that it was half past eight. With a little cunning on her part, she would be able to keep out of sight for the next hour or so then her parents would forget she was still there and she would be able to stay up until quite late. Smiling, she slammed shut the door and turned. What was that? Eyes alert, she scanned the square. Something had caught her attention. Yes, there it was again, over by the entrance. A further movement confirmed her suspicions. Someone was hiding under the archway. Her face cleared and a small giggle escaped her lips. It must be her Dad. He must have crept out after her. Crouching down, Ellie shuffled along the wooden fences skirting the square. Past the Carmichael's and the O'Shea's and on until she reached the end of No. 1. Here, it was completely dark as Vera had not thought to leave a light on. The small child stayed down low, repressing the laughter that threatened to erupt from her shaking body. Suddenly, she sprang and landing squarely in the centre of the entrance, shouted, "BOO! Got you! You don't frighten me, Dad.........oh!"

The face that glared at her was not Jack's. His eyes would never have looked so malevolently at anyone, least of all at his favourite child and never, never would her father have said what this man now hissed. "Piss off, you nosy little bleeder! Go on, bugger off!"

One hand over her mouth, Ellie took two steps back. "Sorry, Mister. I thought it was my Dad." Stuttering and babbling she went on, "We play this game see, trying to scare each other and I thought he was trying to catch me out. I'm sorry, Mr. Ridley. I didn't know it was you." Then turning swiftly, she ran as fast as her legs would carry her back to the safety of Lottie's house. Breathless and wide-eyed, she stood in the hallway with her back to the door and waited until her heart slowed down to an even tempo. Thoughts of what her father would say if he found out she had been springing out on innocent people flitted through her mind. Her only hope was that her father and Seb Ridley did not get on together and hardly ever spoke. So, if she kept quiet and did not mention her misdemeanour, then all should be well. Sighing with relief, she pushed herself away from the door and clutching the cardigan in her hand went in search of her grandmother.

Because of her age and because such things are not discussed openly before any younger member of the family, Ellie was unaware of the Ridley's recent troubles. Therefore, she was ignorant of the search that had been launched to find Seb Ridley and in maintaining her silence, would place Vera and Angela in imminent danger. Now, because of the information that Ellie kept to herself, the plot would run its full, tragic course.

CHAPTER 27

"Sally, Salleeeee! Don't ever wander, away from the alley and me...." Eyes dancing and hands pumping up and down on the keyboard, Sal played the song with gusto. Her neighbours joined in, their voices rising and falling in time to the tune, arms thrown about each others shoulders and feet tapping. To these simple folk there could be nothing better than a full stomach, a few drinks and a good sing-song with one's friends.

At first, Vera and Angela had stayed close together, shy and uncertain, but they had been drawn into the frivolities and their inhibitions had slowly vanished. Now, Vera stood by the piano between Frank and Jack, her arms comfortably looped around each man's waist. She lifted her voice, which was surprisingly clear and sweet, along with the others, her head tilted back and, as Cathy watched, she smiled at the woman's obvious pleasure. Although one eye was blue-black and still half closed and her mouth looked sore and distorted, this did not disguise her happiness. It had been many years, pre-Seb, since Vera had felt so relaxed and at peace and her contentment had an optimistic effect on Angela. The girl stood in the kitchen, talking animatedly to Fay. After the first faltering sentences, the girls had discovered they had more in common than they had believed.

"So, I had a lucky escape and from now on, I'm keeping clear of boys, at least until I'm a bit older. My Nan says there's plenty of time for all that and I'll be able to cope with things better later on." Fay confided.

"It must have been awful, Fay. But you're lucky in a way. You might've learnt the hard way, but you've got your family and they really care about what happens to you." Wistfully, Angela recalled how Jack had sought out his daughter, earlier in the evening, just to see how she was faring. They had talked easily to one another and as he returned to Cathy, Jack had winked at Fay, his affection and concern clearly visible. Angela compared this father-daughter relationship with her own. Seb had often winked at his daughter but there was a completely different meaning behind this gesture. When Angela's father looked at her, his eyes slowly stripped the clothes from her body until she felt naked, vulnerable and utterly defenceless.

Watching the shadows chase across the girl's face, Fay experienced a flash of insight as to Angela's home life.

"Listen, Angela. I know me and you haven't been exactly the best of friends but we could be. I need a friend who won't lead me astray or go along with some of my stupid ideas and I think you need someone you can talk to. You wouldn't have to tell me anything you didn't want to and if you did tell me anything, I wouldn't let on. We might be able to help each other."

Naturally suspicious of this proffered friendship, Angela searched Fay's face for any signs of ridicule. All she found there was a genuine desire to become friends.

"Alright. We'll give it a try. It won't be easy for me, because I've never had a real mate before. Things have been difficult at home, but everything's going to change. I'll be able to have friends come over to my house and I'll be able to join in with things after school." Shyly, she finished, "We could go places together, couldn't we?"

Happily, Fay nodded her head. "Yeah, and we'll start right now and go and find out what the others are up to. Gary's around here somewhere and I haven't seen Billy for a while which probably means he's up to no good. Come on, let's see if we can catch them out." Giggling, the two girls left the kitchen and returned to the fray.

By this time, Sal had retired from playing the piano and an ancient gramophone had been found under the stairs. Records of the day had miraculously appeared and now couples were jiving to the strains of 'Rock around the clock'. Children mingled with the adults, imitating the dance steps, their abundant energy apparent and their performance given with more gusto. Flushed and breathless, Cathy flapped her hand at Jack, shaking her head as she fell laughing into the seat by her mother-in-law.

"Alright, Mother? Enjoying yourself?"

"Who me? I'm having a whale of a time. I might not get up and fling myself around the room any more, but I have a good time watching you lot. And the best sight of today is her." Sal's eyes slid sideways, indicating the small, slight woman in the centre of the room. Frank was currently coaching Vera on the refinements of jiving whilst Eileen and Jack demonstrated. As Vera's faltering attempts grew in confidence, so her feet became lighter and her movements more fluid.

"She's having the time of her life, isn't she? God, when I think of the life she must have led, it makes my blood boil. Anyway, that's all behind her now she's come to her senses and, God willing, things will be better for her and Angela from now on."

Cathy lent over and planted a kiss on Sal's dry cheek. "You're a nice old stick sometimes, Mother." The old woman blushed, pleased in spite of herself at this rare show of affection from a member of her family and replied in blustering tones. "Haven't I always told you that? Don't say it's finally sunk in, my old heart couldn't stand it." Carefully, Cathy picked up one of Sal's gnarled hands and gently placed both her hands over it, her eyes firmly fixed on the gyrating figures before her. Turning her head slightly, Sal looked down with surprise at her hand resting within the warmth of Cathy's clasp. This was a first for the two women who had lived under the same roof for nearly fifteen years. Neither had consciously forged the gap which had grown between them, seemingly becoming wider and deeper as each year passed. In that moment, the chasm was bridged and, feeling Sal's eyes upon her, Cathy swung her gaze from the dance floor and met her mother-in-law's questioning stare. Not a word was spoken between the two of them, but each felt that a truce had been formed, the years of uneasy cohabitation fell away as Cathy squeezed Sal's fingers slightly, then turned her head back to the centre of the room. Standing to one side, his hand raised and glass halfway to his lips, Jack stared at them, his mouth open in disbelief. He watched as his wife smiled quietly at him and his mother winked and looked away. Then slowly a grin spread across his face as he realised that he had witnessed the first intimate and spontaneous contact between the two most prominent women in his life.

"Jack? Did you hear me?"

Vera stood by his side, her hand tugging at his sleeve as she tried to claim his attention. "Sorry, Vera. What did you say?"

"Me and Angela are off home now. It's nearly nine o'clock and we've had a big day. I didn't sleep very well last night and my bed's calling for me now. I just wanted to say goodnight to everyone before I left. I'm just going over to thank Lottie for having us and say cheerio to Ruby, then we're off."

Even though Jack protested that the night was young, Vera insisted and spying Angela in the hallway talking to Gary and Fay, she indicated that it was time to leave. The young girl came quickly to her mother's side and after thanking Lottie for her hospitality, the two gathered their belongings and left the party.

As the door closed softly behind them, Ellie watched, a small sigh on her lips as she sat at the foot of the stairs, elbows propped on her knees and head resting in her hands. She had been sitting there since delivering her grandmother's cardigan, keeping well out of sight, knowing her father would instantly be aware of some problem should he see her face. She dare not confess her mistake to him, even though he might well have seen the funny side of it. All her small life, Jack had drummed into her that she must respect her elders. Her father did not discriminate; all adults should be treated the same regardless of station or status. To the small girl, Seb Ridley fell into this category, not realising that he was the exception to the rule and in this instance there would have been no recriminations.

A shadow fell over the girl as she struggled with her conscience, then Matt nudged her over and sat in the vacant space.

"OK, honey? I thought I hadn't seen you for some time. How long have you been sitting here on your own?"

"Since I got back with Nan's cardigan." Ellie faced the stocky American, her troubled eyes not quite meeting his.

"That must be nearly an hour ago." Placing his arm gently around her shoulders, Matt asked, "Is something troubling you, Ellie? Do you want to tell me about it?"

The child shook her head, then nodded saying almost in a whisper, "I've done something really bad, Matt and if my Dad finds out he'll skin me alive. I didn't mean to do it. Well, I did mean to, but I didn't know I'd got the wrong person."

Puzzled, Matt pulled the girl closer to him, "I'm sure it can't be as bad as that. Your father seems to be a reasonable sort of guy and I'm sure if you made a mistake he wouldn't hold it against you. Why don't you try it out on me first, then we can decide what we should do about it. You just start at the beginning and when you get to the end, if you still don't want to tell anyone else about it, it'll be our secret, OK?"

Slowly at first, then the word's coming out in a rush, Ellie recounted her story. She felt Matt's arm stiffen when she identified her surprised victim and misinterpreted this as a sign of his distaste. "But I thought it was my Dad, not Mr. Ridley, honest Matt. It was dark and I couldn't see very well. See, even you're angry with me, so what's my Dad going to say?"

Taking Ellie's shoulders in his hands, Matt turned the girl roughly and looking directly into her upturned face, noticing the tears shimmering in her clear blue eyes, he spoke urgently to her. "Look Ellie, this is really important. I'm not angry at you and neither will your father be, just answer my questions quickly now. When you say Mr. Ridley, do you mean Vera's husband, Seb Ridley?"

Astonished at his outburst, Ellie nodded her head. Matt looked up over her head, staring into the distance. A picture formed, a 'freeze-frame' of a sinister-looking man stood under a lamppost, his face illuminated in the darkness. It would be too much of a coincidence, after Ellie's encounter, not to assume that the man Ellie had surprised and the man Matt had seen outside the Mews were one and the same person - Seb Ridley. There must only have been a matter of minutes between the two incidents and now Seb must be lurking somewhere in the square. Or, worse still, he might be waiting within the shelter of his own home for the return of his wife and daughter. Matt's thoughts switched and he cast his mind back to his first date with Brenda on the night of the fire. He recalled walking past the 'Rising Sun' and then, suddenly, he remembered the slight figure hunched into the corner of the building. He saw the figure turn as if in slow motion, saw the flame that lit the man's features and instantly the pieces of the puzzle fell into place. "Sweet Jesus! I knew I'd seen him somewhere before. It's the same guy, the same man I saw the night the Rising Sun caught fire." Rising, Matt looked over the bannister, leaning well over the child still sat below him. He scanned the hallway, looking for Brenda. Then, bringing his attention back to Ellie, he spoke quietly but with authority, "Go and find your father. Tell him everything you've told me, remember to say it was Seb Ridley you jumped out on. Go on, quickly now, while I go and find Vera and Angela, they must be in the kitchen."

"No, no, Matt. They've gone. I saw them go just before you came to talk to me." Catching the American's anxiety, Ellie also rose and her small hand clung to his sleeve urgently.

"What! But we've been sitting here for at least fifteen minutes. We could be too late!" Springing from the stairway, Matt leapt up the hall and dashed into the sitting room, his eyes searching frantically for help. He noticed Brenda stood at the far side of the room, but it was Frank who approached him.

"What's up Matt? You look like you've seen a ghost."

"Frank, come with me quickly. There's no time to explain. If I'm right we could already be too late." Grabbing the older man's arm, Matt turned and pulled the surprised man into the hallway, almost colliding with Ellie as she entered the room. Matt's voice had been loud and strident and his last words had brought a hush to the room, coinciding with the silence of the gramophone as a record finished. Matt did not wait. Dragging Frank behind him, he raced from the house, Brenda's astonished face being the last sight he registered as his feet pounded over the cobblestones.

Please God, let me be wrong! Or, at least, let me be in time. He repeated this phrase over and over in his mind, ignoring Frank's pleads to slow down. "For God's sake, Matt. Hold up a minute and tell me what's going on." But Matt had come to an abrupt halt. Lights blazed through the glass panels of the door to No. 1, spilling out onto the pathway, whilst overhead, from the front bedroom, a sudden scream split the night air. Then all was silent once more, except for the hammering of Matt's heart and Frank's loud gasp.

CHAPTER 28

As Ellie had scampered away, her movements jerky from fright, Seb had moved out from the shadows of the archway. Stealthily, he crept past the wooden fence enclosing No. 1 and without a sound had slipped unseen into his house. He stood in the darkness and waited until his eyes adjusted, then chuckling to himself he made his way to the living room. Without turning on any lights, he opened the sideboard door and felt around until his hand found what he wanted. Taking the whisky bottle out, his other hand finding a glass on the top of the cabinet, he poured a large measure and tossed it back. Lips smacking with approval, he refilled his glass, crossed the room and peered from behind the net curtain, out into the square. All was still. Vaguely, he made out the strains of singing followed by the blare of a record player. Sipping his drink steadily, his posture relaxed but senses on full alert, Seb waited. Clouds scurried past overhead, displaying a full moon and by this light, he glanced at his watch, noticing that the time was ten minutes after nine. Just then, a door opened on the far side of the Mews and two people stepped out onto the path of No. 6. The couple linked arms and, their steps brisk, they hurried down the path, onto the cobblestones and past the fountain, heading in Seb's direction. As they approached the front gate, he heard Vera's quiet voice and Angela's answering giggle and, stepping back from the window, he turned and, with measured movements, left the room and returned to the front door. His every action calculated, Seb stationed himself to the left of the doorway, at the base of the stairs, knowing his presence would be obscured when Vera swung open the door. He crouched, muscles tense ready to spring as he heard his wife insert her key and half rotate the lock.

"Old Sal's pretty good on the piano, isn't she Angela?" Her shoulder bumped the door to gain entry and her head turned to address her daughter, Vera reached in and flicked on the hall light. Pushing lightly, she opened wide the door, hiding the preying figure behind it.

"Yeah, she is. I didn't know some of the songs, but it was nice just being there. I've had a really good time, Mum. Everyone was so friendly. Fay's coming over tomorrow and we're going to style each other's hair and play about with some of her make-up." Following her mother, Angela entered the house and stepped to one side to allow room for the door to close. Still chattering, her attention fully on her daughter, Vera leaned back, grasped the edge of the door and pulled it shut, revealing the menace behind her. The reaction on the young girl was immediate. Her eyes opened wide in shock and terror, the colour drained from her face leaving her complexion chalk white and her hands clamped over her mouth as an involuntary gasp of fear escaped her lips. "Mum! Behind you, look behind you!" Bewildered, Vera spun round. Before she had fully turned, her mind reeled as she heard her husband's low, threatening voice.

"Good evening, Ladies. So nice of you to grace me with your presence." Each word was clipped and carefully enunciated and he grinned maliciously as he revelled in the horrified expressions of both his wife and daughter. As quick as lightning and as sure-footed as any wild animal, he moved to the doorway, his back against the portal, blocking the now cowering couple's means of escape. Vera and Angela shuttled backwards, mesmerised, their faces frozen in disbelief. It was Vera who eventually broke the prolonged silence between them.

"Seb! What're you doing here?" Her voice loud with a courage she did not feel, the small woman reached out sideways and pushed her shaking daughter behind her. "You shouldn't have come back, Seb. You should've stayed away. The Police are looking for you. Everyone knows. Do you understand? I've told everyone and not just about this time but about all the other times and all. If you lay one finger on either of us, you'll be sent down." Taking a deep shuddering breath and fighting the tremor in her voice, Vera confronted her husband for the first time. "If you go now, just turn round and walk out the door, we'll not hand you in. It's your only chance, Seb. Get away from here and don't ever come back. I don't wish you any harm, but I warn you, if you start anything, I've only to open my mouth and there'll be people jumping all over you in seconds."

The three faced each other. No-one moved. Angela gripped her mother's coat, staring over the woman's shoulder at the man she had despised all her young life, willing him to leave. Vera also looked at the man before her. She no longer saw the dashing, handsome figure who had swept her off her feet all those years ago. Mind clear, the curtains drawn back fully from her eyes at last, she viewed him as others must. A little, cowardly, bitter man. His ruddy, florid and vein-filled face spoke of the self inflicted alcohol abused life he had led. His hairline was beginning to recede and at his temples, a sprinkling of grey was visible. Fading, red-rimmed, muddy brown eyes looked back at her and in their depths she thought she could detect a glimmer of uncertainty but this vanished as quickly as it came. He sprang. One moment he stood, hands flat on the shut door at his back, the next those same hands held Vera's neck in a vice-like grip. Angela cried out and jumped back, tripping on the bottom step and landing awkwardly at the base of the stairway. She lay there, helpless as she watched her father systematically thrash the life from her mother's frail body. All the while, as his hands worked, beating and punching, pummelling and punishing his wife's flesh, Seb held forth with a steady tirade.

"You mealy-mouthed bitch! Hand me in to the filth, would you? Go round telling everyone what goes on in the privacy of my own sodding home, eh? And then you have the fucking nerve to warn me off and tell me to get out. No-one, *no-one*, tells me what to do, especially not a bleeding, snivelling little cow like you. You can't say I didn't bloody warn you, Vera. You can't say you didn't bring this all on your own stupid head. This time, you've fucking had it. This time I'm going to do what I should've done years ago. You'll never sodding snitch on me again, Vera, never. And when I've finished with you, I'm going to get that poe-faced daughter of yours as well. I'll teach her to prance round here, flashing her body and teasing and tormenting me. I'm going to show her what it's like to have a real man and then I'm going to do for her as well!" By the scruff of her coat, he lifted his semi-conscious wife halfway from the floor until her blood covered face was inches from his own. "Do you hear me, Vera? I'm going to stick it to your daughter good and proper. She'll be crying out for more, begging me not to stop and then I'm going to put her out of her misery, give her some of what you're getting now, understand? But she'll die happy, Vera because she'll have got what she's been fucking angling after for years. Not that all this matters to you, you're not going to be around to tell the take, are you? So say goodbye, my darling wife, say a bloody fond farewell to this bleeding life, because your time's up!" Eyes bulging and voice reduced to a hiss, Seb brought back his head and holding tightly to Vera's coat collar, he slammed his forehead with all his force onto the bridge of her nose.

The sickening sound of snapping bone motivated Angela from her trance-like state. An anguished cry tore from her throat as she watched her mother's whole body stiffen, saw her eyes roll back in her head, then groaned as Vera slumped within Seb's grip, her head lolling to one side. Through dazed and shocked eyes, the girl witnessed her father throw down the lifeless body. With a grunt of satisfaction, he kicked out brutally several times at the inert form and when he was absolutely sure he had completed this task, he straightened up and turned to finish his mission. Not waiting a moment longer, the girl sprang up and, feet scrabbling, she flew up the stairs. She hesitated for a few precious seconds on the landing, then darted into her bedroom, slamming shut the door after her. In the darkness she stumbled over to the bed and lifting the mattress, her hands searched frantically for the concealed weapon she had hid there. It was gone! Kneeling by the side of the bed, she pushed both arms under the mattress and with circular sweeping motions she began to cover the immediate area. It had been there last night but where was it now? Perhaps he had searched her room while they were at the party. He must have found it and removed it. But wait. Was it the window side where she had hidden it or over on the other side by the wall? Time was running out. Outside in the hallway she heard the creak of a stair and her father's maniacal laugh as he approached her bedroom door. Panic stricken, the girl leapt from the floor and scrabbled onto the bed. Knees bent under her chin, her back pushed hard against the headboard and both hands covering her face, she stared at the still closed door through her fingers. In the eerie glow of the moonlight, she watched as the handle slowly turned then with a crash the door was flung wide. Silhouetted in the door frame, black and ominous, Seb stood stock still, legs spread wide and hands on hips. Angela shuddered as his head moved purposefully in her direction whilst his eyes scanned the room.

"There you are, my beauty." He began to steal across the floor, gradually spanning the distance between them. "You can't hide from me, silly girl." She felt the mattress dip as he leant both hands on the end of the bed. "We're going to have some fun, just you and me. And if you're a good girl, daddy's going to give you a nice present, something you've been wanting for a long time. But if you're bad, then daddy'll have to punish you and you're going to get hurt." Bringing both knees up onto the bed, he began to crawl slowly up towards her. "There's nothing to be frightened of, baby. It'll be nice, just you wait and see. With a body like yours, you were made for it and I'm just the bloke to show you how it's done." Crooning softly as one might to a cornered animal, Seb knelt up on the bed and reaching for his belt, began to undo his trousers. Angela watched in horror as his hands fumbled with the zip. She squeezed shut her eyes and wished herself away from here. Far away where there was no Seb and this terrible thing was not happening to her. Somewhere warm and safe where fathers were kind and children were happy. For a moment her mind drifted, falling in on itself and then floated up and out of the danger that was imminent. Reality brought her back to earth with a thud as blunt and callused fingers circled her ankles. She moaned as Seb dragged at her, straightening her legs and pulling her down the bed. Eyes still tightly closed and hands now up over her head, her fingers scrambled for a hold on the headboard. Momentarily she felt the cold smooth contours of the brass bedstead, then it was gone and her hands clutched at empty air. Below, she felt her dress ride up over her thighs as she was pulled further towards the monster who lay in wait for her, felt his legs straddle her hips and then slowly lower his weight upon her. Her brain denounced this obscenity, refused to acknowledge the gross act about to be performed on her. She opened her mouth wide to scream, but her throat was dry with fear and the scream gave vent only in her mind, echoing within her pulsing brain.

Seb looked down on the prostrate form beneath him. She had not uttered a sound since he had first entered the room and he took her silence as acceptance, a quiet surrender to his will. His mouth drooled and his lips pulled back from his teeth in an evil grimace. His eyes travelled slowly up her body, taking in the white gleam of her tender thighs. The soft swell of her young breasts, straining against the tight material of her dress, seemed to beg for release. He brought both hands to her neck and pushing aside the jacket she still wore, he grasped the collar and in one swift movement, ripped the garment down to reveal soft pale skin as yet unsullied by male hands. He heard her sudden intake of breath and mistook the terror etched into her face for expressions of ecstasy. Encouraged by her seeming acquiescence, he bent his head and pulled back the flimsy material of her bra with his teeth, exposing her young flesh. As his lips sought her nipple, hardened by the icy night air, he felt her body grow suddenly rigid beneath him. The taste of her sweet skin inflamed him further and his body responded, the throbbing between his legs becoming almost uncontrollable. Roughly, his hands roved over her, pushing and kneading her, violating her whole being. Savagely he pushed her legs apart and began his exploration of her most intimate places, the wispy fabric of her panties not serving as any protection against his insistent debauchery.

"Not ready for me yet, are you, my lovely? Still, we can't take all night over this, much as I'd like to and the tighter and drier you are, the better it'll be for me. But you might enjoy it more if you relax. God, you're as hard as a board. Like mother, like daughter, I suppose. Never mind, I'll be the first and last, so no other bloke'll have to put up with you, not like I've had to with your mother all these years." With one knee between her thighs to keep her open to him, he raised his hands to his hips and began to slide his trousers down, his eyes glittering with anticipation at the relief that would soon be his. "Here it comes, girl. Get ready for the best thing to ever come your way, what all women want if they'd only admit it."

Through a mind numbed with abject terror, jumbled and distant, the girl battled with her sanity. Desperately she searched for acceptable reasons. Reasons her brain would allow.

This can't be happening! I must be having a nightmare and I'll wake up in a minute. But it feels so real, his hands are really touching me, doing dirty things to me. And I can smell his breath, smell the whisky. Oh my God! He's going to do it and I can't stop him. Please, Mother of God, help me! Make him go away, if not, then let me die before it happens. Hear me, Our Lady, for God's sake answer my prayer!

Angela's silent plea begged for a response. The seconds ticked by and neither of her demands were met. She could still hear the rustle of her father's clothes as he struggled to free himself and she could still hear her own heartbeat hammering in her ears, proving that he had not vanished and she would have to live through the despicable act that would now be inflicted on her. Defeated, the girl allowed her body to go limp. There could be no help now, nothing could save her. There was no God, no benevolent deity to come to her rescue and even if by some strange quirk of fate, she should survive this horror, her life would still be over, she would be dead no matter how the end was written.

CHAPTER 29

Downstairs, all was quiet, as still as any grave. The silence thundered perversely through the lower house, rolling from wall to wall and ricocheted from ceiling to floor.

The crumpled and battered form lay totally immobile. No movement was apparent. The narrow chest did not rise and fall gently with the natural function of breathing. Behind the closed eyelids, there was no flickering of consciousness and the limbs did not twitch or flex as they would in sleep. The head rested on one side and blood trickled slowly from both nose and mouth. A steady stream also formed a pool and congealed in matted hair, the thick sticky substance flowing from the left ear. One arm was flung above the head whilst the other lay at an awkward right angle to the body. The left knee was bent with the foot leaning on the other outstretched leg, caught in a ballerina-type pose.

Vera hovered over the figure, suspended perhaps six feet above. She looked down critically at her broken body and noted the damage it had sustained. She saw her life's blood ebbing away, gently draining into the floorboards staining the grain a stark, vivid scarlet. It would only be a matter of time before she could leave this place and break the tie to her mortal shell. Soon, she would be able to glide into the bright light that beckoned in the distance. She felt an overwhelming sense of peace and happiness envelope her, a sure knowledge that where she was going there was joy and love, contentment and safety. Never again would she have to wonder or doubt; there *was* life after death and it would be more wonderful and awesome than any mere human could describe or fathom.

The spirit that had been, in essence, captured within her earth bound body, floated on towards the brilliant, golden orb, a gateway to the rewards she so richly deserved. She felt the magnetic pull of the light and she welcomed its power over her. Now she would know, now all mysteries would be solved and she would meet her maker. But something halted her progress. Something tugged at her, dragging her back until the light gradually receded and became a small dot on the horizon. Once more she gazed upon the inert figure but now she saw she had not been alone. She watched as Seb turned away from the body he had so brutally destroyed, saw Angela spring up and flee, heard her panicked steps on the stairs and realised with a white heat sense of anger that her evil-minded husband was not yet satisfied. Her work in this world was not over. Somehow she must stop him, finally and for all time. Angela's life depended on her and Vera would need to use her battered, human form to prevent further tragedy.

You must go back, this is not your time, not yet, not now. You must finish with this life first. The words formed in her mind and whispered through the tunnels of her inner brain. With a sudden rush she felt a sharp pull, a swirling sensation and then a deep void opened before her and sucked her down, back into her discarded body.

Blinking rapidly, Vera opened her eyes and stared along the wooden floor. Every groove and scratch was starkly vivid, prominent in their clarity. Slowly, she turned her head until her eyes rested on the cracked ceiling above her and the shining light bulb overhead. She fought down the blackness that again threatened to claim her and willed her lungs to operate. The erratic drum of her heartbeat gave her some courage and then her chest heaved, once and once more and she inhaled, deeply, her body shuddering with the effort. Then came the pain. Wave upon wave of mind-wracking pain. Her brain received messages from nerve endings throughout her body. She suppressed an anguished cry as the signals rushed in from her shattered face, her twisted and broken arm and further down, from her damaged rib-cage and abdomen. With an effort of will rarely found in the stoutest of hearts, Vera reached out and took hold of the banister rail. Teeth gritted in determination, she pulled herself upright and breath coming in ragged bursts, she waited until her quivering back would support her without the aid of her steadying hand. Stretching both legs out straight and apart to gain more stability, she let got of the rail and bringing her good arm across her chest she dragged at her other useless limb until it was hugged tight to her side. Sweat and blood mingled on her brow, dripping onto her lap from her drooped head and threatened to drown her vision. She raised her face and gingerly at first, then with more vigour, shook her head from side to side, clearing her eyes and sending small, bright red droplets spinning in a circle about her.

A sudden noise directly overhead, startled the woman into further action. There was no time to sit here lamenting her fate or to ponder on her injuries. The crash above her head had been caused by the violent opening of her daughter's bedroom door and if she was to be of any help at all, she must stand up, mount the stairway and stop him before all was lost. Demanding her limbs to obey her, she staggered upright and slowly, one agonising step at a time, Vera fought her way up until after what seemed like an age, but was only minutes, she reached the top and stood swaying on the landing. Through the open doorway to her left, she heard the drone of her husband's voice. He was saying something about not being ready and all women wanting it. She moved instinctively towards the noise, feeling her way along the wall until her fingers brushed the door frame. Trembling with shock, Vera stumbled into the room. No light shone in the inky darkness and although she could hear scuffling within the room, she could not see its source. Unthinking, she reached to the side of the doorway and pulled down the knob of the switch. Light flooded the area and she blinked several times to adjust her eyes, then wished she could be blind for evermore. For there, at the far side of the room on the bed, straddling her daughter, was the man who had brought almost total misery to her life. There was the vile creature who had tormented and bullied her, beaten and subjected her to unspeakable acts of degradation and now he was about to force himself on their daughter.

"NO! No, not her as well, you bastard." With wings for feet, Vera flew across the room, unmindful of her injuries and leapt onto the bed. With a strength born of outrage and anger she grabbed a handful of Seb's hair and yanked his head back sharply. Taken completely by surprise, the stocky, half dressed man rolled sideways and fell with a loud thud on the floor, between the bed and the window. Vera knelt on the bed, panting from her exertions, head down and eyes closed whilst Angela scrambled back, pulling her jacket closed over her ripped dress. the girl had still not spoken a word and her eyes were glazed with shock as she stared at her mother. Blood flowed freely now from the various wounds Vera had received and the bedclothes beneath her were splattered with dark red patches. As the girl moved towards her, the natural instinct to help her mother sharply awaked, she felt the bed give and creak. Her body now frozen in fear, she watched as Seb's thunderous face gradually appeared above the level of the mattress. His hand snaked out to grab at the girl's leg. She kicked out swiftly and struck his leering mouth, her shoe making contact and shattering his front teeth with the single erratic blow. Seb fell back out of view, vile obscenities trailing in his wake. Scrabbling to her feet, angela stood in the centre of the bed, her fingers rammed into her mouth, not knowing what to do next.

Vera looked up through pain-filled eyes and reached out her hand. "Get out, love. Go, quick! Don't wait for me, just get out before he comes back for more. Fetch help, Angela, get anyone but for God's sake be quick!" The words were slurred, but their meaning was clear, their urgency piercing the fog engulfing the terrified girl.

"Not so fast, you! I haven't sodding finished with you yet, so stay where you are." Seb staggered up from the side of the bed, his mouth a gaping wound with black gaps where his teeth used to be and blood spitting from the cuts in his gums. "After I've dealt with your whore of a mother, and I mean to do a proper job this time, you'll find I won't be quite as gentle with you. I'm going to really fucking give it to you, no more pussy-footing around. But first I'm going to make sure there's no more interruptions."

With no longer any fight left in her, Vera watched Seb reach across the bed, tears of defeat trickling onto the open skin of her cheeks and flowing into her mouth. She uttered one last helpless plea, not concerned with her own welfare, but desperate to somehow save Angela. "Please Seb, don't touch her. I don't care what you do to me, but for pity's sake don't hurt our daughter. Leave her be, I beg of you, Seb."

Stricken by the sight of her mother begging to this monster, this debased excuse for a father and knowing he would carry out his threats to the full, Angela snapped out of her shocked stupor. Throwing herself to the far side of the bed, to the opposite edge where Seb now crouched, she reached over and thrust her hand under the mattress. Her fingers found what she had frantically searched for earlier. In one movement she pulled her arm out, swung round, found her footing and stood up once more on the bed. With moon-type bounds she leapt across the expanse and, as Seb bent forward his attention rivetted on the quarry knelt before him, she raised both hands above her head, her legs spread wide for balance. Grey steel glittered in the moonlight, then flashed as she plunged the knife down, slicing into the exposed area at the nape of his neck. She screamed once, loud and shrill. A cry from the very depths of her soul, then fell back sobbing.

Seb was unable to cry out. The point of the blade was protruding from an area below his adam's apple and only a gurgling sound issued from his mouth. Staring directly at his daughter he reached up and back and grasped the knife's handle. Slowly he began to withdraw the blade from his neck. He had nearly completed the task when suddenly his body shuddered rippling in one wave from head to toe. He fell forward, face down onto the bed, twitched once, then lay still. In attempting to remove the knife, Seb had unwittingly inflicted more damage than that caused by his daughter. The razor sharp blade had twisted sideways on its return journey and neatly severed his spinal cord causing instant death. His upper torso sprawled haphazardly over the bedclothes, arms stretched wide and head twisted to one side. His eyes stared blindly onto a scene from which he could now play no part.

Downstairs, the sound of breaking glass echoed through the house. Feet pounded on the stairs and Matt and Frank burst through the doorway. They found Vera and Angela huddled in the middle of the bed, the daughter holding her mothers blood covered head tightly to her chest. The girl rocked gently back and forth, crooning a lullaby softly to the unconscious woman and staring blindly at a space in the far distance. On one side to the right, lay the still and silent body of Seb. A knife was firmly embedded in his skin, just under his hairline at the nape. Matt's brain registered the scene, but would not accept the evidence of his own eyes. He moved to the side of the prone man and leaning down, placed his fingers at the pulse point in Seb's neck. Feeling around for a few seconds he removed his hand and, looking over to Frank, shook his head. Then carefully, the American climbed onto the bed and gathering mother and daughter into his arms, he hugged them both to him. With bowed head his shoulders shook and heaved. Frank stood and watched for several minutes, his eyes blurred with tears. Then he turned on his heel and, feet dragging, he left the room quietly closing the door behind him.

EPILOGUE

It was early in the Spring of 1960 before Mermaid Mews and its occupants returned to any sort of normality.

Come April, the weather had improved and on this particular day a brave but ineffectual sun shone down on the fountain. The rays bounced off the surface of the little Mermaid, sprinkling her hair with golden glints. Reformed to her natural hues after the last frost during the previous month, she resumed her occupation of watching over her flock. Although on close inspection her age was evident, there had been some changes. She had been 'overhauled'. As soon as the weather broke, Jack had taken bucket and brush to her scrubbing away layers of over half a century's grime and dirt until her skin shone almost as good as new. Nothing could be done about her chipped mirror and comb nor the gouges and scratches on her body but the fountain bowl had been drained of foul water and cleared of dead leaves and other debris that had accumulated there. Since the initial 'clean up campaign', Jack and Ellie had taken it upon themselves to regularly maintain the fountain and this shared voluntary task had strengthened an already tried and tested relationship.

Now, the pretty statuette basked in the sunlight whilst below her, perched on the fountain's rim, two other ladies of a similar age as she, sat quietly reminiscing. They chatted amiably passing away the time, albeit a precious commodity even to those who have not yet reached their twilight years.

Sal and Lottie had not altered. It was almost one year to the day since they had first met. Neither woman had changed her style of dress nor the way she wore her hair and neither would they at this late stage of their lives. They still held their weekly 'Grapevine' meetings where they were able to air their opinions and let others receive the benefit of their considerable advice. Even though neither woman would admit it, after the excitement of recent events both felt somewhat 'flat'. Of course, they had talked of nothing else for weeks, exploring every avenue until Cathy declared that enough was enough and perhaps it was time for the subject to be dropped. Reluctantly, the two old women had agreed not to mention the Ridleys again, except with regards to present day. Still, when they were alone they indulged themselves, arguing that other than the 'Wars' the Christmas of 1959 had been the most eventful and exciting time of their lives.

On this day, they were alone and would not be overheard and, as if they had never spoken of it before, they began to run through the whole sequence and its consequences. Neither realised that she used the same phrases and had become almost word perfect in the retelling. The context was unimportant, only the content was crucial.

"Vera looked much better today eh, Sal? Better than I've seen her in a long time."

"Well, she still looked a bit peaky to me but after all she's been through, you couldn't expect to find her in the pink, could you?"

"No, I suppose not. Mind you, I can still see her the night they brought her out of that house on a stretcher. It made me go cold all over. All that blood! I didn't think a body could hold that much."

"Me neither. To be honest Lottie, I didn't think she'd make it. It was touch and go there for a while. She was on the critical list for so long, I thought I'd have to get my mourning clothes out. Surprised us all though, didn't she? She might only be little but she's got a lot of fight in her. I still don't understand how that sod could have done so much damage in such a short space of time. He must've been like a madman. Her arm seems to be alright now and the bruises went from her face pretty quick, but her nose doesn't look right to me."

"I know what you mean. It's sort of crooked, isn't it? And Ruby was telling me she's still having trouble with her stomach. He must've given her a hell of a kick to rupture her spleen and break three ribs."

"Bastard. When all's said and done it's not just the damage you see, is it? What about in here?" Sal tapped her forehead, "It'll be a long time until either of them can sleep easy in their beds again. I heard poor Angela still wakes up screaming. I don't know which is worse; screaming her head off every night or not saying a thing day after day. How long was it before she started talking again?"

"Must have been nearly six weeks. She was seeing that shrink for ages and I'm not sure she's stopped going to him yet. They say something like that can ruin you for life and her such a young girl and all." Lottie shook her head as she visualised the pale and nervous creature that Angela had become.

"I'm glad it all went well for her at the trial. Mind you, there would've been a hue and cry and not just from folk round here, if they'd have found her guilty of murder. In all the nationals it was. You couldn't pick up a paper for weeks without seeing a Ridley plastered all over it. I still think they were a bit hard on her though.

She might not have been put in the clink, but for someone who's got years and years in front of them, a suspended sentence for that length of time could cause you a lot of grief in the future."

"You don't have to tell me. I've seen it all before, though not as bad as this case. You remember what that bloody idiot of a Judge said? The sentence wouldn't have been so long if she hadn't kept a knife under the mattress. Bleeding twit! If she hadn't put the knife there, neither of them would be here today, would they?"

"I couldn't agree with you more, Lottie. But think on. If he'd have let her get away with it Scot-free, then twenty thousand teenage girls who've got a grudge against their Dads are going to start hiding knives and things all over the place and bumping men off left, right and centre. No, he had to give her something. I just think five years was a bit strong."

"Well, it doesn't matter, there's nothing anyone can do now. They'll just have to try and pick up the pieces and get on with their lives. That reminds me. Did you hear? The council have found them another place, over Battersea way and they're off next week."

"Yeah, Cathy took great pleasure in telling me. She thinks we'll stop going on about it if they're not around but it'll be a long time until I forget what went on. I hope Vera comes back to visit, not that I'd blame her if she didn't. She must hate this place and as for still living in that house..... well, you wouldn't catch me in there, not even in broad daylight. I know he's six feet under but I wouldn't put it past that bleeder to come back and haunt us all!"

"Oh, Sal! You don't believe in ghosts, do you? There isn't any such thing. He won't be climbing out of any grave to come and get you. He'd have trouble anyway. When that knife went through his neck, it cut all his strings and it's difficult to haunt people when you can't move. He wouldn't even be able to make that moaning sound either, because his voice box got a bit chopped up too!"

"You're bloody wicked, you are Lottie! What a thing to say! Still, I can stop sprinkling the holy water round my bed at night now that I know I'm safe!"

The two women rocked back and forth, their arms clutching their middles, their laughter suppressed for fear an explanation would be called for.

"Here Lottie. What about the day of Seb's funeral? All that thunder and lightning. I thought Old Nick himself had come up to fetch him. Father O'Connell was heard talking on the telephone and he said other than himself and the grave diggers, there wasn't anyone else there. Then he said he knew he should pray for Seb's soul, but he couldn't bring himself to ask God to forgive a beast like him. I was a bit shocked at first. Then I got to thinking. What if God did decide to forgive him? That means that rotten sod would be waiting for me when I get to the Pearly Gates. Over my dead body!"

"How else do you expect your body to be if you're waiting in the queue to get into heaven? You silly moo!"

"You know what I mean. If he's up there, I think I'd rather fry."

"Well! Sarah Treist! I never thought I'd hear the day when you'd swop your place in paradise for that burning inferno that you're always on about."

"Lottie, I don't think I'm ever going to convert you, am I? I think I'd have better luck with old twinkle toes up there," An indication with her thumb towards the Mermaid made Sal's point, "than I'll ever have with you."

"Still, you'd better keep trying, Sal. Otherwise you'll have no-one to play whist with on the other side, will you?"

"Bloody heathen!"

For a while both women were silent, smiling to themselves at the playful banter they often exchanged.

"Looks like Frankie's settled back down again. Poor kid. Eileen told my Jack that that detention place was bloody awful. He was in there with all sorts - kids that'll be hardened criminals before they're much older and he hadn't even done anything. Still, the Police weren't slow in getting him out once Matt had told them the whole story. Of course, I always knew he wasn't guilty. Only a spineless git like Seb Ridley could burn down a man's home and business just because they'd had a few words."

"I liked that Matt bloke. He was nice. I mean, he hardly knew any of us, but look how worried he was over that business. Ruby said he felt guilty because he'd forgotten about seeing Seb on the night of the fire. But he wasn't to know who it was, was he? Anyone can be forgiven for wanting to forget Seb Ridley's ugly mug. He was in tears you know....after he'd broken in with Frank and they'd found Vera and Angela. Sitting on the bed with them he was, holding them and crying. Of course, they can't remember much about it all, once Seb had snuffed it. But Frank said it brought a lump to his throat to see the three of them huddled in the middle of the bed and he's not one to show his emotions."

"Yeah, I quite liked him as well, even if he was a Yank. Did you see Brenda's face Lottie, on the day they got married? She had a grin from ear to ear. And who can blame her? She's a very lucky girl, is Brenda. Landed herself a good bloke and then swanned off to live in American in her own house. And they'll have a car. Young Gary told my Ellie that he's going out to visit them in the summer and Ruby might go for a week or two as well. Matt's going to send them plane tickets. Plane tickets, I ask you? There'll be a man on the moon next."

"Oh yeah and pigs will fly as well. Man on the moon? You do get some funny ideas, Sal. You'll be telling me next that women can be Prime Ministers and film stars can be Presidents."

"Stranger things have happened Lottie, stranger things have happened. Who knows what's around the corner?"

Above them, the Mermaid appeared to smile. She would still be there long after these mere mortals had been and gone. Still she would follow the lives of the people in her domain, detached and unshakeable upon her marble parapet. This was not the end for her, only the closing of another chapter. There would be many more pages to the huge volume of her book. As she sat, queen of all she surveyed, one could be forgiven for fancying that not only did she harbour memories of the distant past but also, perhaps, looked on into the hazy future and knew what lay there.

THE END